FEVER PITCH

Howard shook his head. "This makes no sense to me. How could this bug suddenly become resistant to every antibiotic? Did you test every one?"

"All of the commercially available ones. The only way we could find out for sure what this bug is, would be to stop all antibiotics, let the spores stop hibernating, revert to their natural state, start multiplying and then maybe we could reculture and treat Vicky before . . ."

"No," Howard shouted, starting forward.

The pathologist stood up quickly and snapped off the light under the stage of the microscope, then stared at Howard. "You going to keep her on antibiotics the rest of her life, Doctor? Have her live at the hospital, be a carrier, harboring spores?"

"Goddamn it, Morgue, it's too dangerous."

CONTAGION

CONTAGION

JOHN
DAVID
CONNOR

DIAMOND BOOKS, NEW YORK

CONTAGION

A Diamond Book / published by arrangement with
the author

PRINTING HISTORY
Diamond edition / April 1992

ISBN: 1-55773-684-7

Diamond Books are published by The Berkley Publishing
Group, 200 Madison Avenue, New York, New York 10016.
The name "DIAMOND" and its logo are trademarks
belonging to Charter Communications, Inc.

PRINTED IN THE UNITED STATES OF AMERICA

10 9 8 7 6 5 4 3 2 1

PROLOGUE

The bartender, busily concocting pastel-colored drinks with tiny paper parasols, at first took no notice of the young man who had stepped up to the cash register to pay his bill. The young man, dressed in blue jeans and a crisp red polo shirt, was seemingly the only one of the two dozen customers in the bar who was not sweating. The patrons of the French Quarter saloon were packed tightly together, the alcohol bringing everybody's voice up a notch.

The bartender finally wiped his hands on his apron and moved to the cash register to accept the money from the young man. The bartender's nose twitched as it picked up a scent; the kid smelled like a medicine cabinet. The bartender shrugged. Having worked the French Quarter for years, he was shockproof. The kid, for all he knew, could have been smoking a bush, or had found a way to synthesize cat litter into a mind-altering toke. The residents of the Quarter could be very inventive.

The young man took his change and stepping outside into the oppressive heat, paused for a moment to get his bearings. The route was becoming familiar, and he had already determined that this would be his last practice run. He moved out quickly, heading for Saint Ann Street, forcing his way through the pre-Mardi Gras revelers, whose numbers were growing each day. The young man paused outside a restaurant to glance at the brass plate next to the door: "Marie Le Veau's Restaurant." She was still referred to here in New Orleans as Old Marie, the Voodoo Queen, though her remains had occupied the above-ground tomb in Saint Louis One for almost one hundred years. Local citizens had blamed her for the yellow fever epidemic, and had killed her. It occurred to the young man that Old Marie, in her way, had contributed to the advance of science. Rather like his mission, he thought. He smiled faintly, his hand going under his shirt to finger the cool steel tucked in his belt.

A wall of noise came from Bourbon Street. Thousands of them, both locals and tourists, fought for space along the parade route. They oozed from the sleaze shops and bars and from some of the greatest restaurants and jazz emporiums in the world.

The young man allowed himself to be pushed along by the crowd onto Bourbon Street. He was in no hurry. He took time to look at individual faces. He categorized them, separating them into locals, tourists and local-locals. The locals lived in the fancy Carrollton and Saint Charles areas. They were the "old" families, spending their time at the private clubs with their old-South exclusivity, holding private balls and planning the parades. They tolerated the second group, the tourists, with their pale Northern complexions, who sauntered about the Quarter, plastic convention tags pinned to their shirts.

It was the third group, the local-locals, that the young man had selected as the test group for his experiments. They were the street vendors and sidewalk artists, the bartenders and waiters and clerks. Although many had lived here for years, they had all come from somewhere else. He looked up and saw some of them leaning out over the wrought-iron railings around the small balconies outside their ancient living quarters above the boutiques and bars. Many were attractive and young, skin unblemished and eyes bright and curious, always curious. They were ideal subjects—strong, healthy, self-indulgent, purposeless people who, most notably, wouldn't be missed.

The young man reached the corner of Saint Ann and Bourbon just as the parade was about to start. This parade was short, one of the prelude parades in the weeks before the actual Mardi Gras parade. It was a warm-up. The theme was "drugs." The street was becoming more congested by the minute, and the cops, in Jeeps, preceded the floats, herding the spectators back up on the curb.

The first float was twenty feet long with a huge papier-mâché-and-wire likeness of John Belushi, stark naked on his back with a twelve-inch penis at the highest state of erection, pointed straight at the bright sun. It was matched in height by a large straw in John Belushi's nose. Bare-breasted women, wearing masks, straddled the float and threw plastic Mardi Gras beads and doubloons to the squealing humanity massed on the sidewalk. Some of the women squirted the crowd with scented water fired from toy plastic guns.

The young man moved in behind a short male spectator who was jumping up and down and shrieking, tussling with others for the doubloons like a bridesmaid fighting for a bridal bouquet. The young man made a pistol of his forefinger and 'fired' at the spectator's neck. He nodded in satisfaction and patted the metal injector gun concealed beneath his shirt. Stepping back from the crowd for a moment, he regarded the aimless people with contempt. He had a higher regard for his laboratory rats. Then he moved away, a twinge of excitement quickening his steps as he realized the trial runs were over and his next trip would be the real thing.

CHAPTER 1

Dr. Howard Fletcher was trailed by a coterie of bright young men and women, observers in white coats who someday hoped to emulate him.

They walked briskly into the private suite of the rich sixty-two-year-old man with the brain tumor so large that Howard Fletcher's duty this day was to relay the information that they had not been able "to get it all." But not in so many words. It was not Fletcher's way to pronounce death sentences. He always put the best possible face on the prognosis, leaving unsaid the hard truth.

He told the man in the bed that the neurosurgical team had excised most of the tumor, and further pointed out that there were nonsurgical treatments available to attack "the little" that was left behind. Not mentioned was the part about the tiny tentacles that had curled their way, spiderlike, into the gray crevasses of his brain, malignant seeds that would almost certainly blossom again in a fairly short time. Of course, Fletcher told himself as he looked down at the doomed man, surgery could excise all of the tumor if the patient didn't place a premium on walking, talking or thinking.

Fletcher had delivered the same hopeful speech to others, watching their white faces closely, and tailoring his remarks to what he saw in their frightened eyes. Invariably, no matter the level of intelligence, they read between the lines, either through some deep personal insight or by what their bodies had already told them, the doctor's speech notwithstanding. Fletcher was always amazed at how they would become players in his little charade, nodding agreeably at his optimistic, even breezy, prognosis. Fletcher sometimes had the feeling that they felt sorry for *him* because he didn't have a miracle to offer.

But his sixty-two-year-old patient, a millionaire businessman was having none of it. "What in hell are you trying to say?" he muttered.

Fletcher sighed. The man in the bed had been used to getting his way with men and machines all his life, and could not conceive of any obstacle that he could not move. He was fighting the only way he knew how. "I'm only saying that the location of the growth limited us as to how extensively we could proceed," Fletcher told him patiently. "But there's no reason to think negatively at this point."

The man with the pervasive malignancy spoke to Fletcher as he would to one of his construction superintendents. "I hear bullshit going on here," he said. "I don't have time for bullshit, Doctor. Are you trying to tell me that there's nothing more you can do?"

Fletcher handed the chart to a nurse. He remembered how a medical school professor, in a lecture about bedside manners, cautioned the class that an overbearing boor with a terminal illness didn't necessarily become less obnoxious facing death. "Of course not," Fletcher said quickly. "There are many nonsurgical avenues still open to us. There are new procedures being discovered every day that can bring periods of remission. We have one of the country's top staffs, and we'll use every medical trick known to man." It was not *his* fault, Fletcher wanted to say, that the tumor was not one of those neat, small walnuts, a self-contained lump that could be peeled off like a corn from a big toe. "And we must remember, that every day we see that spontaneous remission. A cure!"

The patient sneered, and Fletcher felt his contempt. A

heavy silence followed as the man looked disdainfully at the white-coated men and women gathered around his bed. "Well, Doctor, you can just let me out of this second-rate, cut-and-slice factory. I'm going someplace where they know what the fuck they're doing."

Fletcher felt his face burn, saw a nurse recoil at the patient's crude belligerency. He fought to keep his voice coolly professional. "Naturally, you are entitled to a second opinion. In fact, I would recommend it. But you'll have to stay with us for a few days. It would be risky to discharge you right now."

The patient, who moved mountains and built skyscrapers and bridges and sprawling shopping centers and convention centers of concrete and steel, rose to his elbows, his face mottled and defiant. "You know how much money I've given to this hospital? Two million dollars. Two goddamned million dollars. And what do I get for my money? A bunch of hand-wringers standing around telling me that all I can do is pray?"

A kind of blinding light flashed inside Howard Fletcher's head, and a red film in front of his eyes filtered the lights in the room and put everything and everybody at a distance. "Shut up, goddamn you," he heard himself growl. His voice rose several notches. "How much money you got, huh? Enough to buy yourself a benign tumor?" The hand of a resident tried to restrain him, but Fletcher pulled away. "You got a billion?" he shouted. "How about a trillion? Write a check. Buy yourself a cure! It's Tuesday; we got half-price days on Tuesday."

Fletcher put his face close to the startled patient while others tried to pull him back. "You don't have enough money, you son of a bitch. You're going to die, do you understand that? We're all going to die."

Hands were grabbing at Fletcher, steering him out the door. He allowed himself to be pulled into the hallway, where he stopped and shrugged off the white coats. His legs went rubbery, and he swayed for a moment. The nurses and residents backed off, and stood apart, watching him with a curious mix of shock and pity. Fletcher stumbled down the hall and into the elevator. He reached the parking lot; he kept on running, coatless in the cold rain.

Howard Fletcher pointed the nose of his car south and drove for ten hours, stopping only for gas.

He felt good behind the wheel, in control, watching unfamiliar scenery float past his windshield. The last two weeks had been a whirl of tedious and painful, though necessary, detail. He had paid off the maid, giving her six months' severance. They had hugged and both had wept. She had been with him and Ellen for eight years. He had closed his private practice abruptly and informed his neurosurgical colleagues at the medical school that he would be leaving. He had put the house up for sale, allowing the realtor wide bargaining latitude on the price.

With all that done, there had been nothing to keep him. But he had hung around for a few days, slouched in furniture draped like ghosts, and, occasionally forgetting himself, calling out to Ellen, and hearing his voice bounce back at him in the empty house. He spent his last mornings sitting in the large airy breakfast room, looking out at the backyard trees denuded by winter. Ellen and he used to take coffee in the window alcove each day before he went to work.

He waited to leave, for whatever reason, until the New Year. He passed New Year's Eve in a chair in front of a television set that he never bothered to turn on, sipping at whatever he came across in the liquor cabinet, not intending to get drunk, but accomplishing it anyway, perhaps for the first time since his army days.

CHAPTER 2

Byron Swinton edged cautiously into the dirty water hole, sloshing through the green slime and making little eddies with his fancy Italian fishing boots. He had been coming here for three weeks, and had come to loathe the trip. Describing this place as a water hole was putting the best possible description on the filthy puddles. His daily companions, the wildebeests and zebras, had come to accept his presence. They were more intent at quenching their thirst, jostling each other to suck a little moisture from the muddy slop.

Suddenly, two of the wildebeests raised their heads, put their noses to the wind and bolted away in full flight. The rest panicked. The beat of their hooves made the ground tremble beneath Swinton's boots. He swiveled his head, instantly alert, and shot a glance at his powerful rifle, propped thirty feet away on an anthill. He started for the gun, a weapon he was not sure he could aim properly. But then he stopped as he saw that the animals had halted their frantic flight and were now placidly milling around in the open plain a hundred yards away from the long grass and scrubby trees that encircled the water hole. Had they been spooked by something harmless, and now realized there was no lion?

Swinton turned back to the water hole. He groped through the layers of mosquito netting, and took a half-dozen small test tubes from his shirt pocket. Three of the tubes were half filled with a preservative solution. He skimmed a layer of water from the top of each tube, then quickly resealed them.

He clambered onto the bank and trudged laboriously to the anthill where he had left his rifle. He gasped for breath in the suffocating heat, which could be seen undulating on the horizon. From his new position, Swinton could see several yards in all directions. No, he satisfied himself, there were no cats. A false alarm. A few of the zebras and wildebeests were returning slowly, almost indolently to the water hole. Any cats in the neighborhood had probably eaten their fill for the day, and were napping in whatever shade they could find.

It was another ironic twist since he had arrived in this bleak, scrabbled land six weeks ago. The lions had proved to be only a minor annoyance. It was the tiny mosquito that he had to fear. The rifle, Swinton mused, was a joke. He rose from a squat and felt his knees creak. He held the tubes to the African sun, and nodded approvingly. There were mosquitoes and larvae captured in all the tubes.

The heat was making him dizzy. The temperature had topped out at 110 degrees, and it was time to get back. At this moment, from where he stood in Zaire, his thoughts went thousands of miles away, to Atlanta, Georgia, where his colleagues were sipping iced tea and talking theory in an air-conditioned room.

It was almost two miles back to camp. Swinton painstakingly began to adjust his clothing. He wore roomy trousers carefully tucked into his boots. The cuffs of his long-sleeved shirt were anchored inside the leather gloves. He put on his old-fashioned pith helmet, making sure the attached mosquito net covered his face and neck, and was tucked into his shirt. Over all of that came another layer of mosquito netting. He had to step into it as he would a spacesuit. The operation took several minutes, and when he was done not an inch of skin lay exposed. Each morning he checked himself carefully in the mirror at this tent. This morning, he had said aloud to his image: "You look like a beekeeper in drag."

The home office had rejected Swinton's request for a genuine, modern spacesuit with its own cooling system. Swinton, inside his cocoon, sniffed the sickening odor of the insect repellent that he had spread on his body this morning.

It was evening and the relentless sun had gone away for a few hours. But Byron Swinton couldn't take advantage of the cool breezes. He was inside his tent at the edge of the village, covered again from head to toe as he packaged the vials for mailing back to Atlanta and the Federal Center for Disease Control. Inside his mosquito-proof shroud, in his mosquito-proof tent, Swinton carried out his evening ritual, carefully labeling each tube and putting the specimens into the packing cases.

Once finished, he ate quickly, spooning the field-ration food from the can up and under the netting and into his mouth, maneuvering the utensil in a sweeping motion while he held the netting away from his body with his other hand.

It was past eleven o'clock when he finally fell onto his cot, making sure that the netting protected the bed from the smallest insect. Swinton rubbed himself with fresh repellent. He was becoming accustomed to smelling like a gas station.

He lay back, wishing the night could last forever. Dawn would come soon. That was the bad news. The good news was that his travels would soon be over, no more trotting around the globe in inhospitable places that never appeared in travel brochures. His son, Swinton thought guiltily, had grown into a young man watching his father board airplanes. The faint noises of the African night were making Swinton drowsy. He burrowed his head into the pillow, sedating himself with the comforting thought of his future life back in the stable and predictable surroundings of a research laboratory.

Swinton was always amazed at transatlantic phone calls. The operator at the Capetown Hilton had one of those sprightly British accents. She had put through his call to Atlanta in less than twenty seconds. The connection was unbelievably clear. He could hear his mother's voice as though she were in the same room. It was one of those times he wished he had gone into chemistry or engineering, or maybe physics. The physical sciences seemed so far ahead of medicine. And more exact.

"I'm bringing out some specimens, Mother," he told her. "I'm coming home. Can you and Robby meet me?"

"I don't think it's a good idea," she said. Her voice, as always, sounded flat and weary.

"Why not?" Despite the good connection, he fairly shouted it and told himself not to sound irritable. After eight weeks in the African bush, it was hard to imagine anyone in the States being tired.

"Robby's started school," his mother said. She paused. "I hate to pull him out, even for a day. He's having a little trouble, and I don't want his grades to suffer."

"What kind of trouble?"

"Oh, it's nothing serious. It's just that he's consumed with that silly laboratory of his. It has nothing to do with his schoolwork. But he'd rather putter around there than study."

His mother was whining again. He knew she regarded Robby's scientific talent as something silly. Swinton glanced around his suite at the Hilton. It was an expense-account luxury rarely granted to other government people. He caught his reflection in the huge mirror on the opposite wall. He looked terrible. Normally, he was one of those thin, rawboned men who look powerful without being muscular. But now he was merely skinny. His eyes bulged out of a face that was pinched and drawn. Eight weeks in the African sun, and no tan.

"Byron, are you still there?"

"Yes, yes, I'm here," he said. "Mother, I don't see how missing a day of his junior year in high school is going to make any difference in Robby's grades."

"Senior," she replied quickly. "A senior. My grandson's in his senior year."

"Yes," he said, recovering quickly. "Of course. I know that. In any case, don't discourage the boy from puttering, as you call it. Working in that lab is almost that boy's reason for living, you know, since Joan . . ." He cleared his throat. "Believe me, he's going to make us proud of him someday. He'll surprise you."

"Nothing my grandson does," his mother replied, "will ever surprise me, Byron."

There was silence and Byron didn't know what to say. His mother had tried her best with Robby. She'd moved in just after Robby's eleventh birthday, a week after her daughter-in-law's funeral. At the time, she'd been a godsend. After Joan's death, Robby had withdrawn into a total silence and Byron had been too disabled by grief to help him. He'd immersed himself in his work, spending evenings and weekends at the C.D.C.

Slowly, though, they'd both come out of it. Robby developed an interest in science, and began emerging from virtual autism. Byron had seized the opportunity to help his son and encouraged Robby's scientific interests, and Robby was soon a familiar figure every weekend at his father's C.D.C. lab. Within a few months, working together, they'd built a laboratory in the basement at home.

But a year later it had all changed. A new disease had been "discovered." Except it wasn't a new disease at all, but rather a disease that had been around for decades waiting to be found. And it was clearly the disease Joan Swinton had died from. The C.D.C. had overlooked it but a small research team of epidemiologists funded by the state of Connecticut discovered it, named it after a Connecticut town, described its effects on humans, its mode of transmission and its relatively simple cure. The nature of the disease made it an epidemiologist's dream. Or nightmare. The findings had been published in the lead article in *The New England Journal of Medicine* exactly one year after his wife's funeral.

Byron had hoped to keep it from Robby, but it had been too late. Robby had begun reading the epidemiology and medical journals on his own, and on the day of the article's publication, Robby had come to his father's office at C.D.C. during school hours. He'd stared at his father with accusing eyes. "That's why she had heart failure," was all he had said and he'd left before Byron could answer. They were the only words ever spoken on the subject.

"Hello? Hello, are you still there?"

Byron was startled back to the present. "Yes, Mother, I'm here. I'll call you when I get back to the U.S.," he said and hung up.

He sat for a long time, thinking. His wife had died from an epidemiologist's disease! The agonizing pain of her death had been rekindled by that particular irony. And he and Robby had become distant again. Byron once more immersed himself in his work, traveling constantly—this African assignment was typical. And Robby had retreated to the basement lab.

He had not remembered what grade Robby was in at school! It was time to put this tragedy behind them. No more trips. He would stay in Atlanta and be a father. His son, he realized, was growing up without him.

CHAPTER 3

An hour inside the Louisiana state line, Howard Fletcher, the BMW kicking up a cloud of dust, pulled into a rundown, two-pump gas station and killed the engine. The sign above the pump—"A Full Service Station"—made him chuckle. No one came out to greet him and nothing, it seemed, was moving in the afternoon sun. Fletcher gave the horn two short blasts, but still no one appeared. It looked like you served yourself at this full-service station. Fletcher climbed stiffly from the car, cramped from driving the last stretch nonstop in three hours. He poked the hose into the BMW and watched the numbers on the gas pump soar at a dizzying pace. His back ached and his arms felt like lead weights. He did a little exercise routine, working the kinks out of his neck and back.

"Y'all a long way from home."

Fletcher turned to see an old guy in an oil-spattered uniform pointing at the BMW's Illinois license plates. "Yeah," Fletcher acknowledged.

The man walked admiringly around the car, wiping his oil-soaked hands on an oil-soaked rag. "I reckon this piece of machinery set you back a few bucks."

"A few," Fletcher replied.

The attendant said, "Hmmm," and spat a brown stream of tobacco at Fletcher's feet. He stuck a finger a knuckle deep into a nose that was peeling from the sun. "On a vacation?" he asked.

"You might say that." Fletcher squinted out over the bayou, watching the heat waves ripple across the concrete highway. "Little warm for this time of year, isn't it?"

The attendant laughed. "Didn't notice. I was born two miles from here. My whole damned life has been living inside a piece of land 'bout ten miles square," he said. " 'Cept for the war, I wouldn't knowed the world was round." He thought for a moment. "I was at Anzio." He clucked. "Bloody mess. A lotta people would like to forget about the war. Not me. I'll be seventy-five years old next birthday and, hell, for me, it was the only thing in my life that ever got the blood circulating."

"I suppose," Fletcher said, "that war is glamorous for some."

"You ever in the service?" the attendant asked.

"Yeah. Medic, First Air Cav, 1969. Vietnam."

The old guy showed brown teeth. "Pitiful is what that war was. Goddamned pitiful." He shook his head and spat again, shifting the wad to the other side of his mouth. "I felt sorry for you boys. Gettin' shot up in them rice paddies and not goin' no place. Shoulda nuked them Communists and got the thing over with."

Fletcher replaced the nozzle in the pump. "I owe you twenty-eight bucks even," he said. "Goddamn car drinks it like water." He had forgotten how to swear in Chicago, and realized cursing at the BMW was an unconscious slip in a patronizing attempt to establish rapport with the old man.

"A camel'd be better out here," the attendant muttered. He eyed Fletcher for a moment. "Yeah. O.K. Whyn't you pull your car off to the side over there and come in and set awhile. Looks like you could use a break. Want a beer?"

Fletcher was grateful. "Well, hell, that'd be nice. Thanks."

It seemed to Fletcher that the beer, out of the cold can was just about the best he'd ever tasted. "Hits the spot," he said appreciatively. He slurped, then wiped the foam from his lips. The two of them sat inside the station, looking out the screen door, their feet propped on empty milk carton crates.

The station was a scene out of *The Grapes of Wrath*. There were two calendars on the wall, one a 1991, courtesy of a local tractor dealer, and the other a Petty Girl, circa 1945. Inside a glass display case, coated with grime, were a few candy bars, a box of cigars and some lighter flints. Atop a counter was the first punchboard—a quarter a punch—that Fletcher had seen since he was a kid.

"Is it O.K.?" Fletcher asked his host.

"What's that?"

"Well, drinking out here in plain sight. If the owner came in—"

The old man snorted gleefully. "This is Louisiana, state of the Big Easy. Shit, we carry guns at wedding receptions. Besides, I'm the owner." He took off his crushed, red-leather cap, and took a long swig. "More's the pity."

They sat in silence for a time—their chairs tilted against the wall, balanced precariously on the back legs. Fletcher felt the tension of the long ride leave him. On the wall, between the two calendars was a mounted display of military campaign ribbons and decorations. Fletcher recognized the Combat Infantry Badge and the Purple Heart.

As the sun sank, his melancholy rose. He and the grease monkey had more in common than Fletcher liked to think about. Vietnam was a long distance and twenty years away. Funny, Chicago now seemed at an equal remove.

Unlike his newfound friend, Fletcher didn't consider *his* war the high point of his life. To him, all the world's lunacy had been packaged and perfected and dropped into that hot green hell that had no good guys or bad guys. Success had been measured by the body count, and the enemy was a shadow, a frail but zealous patriot with a cause. Fletcher had watched newer and newer American military toys introduced into the fighting much as Hitler had done when he used the Spanish Civil War as a dress rehearsal for World War II.

Fletcher had watched as the grunts, those still in one piece, walked away from the jungle after a year, and were whisked back to a place called home, a spot that seemed, for many, as remote as the moon. He supposed, looking back, that he owed the Army something. It had been the catalyst that propelled him into medical school after his discharge. Of all the sights and sounds of Vietnam, the work of the surgeons and nurses had awed him, and provided the only sanity in that lunatic world. He had helped pick up bloody lumps and drop them in helicopters, knowing, just knowing, that nothing or no one on God's earth could save them, and then later see miracles performed. He'd seen his first brain exposed to the air, and six days later watched as the guy grinned from a hospital bed.

The shadows were lengthening outside the gas station. Fletcher's new friend left his chair to pop the tops on a couple more beers. He handed one to Fletcher, who nodded his thanks.

Settling down in his chair again, the old man put his hand to his mouth, too late to muffle a resounding belch. "You're from Illinois, huh?"

"Yeah," Fletcher replied. "Chicago."

"Chicago," the station owner said distantly. He sighed mournfully. "Damn nice town," he said. "Exciting." He glanced sideways at Fletcher. "From all I hear, that is." Fletcher grunted noncommittally. "Whadcha do there? In Chicago, I mean."

Reflecting, Fletcher supposed he owed the old guy some repayment for his hospitality. The man's vision of space and time had a large gap in the middle. He could only see from this two-pump gas station to Anzio and back again. The world ended at the horizon where, for all he knew, the bayou went on forever. Finally Fletcher said, "Well, I was a doctor. I mean, I *am* a doctor."

The old man stirred. "No kiddin'?" he said with a certain

childlike wonder, a tone Fletcher had heard many times and which made him want to groan. That layman's godlike reverence that was thrust upon the medical profession. If the old guy only knew how many people who called themselves 'doctor' should be pumping gas at the two-pump station. Most sick people get well or die, with or without us, Fletcher thought. He wanted to say how he had seen some surgeries performed that the gas station owner could have accomplished with a bent spoon and a tin can. But the old guy wouldn't have believed him.

Fletcher took an oblique glance at his companion who was gazing distastefully around his shabby station. The distance between them, Fletcher noted, had widened appreciably. He sighed. The mystique of his profession had ruined their easy camaraderie. Fletcher polished off his beer and got to his feet, placing the empty can beside his chair on the oil-smeared concrete floor. He patted his stomach. "Good," he announced. "Much obliged."

The station owner roused himself, and crumpled his beer can with one big hand. "Movin' on?" he asked.

"Guess so. Thought I might drive into town. Look over Charlemaigne a bit," Fletcher said, wondering how much it had changed. "Getting a little tired of traveling."

The old man followed Fletcher out the door, stopped and peered up at the fast-fading sun. "You might be able to give 'em a hand," he said.

Fletcher turned. "How's that?"

"The town's a little short on doctors since old Doc Johnson died. Checked out with his boots on. More'n eighty years old. Took care of three generations of my family. The town's down to five doctors now."

"Five? In the whole town?"

"The truth," the old man replied. "Understand the hospital has to send patients outta town."

Fletcher nodded and slid behind the wheel. "Thanks," he called out. "Thanks for the beer." The old man waved, a casual half-salute. Fletcher started the engine of the BMW.

He sat for a moment, reluctant to drive away. "You know," he said finally, "that World War II was one we had to fight." He searched for words. "Had no choice. Might even call it a crusade. Goddamn right."

The old guy nodded vigorously and brightened.

CHAPTER 4

The seventeen-year-old boy, her student, had the longest, softest eyelashes she had ever seen, not to mention the most disconcerting way of looking at you, eyes wide and penetrating, set in an angelic face. He had a full mouth, the corner of his upper lip pulled back in a slight, perpetual curl. It was just short of a smile, as though he were carrying around some huge private joke.

He was too pretty to be a boy, if pretty was the word. The facial bones were too delicate to be called handsome. But he was an indifferent student, achieving far below his potential, a fact that made Miss Lorlene unreasonably angry at times though he was hardly unique these days. Miss Lorlene had seen many merely go through the academic motions.

She watched the boy intently as the rest of the class bent their heads to the grammar test, her lips set as she watched him stare out the window. Miss Lorlene did not believe in coddling her students. She prided herself on her reputation. She had once given a failing grade to the son of Atlanta's superintendent of schools and then had steadfastly held her ground against pressure to reverse her decision.

The boy was gazing around the room again, and Miss Lorlene knew she must talk to him. The hour had gone quickly and the bell signaling the end of class would ring shortly. Miss Lorlene pushed back from her desk, the squeak of the chair bringing up a few heads. She motioned them to continue with the test, tapping her wristwatch to indicate that there was still time. She walked quietly on the balls of her feet to the last row, and bent over the boy's desk. "Robert Swinton," she whispered. He turned his head slowly. "Could you stay for just a moment after class? I want to speak to you about something."

The long lashes flicked at her languidly, his eyes roaming over her face. He nodded. "Sure," he murmured, his tone just a hair from disrespect. Miss Lorlene returned to her desk, feeling an inexplicable warmth on her face. When she sat again to face the class, the boy's eyes were upon her. She looked away and patted her hair, finding it all in place. The bell in the hallway blared its raucous summons to the next class.

Miss Lorlene was forceful when she told the boy about her concerns, not wanting to minimize the seriousness of his situation. He stood next to her desk, his face remaining placid as always. He had an uncanny ability to put you on the defensive without saying a word. He took a long time to answer.

"Why, Miss Lorlene," he said at last. "I knew that I wasn't doing as well as I'd like, but I certainly didn't think I was in any danger of failing." His forehead wrinkled, and she felt a certain empathy when she read the hurt in his eyes. "I've certainly been trying," he said.

It was a lie, she knew, but she let it pass. Lying was part of the teenage makeup. "I'm sure you have, Robert," she heard herself saying, "but you have to work harder." She did not add that it was probably too late to avoid a failing mark. There had also been several absences.

He leaned on her desk, his face drawing near hers. "Miss Lorlene, there's something you must understand. English, of all my subjects, gives me the most trouble. I know I should give it more attention. But, you see, it's not my strength. I'm a scientist. I hope to follow my father, using my talents to fight disease. Microbiology is my goal. It doesn't seem fair that I should be denied getting into college just because I'm not proficient in a subject that I will never have to use professionally."

Miss Lorlene hid her amusement at his youthful pretentiousness. She stood and smoothed her dress over her hips. The boy towered over her. He must be well over six feet, she guessed. They grew them so tall these days. "Yes, but Robert—"

"Ma'am," he interrupted, "I've been meaning to ask you something. I've thought about it for a long time. Even before you asked to speak to me." He paused, reflecting on the ceiling. Finally he looked down at his shoes and then at Miss Lorlene. "I was wondering," he said shyly, "if you might give me a little extra help. Outside of school hours, I mean. I'm trying to understand this stuff as well as I can. But I could get better marks; I know I could. I think I can do much better."

It was a major speech for the boy. It exposed his vulnerability, and her heart went out to him. "Of course, Robert, of course. I'm sure we can arrange something."

CHAPTER 5

Howard Fletcher drove along the back roads around Charlemaigne, revisiting spots that dredged up vignettes of his adolescence. Foliage had grown thick at the entrance to the dead-end farm lane where beer parties were staged after the Friday night football games. One night, somebody had produced a bottle of schnapps to complement the beer, and he hadn't stopped puking until the sun came up.

He drove past the stone quarry where he and his 'gang' had dumped the potted plants they'd swiped off a front porch that Halloween night. And there was the orchard in back of Leslie Hunt's greenhouse, where young Howie Fletcher thought he might have lost his virginity. It was all over so fast, he would go to his grave never quite sure, what with Snooky Jabal squirming under him and giggling all the time like he was some big joke. Afterwards, Snooky, gracious Snooky, had thanked him for "a nice time." Snooky's dad, no longer able to ignore the rumors about the contour of his daughter's heels, eventually shipped her off to Georgia Tech, where she snared the son of a man who owned quite a bit of land down around Macon. Snooky, Howard heard later, fell into contented domesticity, rarely to be heard from again.

He drove back into town, flicking on the air conditioning as the car poked its way through the quiet streets. The day was a sticky 80 degrees that felt more like 95, high for mid-January, as he remembered it. A radio report that morning out of New Orleans smugly told how Chicago had received eight inches of snow overnight. The office workers and bankers and advertising executives would be mushing their way down State Street while the wind off the lake knifed into them and made their eyes water.

Howard took his foot off the gas pedal, and let the BMW coast. Everything was familiar and yet strange. It was true what they said: everything shrank. The streets were narrower than he remembered, the houses smaller. The Ophelia Mann Memorial Park, once a vast playground, was now a scrubby patch of green at the edge of town, hemmed in by a cemetery and a tractor dealership. Several stores had changed hands, but had stayed in the family. The Holiday Inn was new, and some of the majestic old homes were dressed in modern aluminum siding—lovely, aging ladies with taut and shiny face lifts.

The Civil War statues and plaques still stood guard over the old courthouse, paying homage to Lee, Stuart, Jackson, Longstreet and a bunch of other good old boys who, everyone in town believed, would have kicked Yankee ass if they hadn't been so outnumbered.

Howard turned down Carmona Street and into the old neighborhood. He pulled to a quiet stop in front of the old Fletcher house and sat for a moment, letting the BMW idle. The place looked shabby, revealing its age. Maybe it had always looked that way, but he had never noticed while he was growing up. Two dirty-faced kids, no more than six years old, played in the small front yard. For a moment, Howard toyed with the idea of knocking on the door and asking the present occupants if he could just look around inside for a minute. But he decided against it, and drove off.

He supposed Carmona Street was in the wrong neighborhood, on "the wrong side of the tracks," as they still said down here. But when he was a kid no one had ever bothered to tell him that. Townspeople stayed in the house they were born in, or moved across the street or next door, to be close-by to their folks. You went through your life in, or near, the place you were born.

In Chicago, you lived in a different place for each stage of your life. When you were young and without children and first starting work, you lived on the near north shore area, cliff-dwelling in the high-rises as close to the lake as you could afford. With success—and of course, everybody was successful—you inched northward: Park Ridge or Morton Grove for lower middle-class, Evanston for upper-middle since it was closer to the water. Then with Great Success, you moved farther north, still clinging to the shoreline all the way to the mansions in Kenilworth or Winnetka. He and Ellen had lived in Winnetka for a year and a half.

Howard was jerked back to the present by the squeal of tires, but it was too late to avoid the pickup truck that suddenly filled his windshield. He hit the brakes, also much too late. The force of the impact threw him forward, the sudden stop propelling his face into the steering wheel. He cried out sharply and moaned, cursing his stupidity, feeling more embarrassment than pain. He had glided through the red light as though it hadn't been there.

Two very angry men in jeans and feed-store caps bounded from the pickup and surveyed the truck's caved-in side. Then they made for Howard's car, which sat steaming, water boiling from a ruptured radiator. Howard sighed and slid out of the car, wincing as he put a hand to the swelling knot on his forehead. It would be a blue-and-yellow beauty by morning.

He put his arms out at his sides, shaking his head at the men in a signal that acknowledged his blame. The two bore down on him, red-faced, and Howard wondered if people still got physical over traffic accidents in this part of the country.

Just as he was about to invoke a plea for mercy, a black-and-white police car materialized and rolled to a stop in the middle of the intersection, its oscillating red light a warning to other drivers. Out stepped an officer in a brown uniform with gold piping and epaulets on his short-sleeved shirt. He sauntered—that was the only word that fit—up to the two vehicles, fused under the stoplight. Fletcher leaned against his battered car and waited patiently. The cop made his way across the street, nudging broken glass and twisted chrome with his toe. The two guys from the pickup truck descended on the officer, waving their arms wildly. "That a-hole ran that red light just as bold as you please," one of them said, pointing an accusatory finger at Howard. "He came through there without so much as a by-your-leave or kiss-my-ass."

"Simmer down, Ferlin," the officer said. Great, Howard thought, the guy is friends with the cop, probably bosom buddies. The cop walked up to Howard. "That about the way it happened, mister?" He was lean with thinning brown hair, and a thick mustache. About his own age, Howard guessed. The cop squinted his eyes against the sun, wrinkling up his face. He wasn't wearing a hat, and Howard noted, foolishly, his neck wasn't red. The cop smiled pleasantly. The tone of his voice was laid back, a syrupy drawl without the policeman's usual condescension.

"Yessir, officer," Howard said. "All my fault. Wasn't paying attention. I ran the light."

The cop smiled again. "You sure beat the odds. There ain't but a half-dozen stoplights in the whole town." He looked over Fletcher's mangled BMW. "That's a pretty fancy automobile to be playing tag with these boys' old beat-up pickup. You were in an uneven fight, I'd say."

"My insurance will take care of everything, officer. Or if they'd like, they can get the truck repaired and I'll write them a check."

"Just like that, huh?" the cop said.

Howard wanted to bite off his tongue. Shit, he was coming off like a rich Yankee carpetbagger buying his way out of trouble. "What I meant to say, officer, is any way they want to handle it is O.K. with me. I'll be around. I'm not going anywhere."

"Not back to Illinois?" the cop asked, his eyes going to the BMW's license plates.

"Uh, no. I plan on sticking around awhile."

The officer's eyes roved over Howard. "I see," he said finally. "Well, I'll need your driver's license and registration. I'm gonna have to issue you a citation."

"Yes, of course," Howard said, fumbling for his wallet. He got the other forms out of his glove compartment and handed them over.

"You wait right here," the cop said. "I'll go over and cool off these two young tigers." He looked up at the sun. "Which won't be easy. Hottern' a bitch. Humid as hell for January."

Howard watched the cop amble up to the two men standing alongside their pickup truck and talk to them quietly for a few moments, putting a comradely hand on the shoulder of one of them. Apparently mollified for the time being, the two climbed back into the truck. The cop waved goodbye to them as they drove off, then walked back to where Howard stood. "They can drive that old pickup away," he said. "I'm afraid that's out of the question with your automobile. I'll get a wrecker over here, and have it towed to a garage. I'll give you a lift wherever you want to go." He took a forefinger and skimmed off the sweat that had gathered over his eyes. "Don't know why I stay in this evil country."

The cop leaned on the hood of the BMW, writing out a ticket. "Gonna make this for just running the light," he told Howard. "Coulda been more."

"I appreciate that," Howard said.

The cop stopped, his ballpoint pen poised. He waved Howard's license and registration. "Fletcher," he said. "Howard Fletcher." He was comparing Howard with the photo on the license. "Howie Fletcher?" Howard nodded. "Thought you looked familiar. It's been a few years."

"Yes, it has," Howard said, trying to place the man. "I'm sorry, I—"

"You don't remember me," the officer said. "Yeah, well, I was a couple of years behind you in school. Our folks knew each other pretty well, though. I'm Decatur. Beauford Decatur. I'm the sheriff around here." He paused. "But I don't brag on it much."

They shook hands. "Forgive me for not remembering you, Sheriff, er, Beauford. It's been twenty years. Except for when I came back for the funeral. That was just a flying trip. In and out."

Decatur nodded. "Yeah, sorry to hear about your momma."

"That was almost ten years ago," Howard said.

"Uh-huh. Time gets away from you." Decatur fanned himself with his ticket book. "You say you're gonna be around for a while?"

"Well, yeah, I think so. I'm giving some thought to opening a practice here. You see, I'm a doctor."

"Uh-huh, I guess I did hear that you went away to school to be a doctor." Decatur studied Howard for a moment, then looked around at the debris littering the street. "Gotta get somebody down here to clean this up." He handed Howard back his license and registration. "I'll get on the horn and call that wrecker for you." He started for the patrol car, then stopped and turned. "You oughta have a doctor look at that goose egg on your head."

Howard smiled. The sheriff practiced Southern droll.

CHAPTER 6

The boy stretched his arms over his head and yawned. They had been at it for almost two hours, and time was about up. She looked at him, close to her on the couch, and watched those eyelashes sweep over his cheeks as he yawned. "You did very well, Robert," she said. He smiled at her. "You must be a little more alert to your antecedent agreements," she heard herself saying. It was not good to leave them complacent.

"Antecedents," he said in a soft, remote tone. "Three weeks ago I didn't know there was such an animal."

She laughed merrily. "But you do now, Robert. And much more, too. You have been hiding your light under a bushel."

"And I have you to thank for bringing it out," he said solemnly.

He could be so grave sometimes. She laughed self-consciously. "You just needed a little push."

He gazed around the room while she studied him, noting how smooth his skin was. He turned to her, his face so close she seemed to drown in those black pupils. "I'm your project for the semester?" he asked, although in tone it was not a question.

Miss Lorlene felt a catch in her throat, an altogether silly reaction. "I suppose you might call yourself a project," she said with a forced lilt. "But I'm just a teacher trying to do her job." She hesitated, then said. "You are such a special student, Robert."

He nodded. "But I feel," he said after a time, "that we've come to be more than just student and teacher. I would like to think that we have become friends." He lowered his eyelashes. "I would like to be your friend."

He looked so vulnerable. She put her hand on his shoulders. "Of course I'm your friend, Robert." She added: "I hope I'm a friend to all my students."

He brightened. "Good," he said, arranging the books in the crook of his arm. He kissed her on the cheek, a fleeting brush of his lips, the contact so light that Miss Lorlene would go to bed that night unconvinced that it had really happened. But it had left a warm spot on her face. It happened so quickly that he was out the door before she could react. "Same time Tuesday," he called to her.

CHAPTER 7

Byron Swinton watched the face of his son twist in despair, secretly amused at how the young regarded each small disappointment as a Shakespearian tragedy.

"Grandmother has taken my car, Dad. Grounded me. She knew I had planned on going to New Orleans. She's just being spiteful."

"Why New Orleans again, Robby? I've only been back from Africa two months and I'll bet you've been there every weekend." He winked at his pouting son. "Not enough girls in Atlanta for you?"

The boy rolled his brown eyes theatrically in the time-honored look of the teenager that told the world how dense parents were. "It has nothing to do with girls, Dad. This is strictly scientific. It's part of a study I'm doing."

"I see," Byron said. He wished the boy weren't so stifled by his grandmother sometimes. Robby wasn't wild, just imaginative, a creative spirit that needed room to grow, and now his grandmother was constantly badgering him, brooding about him, hovering over him like a hawk. Recently she had even suggested that Robby see a psychiatrist. Byron had nipped that in the bud. He buzzed his secretary to tell her to hold all his calls. "O.K., Robby, so your grandmother has taken away your car."

"Yeah, locked up the keys."

"For what reason?"

"She says I'm away from home too much and I spend too much time down in the basement."

Byron tried to look stern, but didn't quite pull it off. "Well, your grandmother does have a point. You've been running off a lot lately. She worries about you, is all. She loves you. God knows what we'd have done without her these past few years." He got to his feet and came around to give his son a playful chuck on the arm. "Now, what's this scientific expedition you're planning?"

"It's a study I'm doing, Dad. I'm looking over the terrain, studying it for its epidemiologic potential—the crowd density, the population mobility, the sewage system."

"The sewage system? You're going to New Orleans at pre-Mardi Gras time to study the sewage system?"

"Yes, Dad, it's fascinating, especially for intestinal diseases. Your lab people should know that. The entire city is lower than the water table. There's no place like it in America. They even have above-ground tombs. If you dig down a few inches, you hit sea water. It's corroding the sewage pipes. I've read all about it. It's like Paris during the typhus epidemic, before they built the sewers, like London before the plague. The sewage problems, the crowding— the demographics are all there. I want to study it for myself."

"But you've spent weekends down there all fall. Isn't that enough time?"

Robby shook his head quickly. "I've just been doing background work. I need to get down there now, right after New Year's. It's when the pre-Mardi Gras parades really begin. I told you I needed to study crowd densities, and the crowds start to build up, with more and more parades, from New Year's until Fat Tuesday, just before Ash . . ."

"Okay, okay, I understand." Byron held up his hand in the stop position. "Well . . ." He chuckled as he watched his son brighten, instantly aware, Byron knew, when the old man was wavering.

"Please, Dad. It's for a biology paper I'm writing about the great epidemics of the world. You know I've been trying to pull up my grade. A firsthand report would probably get me an A."

Byron nodded. "Robby, you're getting A's in all your science courses. But you're close to flunking English. Going to New Orleans is not going to help your English grade." Robby grimaced with distaste. "Look, son, you're a fourth-generation legacy at Harvard. The only thing that will keep you out will be screwing up again in English. Make you a deal. You pull up that English grade, you can have the car all you want." He watched his son sigh. The kid is handsome, Byron thought. Those genes from his mother. God knows, she was beautiful. Fortunately, Robby had inherited *his* brains. With that combination, the boy could be anything he wanted to be. People just had to get out of his way. Gifted people, Byron told himself, had to be free to operate outside the conventional limits. "Well, do we have a deal?"

The boy shifted his feet. "Oh, Dad, don't worry, I'll get that grade in English pulled up. It's just that I've been awfully busy with my science projects. And Grandmother makes such a big deal out of everything, getting on me for making a mess in the basement."

Byron patted his son on the shoulder. "Now, don't get into a battle with your grandmother."

"Well," the boy asked, "do I get it?"

"What?"

"The car. So I can get to New Orleans this weekend?" He fixed his brown eyes on his father. "I'll get right on that English when I get back. In fact, I'll promise you an A."

Byron chuckled. "Tell her I said to give you the car keys," he told Robby. "Tell her I said it was important. After all, we scientists have to stick together."

Byron walked his son to the main entrance of the C.D.C. and watched the boy jog to the bus stop.

It was a four-block walk from the bus to the Swinton home, and by the time Robby reached the front door he was seething. He stepped into the foyer. "Grandmother?" he called. "You home?"

His grandmother presently came into view. "Is that you, Robby?"

He did not move to meet her. "Come here," he ordered. His grandmother moved toward him warily, trying to sense his mood. She was immaculately groomed. She was *always* immaculately groomed, the boy thought. What for, he wondered, the six o'clock news? That would be about the depth of her comprehension. The thought of his stay-at-home grandmother getting dressed up for a newscast forced a tight smile to his lips.

His grandmother misinterpreted the smile, and she smiled in return. "What is it, Robby?"

His hand shot out to cup her cruelly under the chin, making her cry out. "Listen, you sanctimonious bitch," he said behind clenched teeth, "I've just been down to see Dad, and he says you are to return the car keys to me at once."

With her jaw locked in her grandson's hand, it was almost impossible to speak. "Please, Robby, you're hurting me." Although it was heartbreaking to hear his menacing tone, it was no longer a surprise.

He relaxed his grip, and patted her on the cheek where the impressions of his fingertips would linger for several minutes. He continued patting her face lightly. He saw the terror in her eyes, and he gloated. "I'm going downstairs to check on something," he said in a soft, measured cadence, his eyes flat. He smiled crookedly. "I'll be back in fifteen minutes. That's when I'll expect you to produce the car keys." He stepped around her and was gone.

His grandmother sagged. She watched the stranger, the son of her son, bound down the stairs, and felt reality slip from her. She thought she could easily be losing her mind. Which would be a satisfying refuge under the circumstances.

CHAPTER 8

Robby Swinton hurried down the basement stairs, slamming the door behind him. He hit the light switch at the foot of the stairs.

It was more a cellar than a basement. It was, in fact, a dank, unfinished room of poured cement, and represented only a small part of the area beneath the large Swinton home in Atlanta. Robby, after spending prolonged periods in the low-ceilinged room, would emerge hunched over and blinking. The washer, dryer and sink had been moved upstairs years ago when it was decided to convert the area into a playroom for him. His parents never knew it, but Robby never "played." He did, however, go there alone to sit and think. The toys and sandbox and expensive electric train with its hundreds of feet of track had long since been donated to charity, in mint condition.

The furnace and air-conditioning unit occupied one wall. Workbenches were arranged along the other three walls. The over-bright lighting came from long fluorescent lamps that hung from the ceiling to just three feet above the workbenches. It left the center of the room totally dark, with the workbenches bathed in light, like those dark aquarium buildings where only the water tanks are lighted.

The room seemed built around a boxlike structure on the center workbench. It had a heavy front door, tightly sealed, and resembled a large microwave oven. A simple strip of white adhesive tape on the door bore the printed words: AEROBIC INCUBATOR. There was a small oxygen tank next to it and a vacuum pump. In a corner, where the workbenches joined, there was a larger, heavier box. It looked like a dishwasher and, in fact, had been hooked up to the washing machine outlets. It was an autoclave, which steam-cleaned the instruments and materials.

In the other corner, the basement toilet had been replaced by a disposal basin in which the drainpipe was the size of a large coffee can. A grapefruit could be flushed down it and directly into the Atlanta sewer system.

Along the back of each workbench were arrayed rows of cages, which emitted faint chattering. Most of the cages contained rats, but there were also a few mice, guinea pigs and rabbits. Above the cages, along the three walls and extending to the ceiling, was shelving that held test tubes, Bunsen burners, jars, and glass beakers of every size and shape. But mainly the shelves were filled with petri dishes, dozens of them. Flat, clear plastic containers, they were three inches in diameter and one-half-inch deep. They were stacked like small ashtrays along every unused space.

Robby, bent like Quasimodo, moved under the low ceiling to the central incubator. Blinking under the concentrated cone of light, he sat upon the low stool, and he opened the door of the incubator, its interior heat flooding his face. Inside were five stacks of petri dishes. Covering the bottom of each dish was a thick red waxy material, a mixture of protein broth, vitamins, certain enriching sugars and animal blood. It was used by Robby, as it was the world over, to incubate, nurture and grow colonies of bacteria.

Methodically, he began sorting them, pulling out a stack at a time, and examining each dish before replacing it. Within minutes, the boy's face twisted with rage. "Goddammit!" he shouted. "No growth. I must have put in too much ampicillin." Halfway through the fourth stack he began working quickly, shuffling the plastic dishes in and out of the incubator, muttering curses. He pulled out the last stack, and one slipped from his hand and crashed to the floor. He yelled, a frustrated shriek, and swept the rest of the stack to the cement floor. A putrid odor rose from the shattered dishes.

Robby sat unmoving for a moment, watching the red molasses-like agar ooze around the shards of petri dishes. Was it contaminated? He had inoculated all of them with *Salmonella enteridites*, then put in gradually increasing doses of antibiotic. But that was a week ago and still there was no growth. They should have developed resistance, started to form spores. He checked the incubator for any cracks and openings. It was then that he noticed the thermometer inside the incubator—the reading was 36.2 degrees Celsius. He double-checked it. That was the problem! The incubator temperature should be exactly 37° C. The temperature control was malfunctioning. How the hell was he supposed to grow bacteria with such unreliable equipment? The incubator was a gift from his father, who had 'borrowed' it from the C.D.C. Some gift! But then it occurred to him that the temperature might have fallen temporarily because he had left the door open so long. He should have checked it when he started. He had been distracted, goddamn his grandmother.

He surveyed the mess on the floor. There could be some kind of bacterial growth down there. He'd have to inject an animal to keep the bacterial strain going. With nothing in the petri dishes, he'd have to use a rat. At least the animal would keep a constant body temperature. He eased himself from the stool and went back to the incubator from which he extracted a large syringe with "*Salmonella Enteridites*— pure strain—property C.D.C.*" printed on the barrel. It was filled with a moldy, yellow-green liquid. He carefully examined the syringe. The liquid agar was no longer red. Over the past few weeks it had been replaced by the yellow-green slime. Furious, Robby banged the top of the incubator, seemingly impervious to the pain of his skinned knuckles. The bacteria in the syringes were using up all the agar. The *Salmonella* would keep multiplying rapidly, doubling their population every thirty minutes until they used up all the nutrients and died of starvation. He had to get them subcultured—transferred to another medium—if not the blood agar in a petri dish, then an animal. The animal would be easier, a perfect culture medium. But the infection would kill it, and he would have to sacrifice it in a few days and recover the bacteria again. It would only buy some time, and in the meantime, he could try to grow them again in the petri dishes and add in the antibiotic more slowly. He pulled on a pair of thick rubber gloves and opened the nearest cage. He pulled Champ from the cage. Robby always named the last rat in the cage "Champ." Rats, he had learned, had a pecking order, with one emerging as dominant. It would take for itself the most food, thriving and thereby growing to be the largest, becoming even more dominant. Robby always honored it by selecting it last. It would be honored by being selected for the most important inoculation.

Robby grabbed the rat behind its head, turned it belly up and quickly thrust the needle into its soft underside. A thick brown material oozed into the barrel of the syringe. "Dirty, fuckin' luck," he shouted. His outburst set off a momentary scurrying and chattering in the other cages. "That does it! A lousy end to a perfectly goddamn lousy day. Not even a fuckin' bacteria can make it around here."

Robby pulled the syringe from the abdomen of the rat. He contemplated the rodent for a moment. Then calmly he broke its neck with a quick turn of his hand and threw it into the disposal basin. He examined the syringe. It was half-filled with brown rat shit. It meant he had pushed the syringe too far into the abdomen. The injection was supposed to enter only the sterile peritoneal cavity where the *Salmonella* could grow unmolested. But he'd entered the bowel, and by perforating the intestine, the trillions of organisms living there would give the rat overwhelming peritonitis and kill it before his weak strain of *Salmonella* could get a foothold.

If that wasn't enough, he'd contaminated his syringe, his last one. Robby stomped around the room. "It's full of shit," he screamed down at the disposal basin as he threw in the syringe. "Just like everything else around here."

He went back to the stool. His neck had stiffened from the prolonged stooping under the low ceiling. His back ached. He had, he knew, committed the unpardonable error, an error made by only the most amateur of bacteriologists. He'd allowed his specimen strain to die out. He'd used too high a concentration of antibiotic in the petri dishes.

He felt shame. Mistakes were not tolerated. Now he would have to grovel before his goddamn father. He needed a tougher strain of the bug, one that wouldn't die out so easily when cultured with antibiotics.

CHAPTER 9

Athough the office door was open, Robby paused to rap lightly.

Byron Swinton looked up in surprise. "Why, Robby! What is it? Is something wrong? Why aren't you in school?"

Robby smiled sheepishly. "Oh, Dad, I took the day off." He pointed at the lettering on the door. "Just thought I'd come down and have a chat with 'Byron Swinton, M.D., Ph.D., Director of Intestinal Pathogen Laboratory.'"

Byron looked pleased and laughed heartily. "Buttering up your old man? Robby, did you ever consider going on the road to sell snake oil?" They both laughed.

Robby looked down and dug a sneaker into the thick pile of his father's office carpeting. "Yeah, I skipped school today," he said. "It's just one day. I was bored. Thought I'd just drop in on you." He shrugged, appearing embarrassed. "I was thinking, maybe we could do something together."

Byron was momentarily taken back. "What? I mean, of course I'm delighted. You and I haven't been together enough, son. My fault, of course. Flitting all over the globe, cholera in Bangladesh, typhoid in the Congo, running off every time some Third World country catches diarrhea." He smiled broadly. "Well, now we've got a chance to make up for all those times, right? What would you like to do?"

"I'd like to stay right here, Dad. Go through your lab with you again."

Byron threw up his hands in mock exasperation. "Lord, what a single-minded young man! You've been through that lab a half-dozen times lately." He clapped his hands, and waved for Robby to follow him. "Okay, come on, Pasteur." They went out the door and down the hallway, Byron chuckling.

Inside the lab, Robby bounded in front of his father, squealing like a child at Christmas and pointing to the incubator. "Dad, this one's terrific. Look at it. Fourteen cubic feet, just the right size. Just big enough to fit in our basement."

Byron hushed him. "Hey, buddy, let's not broadcast where we get that equipment for your basement, okay?" The boy turned and exchanged a conspiratorial smile with his father. Robby had pointed out a refrigerator-sized incubator with the words "Salmonella Specimens" scrawled across the front in magic marker. Byron looked around the lab. "Well, let me see what I can do," he said. "But, Robby, are you really certain your temperature control is malfunctioning?"

"Dad, I've told you twice. It's thirty-six degrees one minute and forty-two the next. I shouldn't have to tell you how important a steady thirty-seven degrees is. Besides, my incubator is too small. I can only fit in a few petris. I try to subculture a few of them, the temperature goes blooey, and the bugs die."

Byron lowered his voice. "Uh, Robby, you haven't let that specimen strain—the one I let you sneak out of here—die out, have you?"

Robby swelled up indignantly. "Of course not."

"I'm glad of that. No matter what a big deal it says I am on my office door, I'd get fixed in a minute if I ever got caught sneaking out pathogenic bacteria."

"Jesus, Dad, you think I'm some kind of an amateur?

I've got my bacteria alive and growing. Despite the inferior equipment, my bugs are thriving."

"All right, all right," Byron said, "just checking." He pulled the incubator door open to reveal the usual shelves, not unlike a refrigerator. It was filled with petri dishes containing every kind of salmonella species, with the more virulent strains on the bottom shelf where there was less risk of accident. The shelves were labeled from top to bottom, beginning with *Salmonella enteridites*, down through *Salmonella paratyphi A* and *B* and, at the bottom, *Salmonella typhosa*.

Robby pushed in front of his father, his arm moving to brush a stack of unused petri dishes from the counter to the floor, breaking a few. "Oh, Dad, I'm sorry."

"No catastrophe," Byron said, bending to retrieve the dishes left unbroken. "We'll have it swept up."

In the instant his father was distracted, Robby opened the bottom shelf, snatched one of the petri dishes and thrust it in his pocket.

Byron straightened. "No harm done."

"I've got to go, Dad."

"What? I thought you were going to spend the afternoon with me."

"Just thought of something I have to do," Robby said. "Very important." He hurried from the lab, leaving his father shaking his head.

CHAPTER 10

Ellen lay stretched out on the gurney, her face stark and bloodless, but with features composed and cosmetically touched up as though she had just left a beauty salon. As always, Howard was dressed in a clown's suit patterned in black and white diamonds and festooned with black tassels. He stood looking down, his scalpel poised over his wife. The rest of the surgical team was masked and dressed in traditional operating-room clothing. The members of the team were muttering darkly, impatient at Howard's indecision. "Do something," their muffled voices said behind the masks. Howard's scalpel hand trembled. The harsh light over the operating table blinded him to the mark where he was to make the incision. His hand steeled itself for the move, but seemed stayed by some invisible force. The reassuring blips on Ellen's heart monitor were coming less frequently, almost a straight line now. "Do something," the staff urged in a funereal chant.

Ellen's eyes fluttered, then opened. She smiled up at him dreamily, and motioned Howard to bend his head to hers. Her lips moved, and Howard strained to catch her words. "If it's a boy," she whispered, "we'll name him Howard." Vapors rose from the floor and swirled around her head. The blips on the heart monitor were a counterpoint to the dirge of the surgical team. Howard hushed his wife with a finger against pursed lips. "Close your eyes," he said gently. He guided the gleaming scalpel to the broken line sketched on Ellen's scalp. The blade barely broke the skin, but the head broke open like an overripe melon.

Howard opened his mouth to scream silently. He had botched it again. The same helpless feeling traveled down his arms to his feet, and rooted him to the spot. Ellen shook her head at him disapprovingly, then closed her eyes. The surgical team, obscured by the white vapors, groaned with finality. Howard's clown suit was splattered with gore. He willed himself awake.

His heart thumping against his rib cage, Howard slowly swung his legs over the side of the bed. His chest heaved as though at the end of a marathon run. The dream, Howard's failed attempt to reconstruct reality, had become repetitive. Awake, the mournful cadence of the surgical staff lingered in his brain. When the dream had started, a few days after Ellen's death, he would lie for a time weeping soundlessly. Lately, there had been no tears. He would merely walk woodenly through the following day, dreading the night.

CHAPTER 11

Miss Lorlene, her spirits uplifted for the first time in a week, bustled about, glancing at the clock whose hands scarcely seemed to move. She had been surprised, and had done nothing to hide her pleasure, when Robby phoned, asking if he could resume his tutoring. He was chipper, almost buoyant, and she had smiled and shaken her head at the resiliency of youth. Yesterday's life-crushing disappointment would pale against some trivia that took on monumental importance—an argument with parents considered intrusive baggage, a loss by the football team, the palm-sweating pursuit of a girl. Miss Lorlene stopped. She had never thought in terms of Robby having a girlfriend.

She looked around, satisfied. The house was tidy. And she had baked a raisin pie for Robby. It was his favorite. It was one of the many little things she had learned about him during these past few weeks. She looked up expectantly at the sound of the doorbell chimes.

She opened the door smiling, her smile spreading when she saw him holding the single long-stemmed rose, its petals just beginning to open. He was holding it out to her. A jumble of emotions washed over her, some of which she couldn't identify. "Oh, Robby," she said, "that is so thoughtful of you." His eyes were shining. She gathered herself. "I'll get a vase," she said, heading for the kitchen.

The spotlessly clean window over the sink reflected her wrinkles.

When she returned, Robby was still standing just inside the door where she had left him. He was taking off his windbreaker to reveal his teenage uniform—chinos, open shirt and sneakers. A wisp of black chest hair poked over the top of the shirt. She watched as he threw the wind-breaker casually over a chair in the foyer, and then walked to the living room couch. His walk was somehow different than she remembered; he rolled his lower body, the move-ment something of a swagger. She smiled to herself. Robby collapsed on the couch, his legs sprawled. He grinned at her and, for some reason, his lack of words was unsettling. He hadn't even said hello.

Then Miss Lorlene noticed something missing. "Robby, where are your books—your notebook, your things? We were going to analyze *Childe Harold's Pilgrimage*." His smile was disarming at the same time that it was puzzling. Another boy had a smile like that when *she* was seventeen. She had told herself that she was in love with him. But she never told the boy. It had been 1966, supposedly a time of liberation. But not in her life, not in Atlanta. For the rest of the country, the sixties began in 1963, but for her they'd never begun.

"We don't need the books," Robby said finally. "I memorized the poem."

Sometimes it was difficult to tell if he was teasing. "Oh, really?" She laughed, and was surprised when it came out a girlish giggle.

She watched his grin fade as he began to intone solemnly: "'Oh, schoolboy's tale/The wonder of an hour/Oh happy years/Once more/Who would not be a boy . . .'"

She stared at him, dumbfounded, held by his words, his almost perfect recitation of Lord Byron's poem. She watched his Adam's apple move with Byron's words. Small beads of sweat had appeared on Robby's forehead.

" '. . . No sleep until mourn/When youth and pleasure meet/To chase the glowing hours with flying feet.' "

He finished, and there was an extended stillness in the room. Miss Lorlene had been listening from a wing chair across from the couch, leaning forward to catch the poem. The silence had stretched into a tension. She had wanted to congratulate him on the nuances he had brought to the poetry. Instead, the teacher in her surfaced. "Robert, that was very nice, but in that last stanza it should be 'No sleep *till* mourn/When youth and pleasure meet.' You see, 'until' breaks the meter." She bit her tongue. "It's a beautiful poem, Robby, and you did it beautifully. Thank you. You don't know how delighted I am that you have gained an appreciation for Byron."

"I haven't," he pouted. "I don't like Byron, I learned the poem just for you."

"But you said it with such feeling."

"Because," he said, his eyes cast downward. "I said it—I learned it—for you. The poem is too—too immature. All that glorifying of youth and the joys of being young. The happy years, the wonder of each hour. It's nonsense. I'm young, and I don't like it."

She was startled, upset at his cynicism. "You don't like being young?"

"No," he said firmly. "I want to be serious, do important things. They never take you seriously when you're young. It doesn't matter what you *know*; they don't take you seriously until you've got gray hair. Wrinkles mean wisdom." He stirred impatiently on the couch. "The next few years can't go by fast enough for me. I'm going to be a scientist, a famous scientist." He looked at her pleadingly. "You understand, don't you? I'm wasting my time now. There's no joyous years, happy hours when youth and pleasure meet."

She didn't know what to say. It was 'they' against Robby. Did he include her among the adversarial 'they'? She wanted to say something that would wipe the hurt from his face. "This is a tragedy," she said finally. "You are making yourself a tragedy, Robby. Your sense of responsibility, your sensitivity. You're a . . . a Hamlet." She moved to the couch beside him. She found herself patting him on the shoulder, and then the cheek, comforting him. "Robby, Robby, you're so sensitive. But your dedication, your need to help others—" She searched for the proper words. "You can't assume the obligation for all mankind. You're stifling yourself. You're robbing yourself of your very youth. That would be such a waste."

She had moved close to him in her earnestness. She watched his eyes grow larger, and she could feel his faint breath on her face. When he kissed her full on the lips, she was not surprised. She kissed him back, and couldn't breathe. Her hand traveled to the back of his head, passing the swatch of hair at the base of his throat.

CHAPTER 12

The path leading to the office of Charlemaigne's newest physician was, literally, overgrown with weeds, an unkempt tally of the number of sick people *not* beating a path to his door. Howard Fletcher, lolling in his desk chair and reading a medical journal, reminded himself that he would have to cut the grass. But in the same thought, he decided to do it next week. Indolence, he decided, was sometimes unfairly maligned.

His receptionist, office nurse and bookkeeper, Mrs. Touhy, sat at her desk in the waiting room. She was typing. She was always typing something. "Insurance forms," she said. Howard had seen ten patients in two weeks. Mrs. Touhy might be doing her income tax, or writing a novel, for all he knew.

Mrs. Touhy had been a friend of his mother, and Howard remembered her at Mother's funeral, her Irish face, red and wet, buried in his shoulder. She had been one of the first to greet him on his return to town. Although in her seventies, she had volunteered to help him in the office, and it had worked out well. She was a nice connection to the past. All his patients so far had been her relatives and friends.

Howard rather liked this relaxed beginning. The bank account in Chicago was still fat enough that he could go without a single patient for several years and not lower his standard of living. It was a comfort zone he thought he needed right now.

The lack of business was his own fault, attributable to his sporadic office hours. Twice this week he had closed up at noon, once just to walk over to the park to watch some kids romp around on a swing set and monkey bars.

He laced his hands behind his head and leaned back in the chair, feeling himself entering a level just below sleep. He was aware of the journal sliding from his lap as he entered a twilight zone and was back in Chicago—back in another time when the days weren't long enough to accomplish all that he wanted.

It was their last evening out. God, how could he have known it would be the last? He remembered the drive down the Lake Shore Drive to the party, the silver BMW responding to his fingertips. He was bone-tired and had dreaded going to that dinner party. Though he knew that once there he would have a reasonably good time. The party was being given by his senior partner, a man Howard Fletcher liked and respected.

His partner was a professor and Chief of Neurosurgery at the University, a first-rate teacher and researcher with a lucrative private practice on the side. The wealthy of Chicago liked to have their private neurosurgeon lecture to other doctors about neurosurgery. And Howard, an associate professor himself, knew that he was like a son to this man and was following in his footsteps.

The party guests would include some of their more important patients: a Wrigley, an editor of the *Tribune*, a pitcher for the White Sox. The partner and his wife had a beautiful apartment that occupied one floor of a high-rise with a spectacular view of the lake. They had no children and no need for the schools and lawns of the north-shore suburbs. Childless couples who became rich moved closer to the lake, not north.

"You really don't want to go tonight," she had said.

"Oh no, Ellen," he'd started to protest. "I don't mind, I . . ." He'd flicked a glance at her. There was no deceiving her. She sat against the door of the BMW, turned towards him, her legs drawn up under her, disdaining the seat belt. His mind's eye could picture her as if it had happened an hour ago. She'd worn a simple black knit dress, quite short, the hem riding up to mid-thigh. The dress was tight enough that he could see the beginnings of the bulge of her first pregnancy. A single strand of pearls and a wedding ring were her only jewelry. Even in the dim green light of the dashboard she'd looked incredibly beautiful—and sexy. "Just a little tired," he'd said.

"Right now you think you're working too hard and spending too much time on the North Shore Drive," Ellen had said. "And you really don't want to go to this party."

It was a statement, not a question. She had always been able to do that, guess what he was thinking, then take his disjointed thoughts and summarize them, crystallize them. Some sort of clairvoyance, he'd decided. "Yeah," he'd said with a long sigh. "Sometimes I do wonder about the big city neurosurgeon-professor scene. But I don't wonder about you. You make it all okay."

And suddenly she had scooted over and was next to him. Her hand had reached down and grabbed his crotch. "You need a stress reliever," she'd said. And before he could say anything, she had unzipped him and her soft black hair was in his lap.

The sound of the front door chimes floated through the old house that Howard had converted into an office. He lifted his feet off the desk and shrugged into his white coat; his stethoscope was already draped around his neck. A doctor, even in Charlemaigne, had to look the part. He could hear Mrs. Touhy's soft voice and the visitor's muffled replies. Howard stood at the doorway, not wanting to seem too eager to greet his first patient of the day.

Standing at the receptionist's desk in the waiting room was a tall woman, maybe five foot nine, in her mid-thirties. Attractive, if you ignored a certain hardness around her green eyes. Shiny brown hair fell to just above her shoulders. He wondered how she stayed so pale in this climate. Mrs. Touhy finished her forms, and ushered the woman toward Howard's office. He realized he was staring. He ducked into the office and sat quickly behind his desk. He rose and extended his hand. "Good morning." Mrs. Touhy handed over the medical history form with the personal information across the top, then returned to the outer office.

"Uh, yes, Miss Marva Langston. What seems to be the problem?"

"Mrs.," she corrected him.

"Oh, sorry."

"Don't be. I'm divorced. For three years."

"I see."

Howard nodded. He took her through her medical history, childhood illnesses and family history. "You'll excuse me for mentioning it," he said, "but you don't sound like a . . ."

"A Louisianan? That's right. I'm from Pennsylvania. This is my ex-husband's home town. I came down here with him and stayed on when we split. I have a daughter in high school here. She'll graduate this year."

"I see." Howard stopped and allowed a slight smile. "And you list your occupation as barmaid?" He said it with just a hint of disbelief.

"Right now, I'm the night manager at the Amble Inn. That's a bar and restaurant outside of town." She said it pridefully as though expecting to be challenged. "I go to school in the afternoon, at the Community College."

That explained the lack of tan. He picked up a pen and hunched over his desk. "What seems to be the trouble?"

She drew in a breath. "My hand, my right one. It's painful, bothering me at work whenever I try to pick anything up. It even seems to be getting a little weak. I've been dropping beer mugs." She smiled. "Very troublesome in my line of work."

Howard couldn't imagine this woman lugging beer mugs around. "When this first began," he asked, "was your hand tingling, falling asleep?"

She nodded thoughtfully. "Yes, I guess it was."

"And then the tingling became more pronounced until it was actually painful?" She nodded again. "And worse at night? Maybe aggravated by lifting, uh, beer mugs at work, but worse at night?"

"You've got it."

"Have you been using your hand more than usual? Maybe taken up horseback riding or jai alai?"

Howard saw the green eyes snap. "Well, only in the morning," she said, her lips curling. "It's polo in the afternoon, and then a massage at the club before dinner, of course. The day just flies by."

Howard was startled at her quick repartee and tried to suppress his smile. This was a quick, tough woman sitting across from him.

"I don't have time for much recreation," she said. "As I said, I work at the bar nights, and go to school during the day. I'm taking accounting, and I do use an adding machine quite a bit."

Howard returned to his sober professionalism. "Tell me, is the pain in this area of your hand?" He held up his own hand, and traced an area.

"Yes. So what is it?"

He shrugged. "A carpal tunnel syndrome. But let me check you over, do a neurological." He buzzed Mrs. Touhy to come in, and told her to prepare Marva Langston for a limited exam.

He counted to twenty outside the examining room door allowing his patient time to change her clothes, then entered and began checking the reflexes in her arm. "How long has this bothered you?" he asked.

"Four months."

"And you haven't done anything about it until now? You're beginning to have motor weakness—a slight paralysis from the pinched nerve. Haven't you seen anybody about it?"

He saw the quick flush. "Well, actually . . ." she began slowly, "I went to the Ochsner Clinic in New Orleans. I've been seeing, well, different doctors there and . . ."

Howard grunted. "Ah yes, the old medical-center runaround. You went to a general medical clinic where they did an examination and did tests and referred you to the internal medicine clinic, and they did more tests and referred you to the neurology clinic where they did more tests, and you are still waiting."

He could see she was getting annoyed, and he told himself not to patronize her. "I was at a medical center myself. It's an old story," he said, shrugging. "What did they tell you?"

"That I've got a pinched nerve in my neck."

"Have they done an EMG, an electromyogram?"

"You seem to know everything. It's scheduled for next week. That's why I'm here. I guess I want a second opinion. I'm told the EMG is painful and, well, they've been doing all these tests and don't seem to . . ."

"Have the EMG done. It's the one test you really do need. The nerve in your hand is being pinched, and theoretically it could be anywhere along the course of the nerve—from the neck to the wrist. They may think the pinch is in the neck, but the EMG will show they're wrong; it's in the wrist. And you'll need an operation."

"Just like that. Are you always so sure?"

"Only when I'm right."

"And all those doctors at the clinic are wrong?"

"Mrs. Langston, you haven't seen any doctors. You've been seeing residents, doctors in training. Did you see any doctor over thirty?"

"Well, now that you mention it, they were all kind of

young." She bit her lower lip. "Can you recommend a surgeon?"

"Well, how about me?"

"You?"

"That's right." He was tempted to tell her that he had done maybe a thousand carpal tunnels, the last one on a pitcher for the Chicago White Sox. He wanted to boast a little; for some reason wanted to impress her. "I really could fix it for you if you'd like. It's just an outpatient procedure, no worse than going to the dentist."

She gathered the shapeless examining gown around her. "Isn't that sort of thing done by a specialist? Like a neurosurgeon?"

"That's right." She looked skeptical. "On my honor," he said, smiling. "A board certified neurosurgeon." He looked around. "Don't let the humble surroundings fool you." She began to smile. The hardness around her eyes softened, and she looked almost vulnerable. "I'll leave it up to you," Howard said. "Have the EMG, and then decide. The Ochsner Clinic people can fix it, or I can do it here. It was a pleasure meeting you." He wheeled and walked out of the room.

Howard pulled the waiting-room window drapes aside, and watched Marva Langston walk to her car. Her stride was purposeful, almost manly, with shoulders back and braced. Her hair, the tone of walnut, swirled about her face. Howard looked around to see Mrs. Touhy watching him. He was a beat too late to catch her smile, but the traces of one lingered in her eyes. He felt himself flush. He hurried past her, avoiding her eyes, closed his office door and resettled himself in his leather chair. The sharp pain that he had felt last October, on the day Ellen died, stabbed at him again, a searing knife that started low in his gut, then sliced through his heart to lodge in his throat and make swallowing impossible. He had thought that enough time had passed that he could live with a dull ache.

It was true what they said when you got the news. Reality left you, and there was an overpowering urge to run, or to will yourself into unconsciousness. A numbness took over so when you heard the words, you were insulated from their meaning.

The neurosurgeon, who was also a close friend, had never used the word 'dead.' Howard had done the same thing countless times, confronting the families huddled together in hospital waiting rooms, who searched his face for signs of a miracle but found none there.

"I'm sorry, Howard," his friend had said, his surgical mask a limp piece of cloth rumpled around his neck. "We did everything we could." His eyes swam with angry frustration as he choked out a stream of phrases. "It was a huge subdural hematoma . . . some intracerebral bleeding also . . . lot of brain-stem compression . . . arrested." His despair had been almost as deep as Howard's.

Howard had wound up consoling the other man. He patted his friend on the arm. "I know you did everything," he had mumbled.

He'd left home in the morning and four hours later life had changed completely and irreversibly. Ellen had fallen down the stairs, the stupid little goddamn six steps that she had negotiated two at a time, hundreds, maybe thousands, of times since she had decided that the sun room off the master bedroom would make a perfect nursery.

Howard had driven out to Navy Pier and parked for hours, watching a wild Lake Michigan, its surf turned into a green and gray sea by a late-October minigale. Sleet pelted his windshield. No one had told him, and he had never asked, whether it would have been a boy or a girl.

Afterwards, the days had crawled by with everybody assuring him that time would eventually heal him, that the pain would go away. Everybody, he knew now, had been wrong. Friends had told him how glad they were to see that he was 'taking it so well.' They had reminded him that he was 'still a young man,' and that 'there will be others.'

They had coaxed him into their inner circle. But the chairs around the table were always an odd number. Howard felt embarrassed for them and their forced efforts on his behalf. Little by little, he had found excuses to decline their invitations until the invitations had stopped coming.

CHAPTER 13

The Saturday morning "special conference" with the principal had exhausted Miss Lorlene and she lay in bed all day Sunday. She called in sick on Monday, and then again on Tuesday. And so on, each day for almost two weeks. Each night she had fallen into a fitful sleep, resolved that she would go to work the next day to face the principal and her students. And Robby. And each morning, she would begin the ritual, moving against the oppressive depression that added weight to her legs, plodding to the shower, struggling into her clothes. Nauseated, she could only nibble at a breakfast that turned to cardboard inside her mouth. And each morning she had gotten no farther than the front door. Then she had gone to the phone, called in sick again, and retreated to her bed where she would spend the day, the comforter pulled up to her chin, sometimes staring at the ceiling and in a self-delusional exercise, turning back the clock to a time before Robby. At other times she sobbed uncontrollably at the harsh reality.

The principal had shown his usual waffling obsequiousness, apologizing profusely about calling her in on a Saturday. "What we have here," he'd said, clearing his throat several times and avoiding her gaze, "is a situation." She could tell he'd wanted her to help him out, take over the conversation, saying something like, yes, she knew what he was referring to, and that there would be no repetition of her actions. But she'd said nothing. The principal had taken a deep breath and plunged ahead. Miss Lorlene remembered that he was, under stress, given to partial and incomplete sentences. "It has come to our attention . . . that is, the school board and the administration feel . . . part of my responsibility is to protect the reputation of the staff, our school . . ." He'd struggled mightily and then was silent for a minute, then swiveled his chair away and stared at the wall behind him. "It has come to our attention that you are tutoring the Swinton boy in your home." He had flinched against an outburst that never came. Miss Lorlene had been aware only that her eyelashes had flicked rapidly several times. That had given him courage to continue. "There has been talk . . . I want you to know that, personally, I have every faith that this, uh, situation is a result of your dedication as a teacher . . . Personally, I don't believe there is anything . . ." There was an agonizing pause. She had stopped him by getting quickly to her feet. "Thank you," she had said, her first and last words of the meeting, and was gone before he could say more.

It was during one of those long mornings with the comforter tucked under her chin that Miss Lorlene settled on a course of action. The decision lifted her depression to the point where she had once even caught herself humming as she went about her preparations. Serenity could be achieved when one was in control of one's own fate.

She had been very systematic in her planning. She had updated her will, filing one copy with her attorney and putting another in her safety deposit box at the bank. Almost everything she owned would go to her alma mater, Emory University. The money was to go to establish a scholarship in her name. The few cousins who were her only living relatives had long been scattered like autumn leaves, and she had not heard from them in years.

Miss Lorlene descended the stairs into the cellar, pausing to let the wave of nausea pass before making her way to the cedar chest in the corner next to the furnace. The nausea

was followed by another lower abdominal cramp and she
thought she might need to use the bathroom again. The
nausea, along with the tenderness in her breasts, had been
expected. But the severe diarrhea had been a surprise, and
she'd considered seeing her physician about it. Now there
would be no need for that particular humiliation. She ran
her hand across the polished lid of the cedar chest and
slowly opened it, an airtight container with a box of baking
soda tucked into a corner among the treasured books,
bringing the humidity to zero. The chest was as good as any
dust-proof display case. She fingered the volumes lovingly.
Here was one of the original treatises on the Civil War, there
some letters of the period, one of them from Jeb Stuart to
his wife. The historical collection would also go to Emory
University.

Miss Lorlene lifted out Byron's first work, published in
1831 and brought over from England by Miss Lorlene's
great-great-grandmother. Ah, and here was Byron's fourth
work: *Childe Harold's Pilgrimage*, in a single volume, date
of 1837. Both were in excellent condition. She had no idea
of their monetary value, but it was probably considerable.
Whatever it was, it was nothing to their true value. And it
was a comfort to know that they would be going to Robby.
He would hold them in trust, perhaps to pass them on to his
own children. A wave of melancholy broke over Miss
Lorlene when she thought of Robby as a grown man with
children. With great care she replaced the books, and closed
the lid on the cedar chest. She regretted she would not be
here to see Robby's excitement when they were turned over
to him. Dear Robby. His enthusiasm was so endearing. She
could still picture that excited face when she'd allowed him
to "inject" her as part of his science experiments. The
sweet, foolish boy. He hadn't even used a needle, only what
seemed to be a silly water gun. It had barely broken the skin
and had left a small pimple where he'd used it on her arm.
She'd been careful not to laugh or make fun of him or his
"experiments."

Miss Lorlene saved the housework for last. When they found her, even the glass that she had used to wash down the pills would have been rinsed and returned to its place in the cupboard. The house would be spotless. She dressed slowly and carefully, finishing with a subtle dash of perfume behind each ear. She had never worn perfume in the classroom. Then she wrote the note.

"I have been neither a coward or a namby-pamby," she began. "I have soberly studied the alternatives. I considered running away, to be gone. But that would be an act of cowardice even more reprehensible than the one I have chosen. At least this way, I will not be around to see the leers or hear the snickers when that 'foolish and frustrated spinster teacher' passes on. I plead guilty to foolishness. The brain does not rule the heart. I can only hope that there will be some forgiveness. I cannot depend on that, of course, so I have chosen this countermove to ensure that I won't have to face the shame and embarrassment in a community in which I have established a reputation for integrity and moral values, values that I hope I have imparted to the hundreds of students whom I have been privileged to guide. But I have betrayed that trust, and it is too much to believe that there will be understanding."

Miss Lorlene folded the note and placed it in an envelope, which she propped in plain view against the pen and pencil holder on her living room desk, next to the note she had left for Robby.

She walked to the couch, feeling nothing. It shouldn't be too long now. The pills should begin their work within thirty minutes. She had researched the subject thoroughly. She stretched out on the couch, smoothing the turquoise party dress over her knees. She had worn it only once, last year when she was a chaperone at the junior-senior prom. She had left instructions to be buried in it. She closed her eyes and began to construct a scenario of her funeral. Would there be any mourners?

The thought was too depressing. She opened her eyes and

ran a hand over her face. There was no numbness yet, or any other sign that would presage the coma. The heart, she knew would merely come to a stop. She wished she could speed things along. In her head, she began to conjugate verbs, at the same time recalling their Latin roots. The mental exercise would lead her into it. Into what? She turned her head languidly, fixing her eyes on the note on the desk. Had she said it in the right way? Whatever the words, they were inadequate to what she felt. She was certainly no poet, but she knew the proper use of the language, and she had always taken fierce pride in that. She supposed, as a grammarian, she would have been regarded as first rank. That's the way the British would have said it. Ah, the British, with their impeccable speech. The slovenly Americans at the worst had bastardized the language, at best had allowed it to fall into imprecision.

She settled her head deeper into the pillow and sighed. Dying, she thought analytically, closing her eyes once more, was one of the few things a person was forced to do alone. Miss Lorlene, as during most of her life, was going without an escort.

She was having trouble getting comfortable. Something was nagging at one corner of her brain, something left undone. She sat up slowly, and rechecked her preparations. Everything seemed to be in order. The note to Robby was perfect, but something drew her attention to the suicide note. She arose heavily and went to the desk. She opened the envelope and quickly scanned the note. Of course. In the opening sentence there was a grave error. She smiled. She had always had an uncanny instinct when something was out of place. "I have been neither a coward or a namby-pamby," she had written. She had no time to rewrite the entire message. Her ballpoint pen ran a line through the word 'or' and substituted 'nor.'

Satisfied, she returned to the couch, reminding herself: Correlative conjunctions are coordinating conjunctions used in pairs. The constructions following correlations should be parallel in form.

She closed her eyes awaiting the blackness. Regrets and guilt, she reminded herself, were totally useless emotions. Still, she regretted that she would not be there to see Robby's face when he got his A.

CHAPTER 14

Robby Swinton was in a high state of excitement, his breathing so labored that he thought he was hyperventilating. The people and buildings swam before his eyes, and the sidewalk seemed to buckle beneath his feet. He slowed his steps and finally came to a stop. He had just entered the French Quarter, across the street from Brennan's. A long line of tourists snaked down the block and out of sight around the corner, waiting for the traditional breakfast they could name-drop to the folks back home.

Robby counted slowly to himself, stabilizing his breathing, and moved slowly toward Saint Ann and Bourbon. He had arrived much too early, and had several hours to kill. He had planned the first experimental operation for evening, when the crowds in the Quarter were at their height and when abnormal behavior was the accepted norm. Robby pressed his forearm to his side to make sure the injector gun was tucked securely in his waistband. Making sure no one was watching, he reached inside his belt and felt along the cool metallic smoothness of the barrel. The gun, he reminded himself, was another example of his genius. The 'med-injector' had been developed for patients with a phobia for needles. It was a relatively new device, somewhat experimental, being tried by some pediatricians and used by certain types of diabetics. It shot a fine aerosol spray at such high speed that its contents penetrated the skin with little or no sensation. He had fit the med-injector device into the empty casing of a BB pistol, with the trigger activating the injector apparatus at the tip of the barrel. It resembled an oversized watergun.

The crowd was building on the corner. He must be certain he didn't pick tourists. This was, after all, a controlled experiment. He meandered through the clogged streets. The agitated excitement he had felt earlier was gone. A calm had settled over him, now that he felt confident of his plan. He sauntered along, gaping like any tourist. The air was heavy with pungent odors—warm beer, sweaty bodies, spicy food. His watch told him it was just past noon. He decided to wander down to Jackson Square and watch the sidewalk artists.

The sixty-year-old salesman had raced back from his regular territory, driving all night from the Florida panhandle where he had spent the past week kissing the backsides of customers, without a dime in commissions to show for it. Since no one expected him back until tomorrow, he had snuck into town and rented a room down the street at the Royal Orleans Hotel. Despite living six miles away across Lake Pontchartrain, in the suburb of Slidell, he rarely got to the Quarter around Mardi Gras time because his wife spent most of her time trying to run his life and the lives of his four grown children. His greatest fear was that he would meet one of them, or someone he knew, here in the middle of the Quarter. He tried to reassure himself no one would recognize him wearing an open collar and Bermuda shorts.

There was something deliciously naughty about playing hooky from job and home, adopting new identities for the young men he would invariably meet. He had been, at various times, a private investigator, the captain of an oceangoing liner, an oilfield wildcatter, a foreign service diplomat. If the young men did not believe him, they usually played along with the charade; in fact, they usually appeared dutifully impressed. They were interested only in the money anyway and, besides, the salesman's little game heightened the excitement.

The salesman lingered over his overpriced beer, and regarded the frolicking crowd with some distaste. Men dancing with men. The salesman had his own standards, old-fashioned though they might be. The bar had been a waste of time. Eye contact had been fleeting, interest cool.

Then the salesman's roving eye settled on a young man sitting at a table just a few feet away who was staring at him intently. He smiled at the handsome boy, who was delicately featured and who had the most luxurious, longest eyelashes the salesman had ever seen. The salesman nodded, and the boy smiled back. "You a stranger to New Orleans?" the salesman called over. The boy nodded amiably. The salesman got to his feet, taking his beer along. "Mind if I join you?"

"Please do," the young man said.

Robby listened to the man's inane, feverish chatter with a studied attention. In the space of a few minutes, the man had edged his chair ever closer until they were thigh to thigh.

"How old are you, anyway," the salesman wanted to know. "Eighteen, nineteen?"

"As old as the ages," Robby replied, delighted at the old fool's puzzled, waxy smile.

"Tell you what," the man proposed eagerly. "Why don't we get a bite to eat, my treat. We'll go to Arnaud's. It's excellent, a local favorite. Then I'll show you around town. Born and raised here. Know all the best spots."

"Sounds like fun," Robby said. Under the table, he pulled the injector gun. Then he put a hand on the man's arm, the intimate pressure drawing attention from the light touch of the injector gun against the man's bare leg. He pulled the trigger, then wagged a finger at the man. "Wait for me while I make a little trip to the powder room."

Robby crossed the darkened dance floor, and ducked out

the back door, leaving the deluded salesman to contemplate what might have been. He was exultant. It had all been so easy. He stepped into the muggy evening, back among the bizarre costumes, dyed hair and painted faces. The sidewalk crowd at Saint Ann and Bourbon was five and six deep. Robby palmed the injector gun and moved in among them. He picked out a young man whose hair was pulled into a ponytail and secured by a rubber band. He stood with his back to Robby, taking pulls from a bottle inside a brown paper bag. Robby pressed the muzzle against his neck. So easy. The young man's companion, a gaunt boy, was jostled into Robby, and he shot him in the back of his bare left arm.

Robby crossed the street and stationed himself under the balcony of an apartment from which drunken local-locals were hooting at passersby. Sandwiched between bodies, he held the gun poised at waist level. There was enough serum for one more subject. Robby felt exhausted by the tension of the day. The air was sweet with marijuana smoke. Out of the street door of the apartment staggered a young man, his eyes glazed and unfocused. He groped blindly, grabbing at Robby for support, clutching a handful of his shirt to keep from falling down. Enraged, Robby raised the injector gun and aimed for a spot behind the young man's ear.

Robby's wrist was suddenly caught in a vise, and bent painfully backward. He was spun around to come face to face with a huge cop. "What in hell you doing?" the cop demanded. He wrested the aerosol injector gun from Robby and stuck it under his nose. "What do you call this?"

Robby froze, but only for a moment. He winked at the cop. "Oh, a guardian of the peace. It is so comforting to know you're on the job, officer." He bent and kissed the cop's badge. The cop recoiled in disgust. Robby rubbed the hand that had been in the cop's grip. "You're very strong."

The cop sighed. "Never mind that shit." He turned the injector gun over, examining it. "What is this thing?"

Robby cackled. "Can't you see? It's a very, very special water pistol, full of the finest French perfume."

The cop held the gun to his nose. "Phew. You call this perfume?"

Robby lowered his eyes. "Ran out of perfume. I had to pee in it."

The cop rolled his eyes skyward. "Jesus," he muttered. He thrust the injector gun at Robby. "Put that thing back in your pocket and get the hell out of here. At least get out of my sight."

Robby pouted and began moving away. "Why don't you get into the spirit, you big thing," he called back to the cop.

Around the corner, he ducked into a courtyard restaurant. He was sweating profusely. He was spent. He put away the injector gun and smiled, congratulating himself on his impromptu theatrics.

Something gnawed at him, and he realized he was hungry, famished in fact. He sat down at a table, ordered, and ravenously cleaned up three bowls of shrimp gumbo.

CHAPTER 15

The director of the C.D.C. watched the ancient DC-3 descend toward Dobbins Air Force Base. The Surgeon General had been quite explicit; he would be using the small Air Force facility rather than the Atlanta Metropolitan Airport, where his presence was sure to be noted and questions raised.

The plane taxied off onto a side tarmac and the pilot killed the engines. The Surgeon General was trundled over in a jeep.

"What did you tell them in Washington?" the director asked as he transferred the Surgeon General to a C.D.C. car.

"I told them nothing," the Surgeon General replied, "other than it was a routine trip to visit my friends at the C.D.C." He looked out the back window, then grunted and chuckled. "Can you believe that airplane?" he said. "My ears are still ringing. Haven't flown in a DC-3 since I was an ensign." He settled his considerable bulk into the backrest. "A nice little cloak-and-dagger touch, though, don't you think?"

The director refrained from saying that the subterfuge was probably an exercise in frustration given the Surgeon General's resemblance to Captain Ahab, a visage that had looked out gravely from TV sets all over America while he cast dire warnings about AIDS and the hazards of smoking.

"I thought you should stay at my place," the director said. "We can go straight there; you can get some rest."

"No," was the sharp response. "Let's go right to your lab. I want to look at those bugs myself."

"At this hour? It's after midnight!"

The Surgeon General nodded, his salt and pepper under-the-chin beard bobbing inside the darkened car. "I know it's late, but it's probably the best time for me to be at the C.D.C." He turned to the director. "Where are you keeping the slides from New Orleans?"

"Locked in my office. I have a microscope on my desk. It will be private."

The Surgeon General sighed and spoke softly. "I don't like it, don't like it at all. From what you've told me, it doesn't sound good. Hell, it sounds horrific."

The director could only nod his agreement.

It was three o'clock in the morning, and except for some janitors and night watchmen, it was deserted in the C.D.C. The director was tired. And bored. He had brought the Surgeon General to his private office where the slides from New Orleans were locked away. And now he'd spent the last hour fidgeting and pacing around his office while the Surgeon General meticulously studied each slide under the huge binocular microscope. Of course he would do that, the director now realized. The Surgeon General was a top-notch clinician, not some hack bureaucrat who had risen through the ranks by shuffling papers and toadying to the right congressmen. The director knew this particular Surgeon General was not about to take someone else's word for something as important as this.

The director cleared his throat. "If I didn't know you better," he said, breaking the long silence, "I'd be insulted. I'm considered one of the best microscope men in the business." He tried to say it lightly, and watched the Surgeon General's slight smile. "I've been known to tell a baceterium from a pinworm," the director continued. "Are you going to check all twenty cases?"

The Surgeon General backed away from the microscope, rubbing his eyes. He looked weary. "O.K.," he said to the director, "you're right. They're spores." He gave the director a wry smile, biting the inside of his lip as he spoke. Then he added softly, "Except that bacteria that cause acute illnesses don't form spores." There was a long silence, then the Surgeon General spoke again. "You say they're resistant to antibiotics? Which antibiotics?"

"All of them, all of the ones we've tested."

The Surgeon General buried his eyes back into the eyepieces of the microscope. He played with the sub-stage lamp, the powerful light source under the barrel of the scope. He snorted. "Maybe if I turn the light off they'll go away."

The whistling of a night watchman could be heard down the hall, then the clang of a mop bucket.

"You know I never realized how much spores looked like commas," the Surgeon General said. "I'd always heard them described as being club-shaped, like exclamation points, never as commas."

The director of the C.D.C. shook his head. His clothes were sticking to him from wearing them almost twenty-four hours in the Atlanta heat. He sat on the edge of his desk, not quite believing he was here in his office at three in the morning, dead tired, clothes rancid, listening to the Surgeon General of the United States indulge in this inane chatter.

But he understood. He'd done the same thing a week ago when the slides from New Orleans first began arriving. He'd been totally preoccupied, constantly returning to the microscope and unable to do any other work. Like the Surgeon General, he couldn't believe it, and stared for hours at the unmoving bacteria on the slides, noticing miniscule differences of shape among the different bugs. He'd read that suicidally depressed people on window ledges scrutinized the cars and people below in the same way. The director remembered how he'd started naming the individual bacteria; one was Sarah, one Jane, and one, a little larger than the others, was Vera. He knew a lady named Vera and she was fat.

"Are you O.K.?"

The director suddenly realized the Surgeon General had been speaking to him.

"I said, are you O.K.? Your lips are moving. You're talking to yourself."

The director smiled. "Sorry. A little woolgathering. Tired."

"We're both a little tired," the Surgeon General said. "Time for us to do a little hibernating ourselves." He began putting the slides away, carefully placing them in a slide box, then placing the box in the bottom drawer of the director's desk.

The director smiled. Hibernation was the word most often used to describe spore formation in bacteria. Certain bacteria, when threatened, could round up into irregular little balls and survive a hostile environment. In this state they could survive excessive heat or cold or lack of nutrition. Or the presence of antibiotics. They couldn't grow or multiply—antibiotics kill bacteria when they're reproducing—but they could stay alive. Evolution had dictated that spore formation be limited to specific bacteria that had to lie dormant for long periods of time, usually soil bacteria such as the tetanus or gangrene bacillus. Only when these bacteria found themselves in favorable environments such as a human wound, could they break out of their spore state and become invasive.

"Did you check with the germ warfare people?" the director asked.

The Surgeon General nodded. "Just before I left Washington. I know spores are their favorite toys these days—they're the toughest bacteria around—but there've been no leaks, no accidents of any kind. Believe me, I'd know about it."

"What about the astronauts? Do you think we've become too lax with them?" the director asked.

The Surgeon General grimaced. "I *know* we have. We've become too lax with the whole space program. I was thinking about that on the flight down here. You know we used to clean everything off a lot better than we do now: the spaceships, the suits, all the equipment, even the astronauts—hell, *especially* the astronauts. Scrubbed everything down with disinfectant."

The director leaned wearily against his desk. He didn't want to think about that possibility. Spores from outer space had been a definite concern in the early days of the space program. Since spores can lie dormant for hundreds of years, there was concern that some of them might be brought in from space; different kinds that had not evolved with the life species on earth. In theory they could be a calamity, but the first space explorations had brought back no life forms, so the practice of cleansing and sterilizing the spaceships, and their occupants, had been abandoned by NASA.

There was another silence. The Surgeon General put his hands flat on the top of the director's desk and wearily pushed himself up from the chair. "I want to see the chickens," he said abruptly.

The director nodded. "O.K., but they're not causing this epidemic. This epidemic's a carrier. Has to be. Look at the way it's spreading—all from that one central locus. There's got to be a carrier down in the French Quarter."

The Surgeon General nodded. "I agree. But we can't take any chances now, can we? I mean, we'll be forgiven if the space program brought back some resistant bugs or if the germ warfare people had an accident. We'll even be forgiven if there's a disease carrier in the New Orleans French Quarter. None of that's exactly our fault. But a contaminated food processing plant? That's our line of work. *Sixty Minutes* would kill us on that one."

The director winced at the mention of that name. *Sixty*

Minutes had devoted two shows to chicken-processing plants and how the automated cleaning processors tore open the bowel of the animals and contaminated the meat. There had been a lot of flak about them, and the C.D.C. had received thousands of letters. The director could only imagine what *Sixty Minutes* would do if these plants were causing some new deadly disease.

"There's another reason I want to see that chicken processing plant," the Surgeon General said. "It might explain the resistance of these bugs to antibiotics. The food processing people have been feeding low levels of antibiotics to chickens for years and these spores are acting as though they've been exposed to low levels of antibiotics. Maybe there's a connection. Maybe these bugs *have* come from contaminated chickens. Maybe it's just some common intestinal bacteria that lives in the gut of the chicken, and it's learned to form spores and become resistant to our best wonder drugs."

The director held the office door open for the Surgeon General. "Dangerous," the Surgeon General muttered as he walked past. "Spores are supposed to live in the ground where they belong. They're opportunistic bugs that cause trouble only under specific circumstances. Look at the gangrene bacillus. It's a spore, but it knows its place. Only when there's dead tissue do gangrene bugs break out of their spore state and become invasive. Spores have never caused an acute illness with fever and diarrhea and dehydration."

Their heels made loud clacking sounds as they walked slowly through the empty hallways of the C.D.C. "Damn, goddamn," the Surgeon General said. "We've got a bunch of spores acting like some wild animal that's no longer afraid of man."

The director shrugged. "When do you want to go see the chickens?"

"We'll leave at seven A.M. That'll give us a couple hours of sleep."

They left the main entrance of the C.D.C. and headed for

the director's lone car in the parking lot. Once outside the air-conditioned offices, the muggy heat of Atlanta—even at three-thirty in the morning—enveloped them. The Surgeon General stopped and turned to the director. "You know, it's occurred to me that maybe we should take a bacteriologist down there with us. Since we're both mainly epidemiologists, we probably ought to have a genuine bug man come along. Tell me, who's your man that just got back from Africa, the one who proved AIDS wasn't being spread by mosquitoes? A nice piece of work."

"You mean Swinton? He's a bacteriologist and an epidemiologist, a Ph.D. in both."

"Yeah, let's take him. Is he back here in Atlanta?"

The director nodded, then grimaced. "But I promised him that he wouldn't have to go on any more field trips."

"Hell, man, this is just a one day-trip to a food-processing plant in the New Orleans area, not Katmandu. Isn't he your best bacteriologist? We'll need cultures from the chickens, the holding tanks, all through the processing plant. We need him."

The director nodded again.

"Well then, wake him up. Tell him we're leaving—crack of dawn."

They tried to ignore the stench and the curious glances of the workers who, the director thought, might not readily recognize the Surgeon General out of uniform. The three of them, accompanied by the plant manager, were working their way down the mile-long production line. It was not unlike other assembly lines in this age of the robot, the workers doing little physical labor. The workers watched, inspected, and occasionally threw a switch; the main focus of their attention was to make sure the line never stopped.

The plant manager was a man plainly ill at ease this day. He had begun the tour at the "holding pens," several acres where tens of thousands of chickens were confined, the birds' cackling a constant din. They'd watched as two dozen workers grabbed the chickens, one in each hand, and quickly stuck their heads in looped nooses on the moving conveyer belt. The noose automatically tightened, strangling the chickens and sending them on their journey through the production line.

They had watched the process for more than thirty minutes while the Surgeon General fired questions at the plant manager: Where had the chickens come from? What regions of the U.S. were supplied by this processing plant? What was the nature of the chickens' feed while they were held here? What was the precise dosage in milligrams, of tetracycline and other antibiotics in the feed?

The Surgeon General found it hard to believe that the chickens had come from so many neighboring states, and found it incredible that this one plant supplied the entire mid-South. The plant manager had been ordered to produce shipping invoices documenting the origins of the chickens and their final destinations.

Then the questions had ceased and the four of them walked single file, the nervous plant manager leading the way. They observed how the heads of the chickens were cut off surgically just above the noose by a computerized robot that measured the length of each bird, and, according to the length, removed the head at a point that would leave a maximum length of neck. If the chicken was 50 centimeters long, the neck was cut 4.8 centimeters below the top of the head. If it was 60 centimeters, the cut was 5.3 centimeters from the top. It never missed cutting just below the bony structure that constitutes a chicken's cranium.

The robot then turned the chicken upside down while the body was gently compressed, not enough to tear the meat but just enough to drain the last dregs of blood from the open carotid arteries.

The carcasses then moved along the line to another machine which, after dipping them in a mild acidic solution, cleanly took off the feathers, pulling them out within a micron of the surface of the skin. The carcasses were then dipped and washed in several solutions to remove any residue of feathers. The neck was cut off at the torso and, like the feathers, was shunted off away from the production line, the feathers to be salvaged for mattresses and pillows, most of the necks to be ground into cat food.

Most of this was ignored by the three men following the plant manager, who was giving a proud travelogue of his operation, citing the plant's cleanliness, order and efficiency. The Surgeon General, the director and Byron Swinton had walked two-thirds of the line without saying a word. They reached a point where each carcass was held upside down in the conveyer belt while a large rotary blade cut through the abdominal wall. As the lower abdominal wall opened, a huge suction machine entered the cavity, vacuuming out the intestinal contents. It was all done in a split second. "Our evisceration machine," the plant manager proclaimed. The Surgeon General said nothing, his eyes glued to the operation. He made a quick movement. "That was one," he said to the director. Another fifteen minutes passed before the Surgeon General stirred again. "That's another one," he said. "A definite tear." He and the director watched intently, beginning to move slowly as the plant manager checked his watch. They watched the conveyer belt take the gutted chickens down into a huge vat, the conveyer mechanism stopping at measured intervals to allow each carcass to bathe for several minutes.

"How many chickens in the vat at one time?" the Surgeon General asked.

The plant manager jumped. "About three hundred, sir."

"And how long do they stay in the vat?"

"About an hour, sir. We wash them very carefully."

"And the temperature of the fluid?"

"It's cool, sixteen degrees Celsius." He paused. "That's sixty-one degrees Fahrenheit." The Surgeon General gave him a glance that asked, Do you think I'm *that* dense?

• • •

Byron Swinton, the Surgeon General and the director were alone in the back of the DC-3 which was parked out of sight behind a hangar. "One more time," the Surgeon General was saying. "You're sure every chicken in the New Orleans area comes through that plant."

The director nodded. "All but the frozen ones. That plant cleans all the chickens in the mid-South."

"Clean?" the Surgeon General said incredulously.

"Bad choice of words," conceded the director.

"That's the most chickenshit I've seen since boot camp." He shrugged and then sagged, the long night and day finally sapping his energy. He turned to Byron. "What do you think?"

Swinton carefully measured his words. "It's not contaminated chickens," he said sharply. "Those eviscerating machines *do* tear the bowel and spill feces into the holding tanks. They may contaminate everything in sight, but they're *not* causing an epidemic in New Orleans. It's a carrier."

Swinton's response drew a reproachful eye from the director. The director's look said, *Don't patronize the Surgeon General of The United States of America*. But Swinton was boiling with anger. After a promise of no more field trips, he had been roused out at five A.M. for this foolishness. He had long been wary of the 'science' of epidemiology. Following his graduation from Harvard Medical School, Swinton had done graduate work at the famed Harvard School of Public Health, obtaining a Ph.D. in epidemiology. Then he found he didn't like the work. It was too subjective and he'd become bored. Epidemiologists were accountants, collectors of data and information, not real scientists. He'd gone back to graduate school and obtained another Ph.D. in bacteriology and had spent his career in both fields. As someone who knew both fields, he now questioned the methods of any and all epidemiologists.

This trip had confirmed those feelings. Here he sat with the two most renowned epidemiologists in the world, and they were stumbling over the obvious. He had studied the demographics of the New Orleans epidemic on the DC-3 during the ride down from Atlanta. It was clearly a carrier that was causing the epidemic. All the cases were coming from one area in the French Quarter. One area, nonsense— one *street corner*. No satellite cases, even. There was an index case living near the corner of Bourbon and Saint Ann Streets. It was that simple. "A carrier," he repeated. "Couldn't be anything else. Not these—these—chickens," he said disdainfully sweeping his arm in the direction they'd just come from. "The whole idea that they could be causing . . ." He stopped abruptly as the director stared bullets at him.

The Surgeon General chortled, ignoring Swinton's sarcasm. He had opened a flask and offered Swinton some, but he refused.

There was a burst of noise as one of the DC-3 engines started. The second one turned over, the noise hammering at Swinton's brain. He wondered if the noise level in the passenger cabin was below the 80-decibel level allowed by OSHA. His ears had been ringing all day from the trip down here.

The Surgeon General ignored the noise. "You're right, of course," he yelled. "There's an index case down there. And it's got to be stopped." He turned to the director. "How long do you think we've got?

The director tightened his lips. "Not long. We've instructed all the labs in the New Orleans area to send all their specimens straight to the C.D.C. So far we've been able to cover it up in the New Orleans area. And I'm doing the species identification personally, so no one else at the C.D.C. knows . . . just the three of us." The director gave a short grunt of a laugh and shook his head sadly. "All the cases we've been getting from the New Orleans area are from patients with spores. As bad as that is, it will at least make it nearly impossible for any local labs to identify what the bug is, since all spores look the same."

The Surgeon General took a long pull on the flask. "So, we have a Gaeton Dugas." He had said it softly, barely audible above the engines.

Swinton and the director stared at him. The director slowly nodded and said, "Yes, I guess we do."

They sat in silence. Another Gaeton Dugas, Swinton thought. Dugas was the index case for AIDS. A homosexual airline steward, he had in the opinion of most epidemiologists been largely responsible for the spread of AIDS in the U.S. His work schedule included frequent trips to Africa. He had a voracious appetite for sex, with over a thousand contacts a year. And he was infectious for over six years before he succumbed to the disease. Most of the initial cases in the U.S. could be traced to him.

The Surgeon General leaned forward and in a conspiratorial tone said, "You know, the Public Health Service knew about Dugas but they couldn't stop him. Oh, they warned him—told him what he was doing to people—but he wouldn't stop having sex." The Surgeon General leaned a little closer, his voice barely audible. "They should have killed him—assassinated him."

Byron Swinton was shocked. But the director, after a minute of thought, began nodding his head. They rode the rest of the way to Atlanta in silence.

CHAPTER 16

Howard Fletcher guided the car into the doctors' parking lot at Charlemaigne General Hospital and parked it near the emergency entrance, next to the hospital's only ambulance. The sight of the emergency vehicle fostered a smile. The word, 'ambulance' was a Charlemaigne euphemism. The vehicle was a converted hearse. The only equipment it carried was a bulky, green-tube oxygen tank with a flow meter and a mask. There were no IV solutions because the drivers didn't know how to administer them. Fletcher, as a combat medic, had carried more medications with him when he was in Vietnam. He probably wouldn't live long enough to see the town of Charlemaigne get any advanced life-support systems.

The patient was a boy, nearly a man, about eighteen years old. His skin was hot and dry and his lips had a bluish tinge. He was grunting his respirations, explosive bursts of noise that made the nurses wince. His chart identified him as Samuel Avignon, the son of Grace Avignon, one of Howard's private patients, a pleasant self-effacing woman, a widow schoolteacher whom he had treated on occasion.

The nurses had undressed the young man, putting on the hospital gown backwards so that it gaped open in front. If the kid hadn't been so sick, he probably would have been humiliated exposing himself to the mixed company in the emergency room. Howard turned to the nurse next to him. She was a short dark Cajun in her mid-twenties. She was chewing gum, and the sight angered Howard. He felt like prying it from her mouth and sticking it behind her ear. "You're sure there haven't been any chest pains or cardiac symptoms?" he asked. It would be rare in one so young, but he had to check it out.

"Positive," the nurse replied. "I double-checked it with the mother."

Howard nodded. If this were cardiac, the young man would have been pale and sweaty, and also cold from diminished circulation. Instead, he was hot to the touch. "What's the temperature here?" he asked the nurse.

"A hundred 'n five."

"A hundred *point* five?" he asked irritably.

"No, Doctor, a hundred *and* five."

He smiled down at Sam Avignon. "Diarrhea? Did you tell the nurse you had diarrhea, nothing else?"

The young man nodded weakly, whispering through parched lips. "That's all, Doctor, diarrhea. Terrible."

"No chest pains or shortness of breath? No vomiting?" Sam Avignon shook his head. "How about cramps?" The boy opened his mouth, but nothing came forth. "Cramps," Howard prompted, trying to help him out. "Just before you have to, uh, go?" Sam Avignon nodded.

Howard proceeded with a careful examination, obtaining as much information as he could while he checked the heart and lungs. Sam Avignon managed, with supreme effort, to explain how his illness had begun two days ago with cramps and diarrhea, and that the diarrhea weakened him to the point that he could barely walk. Over the past twenty-four hours, the bathroom had become his home. His mother had found him passed out there this afternoon, and had driven him to the emergency room.

Howard palpated the abdomen. The hot skin had that peculiar doughy feel characteristic of severe dehydration and protein-wasting. It was like kneading flour without enough water. Howard lifted his hand from the abdomen and noticed the spots for the first time, some sort of rash, brilliant red across the lower abdomen. He had never seen anything like them before.

"Sam," he asked, "have you eaten anything lately, that is, something out of the ordinary, at some restaurant, maybe, that you haven't been to before?" The young man shook his head, his eyes wide and frightened. "Changed your normal routine, been anyplace different in the past few days?"

"Went to New Orleans with some friends last Saturday," the boy croaked. "Just went down to watch the parades. But we didn't do nuthin', I mean, eat anyplace or anything. Just got us a spot at Saint Ann and Bourbon and watched the parade. Then we came home. Had supper at home."

Howard shrugged. He patted Sam's arm. "Don't worry, you're going to be O.K."

The nurse had herded the family into a corner of the E.R. waiting room, and Howard joined them there. Grace Avignon was flanked by her two other teenage children, another son and a girl. The boy, about sixteen, wore overalls. He and his brother worked the family's small sugar cane farm. Nice looking kids, a decent hard-working family right out of Norman Rockwell.

Mrs. Avignon was working her hands together. "What is it, Doctor?"

"I'm not sure," Howard said. "Tell me, Mrs. Avignon, your son said he began feeling ill just two days ago, is that right?"

"Yes, that's right, Doctor. It all began so suddenly; must have gone to the bathroom twenty times."

Howard glanced at his watch. "He got this sick in just two days?" Grace Avignon shrugged helplessly.

"You have a well?" Howard asked.

She shook her head. "We were hooked up to city water last year."

"I see." Howard was grasping for straws. "Any complaints with the rest of the family? I mean, do the rest of you feel all right? Has anyone had any intestinal complaints?"

Mrs. Avignon looked at her other children, who shook their heads. "No, Doctor," she said. "Is Sam going to be all right?"

Howard nodded reassuringly. "Yes, of course. He's pretty sick right now, dehydrated from all the diarrhea. We'll start antibiotics, and give him some fluids intravenously. Probably be out in a few days." They looked relieved.

Howard sat in the doctors' lounge writing orders on Sam Avignon. The lounge, a Spartan room located just off the E.R., was just large enough to accommodate a Formica-top table with a dozen molded plastic chairs around it. A coffee machine was in one corner on a small table cluttered with dirty plastic spoons and Styrofoam cups half-filled with the dregs of cold coffee and floating cigarette butts. A neatly lettered sign hung on the wall above the table: "We thank you for not smoking."

He looked down at the inadequate orders he had written. A flat film of the abdomen instead of an abdominal CAT scan, and old-fashioned twelve-lead EKG instead of an echocardiogram. At least he would get reliable bacteriology cultures. There was no local bacteriologist and only a part-time pathologist, but Howard had been told that certain bacteriology cultures were being sent away to some Government lab at Charity Hospital in New Orleans. He'd have to check on that later. Charlemaigne General Hospital had lost out in the competition for new equipment. These days hospitals were dependent upon allocations from state bureaucracies. One had to have a CON from the HPA or the RHC, a Certificate of Need from the Hospital Planning Authority of the Regional Health Council, both located at the capital in Baton Rouge.

Unfortunately, Charlemaigne was located off the medical Main Street of America, off the expressway between the

U.S. Public Health Center leprosarium in Carville, and New Orleans, with its huge Charity Hospital. Howard mused that the only physicians in town were local boys who, like himself, had 'come home.' The bureaucrats, in their infinite and unassailable wisdom, had deemed that the grants for new equipment go to one of the two larger institutions. Charlemaigne Hospital got no CAT scan monies nor angiogram facilities, nor operating microscopes. A glorified infirmary, Howard thought.

The E.R. consisted of one large area with room for six gurney cots separated by curtains. There was a door that led to the nurses' station and, just beyond that, a door to this doctors' lounge.

Howard would simply have to make do, although he wished he had a CAT scan of Sam Avignon's abdomen. But then he reminded himself that 85 per cent of all diagnoses came from taking the patient's history and from the physical exam. The time-honored H and P was still the most reliable. He hoped for Sam Avignon's sake that that was still true. He finished writing orders and got to his feet. There was still the business of that rash. He headed for the library. It was a reflex, kind of a hobby, reading about unusual cases right on the spot.

But then he stopped, and remembered where he was. He was in Charlemaigne General Hospital in Charlemaigne, Louisiana. And the doctors' lounge doubled as the hospital library. Get real, Howard, he told himself. Remember where you are. The bulletin board opposite the "library" told him. There was his name on the roster of the call schedule for the E.R. In order to build up his practice, he'd volunteered to cover the E.R., to take the dregs—the patients who couldn't afford a private physician; the welfares, the Medicaids, the drug addicts, the drunken Creoles and the spillover medical flotsam from New Orleans. He'd seen the same indigents many times over. As the burlesque comedian would say, the place was so small, people had to take turns being the town drunk.

Howard headed back to the E.R., hoping some of the lab work would be back. At the entrance, he almost collided with the E.R. nurse coming out the door. She thrust a handful of lab slides at him and shrugged. "About what you'd expect," she said, "except that his white count is twenty-eight thousand."

Howard nodded. "That's high," he conceded. He drew a breath. "This is one hell of an infection." He walked over to where the Avignon boy lay. He looked better. The IV, which had been running since his admission, was already helping. He seemed less dehydrated, and he even managed a weak smile for Howard. Howard checked the catheter drainage in the bag hanging alongside the cot, and noted the urine output was improving. He raised the sheet covering the abdomen. The red rash was gone. Probably nothing. Maybe it was just irritated skin from the dehydration.

The nurse touched his arm. "Dr. Fletcher, is it okay if we take him to his room? Have you finished writing orders?" Howard nodded his permission.

CHAPTER 17

The Amble Inn was easy to find, nestled as it was in an elbow of State Highway 20, the main thoroughfare in this part of the country when Howard Fletcher was a boy, but now only a two-lane extension of Charlemaigne's main street and rendered obsolete by the expressway that carried the world past the town's front door. Howard pulled into the parking lot, which held only a few cars at this late hour. He had planned on getting here earlier, but had spent a couple of hours suturing up a kid who had put a motorcycle on its side for almost a half-block while showing off for the downtown Saturday night crowd. The kid would be all right. He'd be out of the hospital in a couple of days, proudly showing off his battle scars to his fellow daredevils.

Howard had his choice of bar stools. Through an arch, he could see a few late diners finishing up in the restaurant. A guy sat behind a piano in one corner playing Gershwin and Cole Porter, soft, easy and faithful to the composers. All in all, a relaxing place, probably what passed for a nightspot in Charlemaigne. He ordered an Old-Fashioned from a girl in a black uniform with a white plastic name tag that said she wanted to be addressed as 'Debbie.' So he did. "Thanks, Debbie," he told her when the drink was set in front of him. She smiled at him and moved to a tall chair at the end of the bar. The drink had proper bite, and seemed to perk him up.

It was several minutes before he caught sight of Marva Langston. Wearing a rose cocktail dress, she emerged from a door at the rear of the dining room. She stopped to say a few words to a waitress laden with a tray of dirty dishes, then stepped behind the bar, and their eyes met. Howard gave her a little wave, but received no sign of recognition. A guy in a gaudy Hawaiian shirt three stools away raised his face out of his drink and called her over. Howard turned away, but bent his ear to catch their conversation.

"Another beer," the guy ordered in a tone that suggested he was anticipating a turndown. "And two fingers of my good friend, Jack Daniels, on the side."

Marva Langston shook her head. "No. That's enough. That one," she said, pointing at the empty shot glass, "was your last call."

"I'm O.K.," he protested.

"Sure you are," she said mockingly. "Your eyes crossed an hour ago. I've seen guys embalmed that were in better shape."

Howard hid his smile behind his glass. The guy shook his finger at Marva. "You, Marva Langston, are a despot. Worse than that, you have taken this job under false pretenses. You don't know the difference between mellow and drunk."

"Sure, sure," she said. She eased down the bar. "Good evening, Doctor."

Howard nodded. "Good evening. Nice place you have here."

She surveyed the room. The Amble Inn was winding down. "It'll do," she said. "To what do we owe the pleasure?"

"Just passing by. A little unwinding time." She nodded, playing the tip of her tongue along the edge of her teeth the way she'd done at his office, a playfully cynical gesture suggesting instinctive wariness more than seductiveness.

"Well, you came to the right town," she said. "I can't think of a more wound-down spot on the face of the earth than Charlemaigne. It's so relaxed, it's almost comatose."

He smiled. "Oh, I don't know. I kind of like it around here." He took a sip of his drink, meeting her eyes over the top of the glass. "In fact, I'm liking it better each day."

He saw that he'd put her a bit on the defensive—her body language told him so—and it rather pleased him. But she dug in and came back. "You need help, Doctor. Where did you come from, New Guinea?"

He laughed and shook his head. "Chicago."

"Chicago?" she squeaked. "Oh, God." She giggled at his folly, putting a hand to her mouth. "Talk about a change of scenery. You need another drink?"

He raised his glass. "No, this'll do for now."

"Well, if you change your mind—It's almost closing time."

The drink had warmed him. "The real reason I stopped in was to see if you were still lifting heavy beer mugs."

"What?"

"Your hand. How is it?"

A small spot of red embarrassment appeared on her cheek, and disappeared just as quickly. "Oh, yes. You were right. I went to the clinic. It *is* carpal tunnel, and I'll have to have it taken care of."

"I'll be glad to do it. Guaranteed little strain, little pain. I'll even let you look at my diploma to prove I'm qualified."

Marva Langston laughed, an unaffected nasal giggle that surprised him. He would have expected something throaty and dusky. "O.K., I believe you. I'll call for an appointment."

They turned as the drunk down the bar called to Marva. "I've given you ample time to reconsider. A little one," he pleaded, holding his thumb and forefinger an inch apart. "For the road."

It was only then that Howard recognized the face of the

sheriff. "Beauford, quiet," she ordered. "Your one for the road is coffee. Come on, I'm buying."

Howard masked his surprise. "Evening, Sheriff. Nice to see you again." Howard looked around. The place was almost deserted.

Beauford Decatur squinted down the bar. "Whozit?" He leaned closer. "Ah, Dr. Fletcher, the prodigal son. How are you finding the old place, Doctor? Somewhat tired and bedraggled, I'd venture. Yessir, poor old Charlemaigne. Ridden hard and put away wet."

The sheriff's speech, a down-home country vernacular when sober, was grammatically perfect, even cultured, when oiled by liquor. "Haven't quite made up my mind yet," Howard replied.

"Given time," Decatur said, "I think you'll come to agree with me that our little hamlet is practically moribund, though you wouldn't know it by the fatuous smiles that adorn many of our most illustrious citizens."

Marva went around the bar, talked quietly to Decatur for a few moments, then escorted him to a corner booth and set a pot of coffee in front of him. The piano player waved good night, and the last of the waitresses were also checking out. Marva came and sat next to Howard. "He's a nice guy," she said. "He'll do this maybe once every couple of months, that's all. Don't know why. I think he thinks he's not appreciated. Small town. Everybody thinks they own a piece of the local sheriff."

Howard nodded. "What now?"

"I have to get him out of here. And he's in no shape to drive."

"I'll be glad to help you get him home," Howard offered.

"Well, thanks. Yes, that'd be nice of you," she said. "He doesn't live too far from here."

Howard polished off his drink and stood. "Shall we? We can take my car."

• • •

Beauford Decatur, propped between the two of them, managed to negotiate his front stoop without too much trouble. Marva and Howard got him into the living room of the small house, where the sheriff shrugged them off and collapsed on a couch. He sighed deeply and flung an arm across his eyes. "Let's go, Beauford," Marva urged. "Let's get you into the bedroom or you'll spend all night out here." She bent over him, and Beauford tugged at her.

"You gonna tuck me in, Mommy?" he asked, a clown's grin plastered on his face.

"He lives alone?" Howard asked.

"Yeah," Marva answered. "He never married. Folks are gone." She turned back to the sheriff, exasperated. "Up, Beauford, or we're going to leave you here." Her face was flushed, and she was breathing hard from her exertions. "Oh, God, Beauford, I'm glad you don't do this very often."

"How about a little good night kiss?" Beauford said, his crooked grin in place.

She smiled wearily. "Inappropriate, Sheriff. I think of you as an older brother."

"Gimmee a big wet kiss, sis."

Marva straightened and put her hand to her lips. "Lips that touch liquor shall never touch mine."

Beauford giggled. "You're quick, Marva. A tad old-fashioned, but quick. A little tenderness would do wonders for my morale. Soon I sally forth into the streets to do battle with the evil criminal element so you will remain safe in your homes." He waved an arm grandly and sank deeper into the couch cushions, closing his eyes. In a few moments, he was asleep.

Marva turned to Howard, pushing the damp hair out of her eyes. "Let's leave him," she said. "We've done our good deed for tonight."

"Where do you live?" Howard asked.

Marva was running her hand over the plush front seat

upholstery of the BMW. "Take me back to the bar. I left my car there." She looked over at Howard. "Doctors, as a rule, go first-class, I guess."

"What?"

"Elegant automobile," she said.

"Well, yeah, I made a lot of money once." He shifted uneasily behind the wheel.

"You sound embarrassed about it."

He gave her a quick glance. "I suppose I am. I liked making the money, don't get me wrong. I liked it and all the things it could get me. At the same time, I guess I always felt a little uncomfortable with it."

"Guilt," she pronounced. "People come from nowhere, get someplace and then torture themselves because they don't think they deserve it."

"I didn't say I tortured myself over it."

She made a derisive sound. "Well, just give me a crack at it and see how tortured I am. Like the man said, 'It's no sin to be poor but on the other hand, it's nothing to brag about either.'"

Howard turned into the deserted parking lot of the Amble Inn. Marva opened the door. "Thanks for the lift," she said. She stepped out of the car. "And thanks for the help with Beauford."

Howard leaned across the seat. "The sheriff has a good friend. I hope if I'm ever in such a state, somebody like you will take pity on me."

CHAPTER 18

Beauford Decatur had been a Rotarian since he'd been old enough to vote, just as his daddy before him. But he'd always felt a little out of place, kind of like transferring from Boys' Town to a private prep school. He got along with all of the members well enough, but they took different routes when leaving the Holiday Inn every Thursday after lunch. They went back to their white-collar jobs or to the country club. Beauford had never been inside the country club, never. His education had been incomplete. Then again, none of his fellow Rotarians had ever tried to put a drunk in a cell on a Saturday night while the drunk ("Jes' lemme sleep it off, Sheriff"), thank you, was concurrently shitting his pants. There were other things, subtle things, that set Beauford Decatur apart from the others. Beauford hitched self-consciously at his gun belt, and looked around at the other Rotarians and thought that he had only two business suits, one serviceable, and that two were all he would ever need. He could not suppress the feeling that he was regarded, with unfailing politeness of course, merely as a necessary functionary to keep the peace. He'd gone to high school with most of them, and it struck him just now that he had never been inside any of their homes. Beauford knew, even as he compared himself with them, that one of his feelings, however slight, was one of envy, and he didn't like himself very much for it. A childhood chip on the shoulder, carried over to the present because his family, had there been any railroad tracks in Charlemaigne, Louisiana, would have lived on the other side. Beauford shrugged and turned his attention to the speaker's table.

The Charlemaigne Rotary Club's budget didn't stretch to the point where it could hire outside speakers, so it was forced to turn to prominent local citizens who, if not exactly spellbinders, came cheap. The club called upon H. T. Mann at least three times a year. Mann, like the other luncheon speakers, didn't vary the talks a great deal. But the audience didn't necessarily come to be inspired. The speeches served to fill the time between the chicken à la king and the sherbet.

In fact, the Rotarians seemed to derive some comfort in the sameness of the words, which rarely dwelled on the negative. The words left them feeling lucky to be citizens of Charlemaigne. And they paid particular attention to Mann, whose influence as the publisher of *The Charlemaigne Advance* was a given.

Mann waited until the tinkle of the forks and cups and the noontime babble had subsided. He looked down over his glasses at the twenty or thirty white male Protestant faces. "There is talk going around," he began slowly. "No, grumbling, really, that Charlemaigne is living in the dark ages. That there is some kind of old-boy conspiracy to purposely stifle industrial progress.

"The *Advance* has been accused in some quarters as being obstructionist. Economic development is discouraged in Charlemaigne, they say."

Mann went on darkly for several minutes without saying who 'they' were. Then he paused and let his eyes sweep the room. "I submit to you, my friends, that progress is a two-edged sword. Remember, growth and bigness are not inherently good, nor smallness inherently bad.

"Unbridled and unchecked growth"—Mann raised a finger for emphasis—"that mindless appetite for the quick buck, comes at a heavy price." He leaned over the lectern and lowered his voice. "Its price is zoning chaos; its price is dirty air and crime; its price is an influx of outsiders who have no appreciation of what we have built here."

Mann straightened and paused. He smiled. "Today, we have a positive example of what I'm speaking about. Please allow me to welcome and extend the Charlemaigne hand of friendship to our newest citizen. One of the dedicated group of public health officials who have seen fit to grace our town. We're all aware of the U.S. Government's public health group of homes just west of town, fine homes built for the doctors and scientists of the U.S. Public Health Service in Carville. That addition is just the kind of growth I'm speaking about. In this case, distinguished men and women of science, people who add immeasurably to the image of our community. These are the kind of people who can bring honor to Charlemaigne. Let us hope others will follow. Let us encourage *that* kind of growth, and guard against opening ourselves to undesirable industrial expansion in which smokestacks dot our skyline, bringing with it an influx of people who have little in common with the history and traditions of our city."

People, Beauford Decatur surmised, who talked funny and came from where it snowed occasionally. Decatur glanced at his fellow Rotarians, and wondered how many remembered that no industrial plant had come to town since the cigar-wrapping factory thirty-five years ago, and that the skyline of Charlemaigne was dominated by the three floors of the Holiday Inn where they were sitting. And the public health-owned group of homes had been started in the twenties, when the Government took over the leper colony at nearby Carville.

Mann was introducing somebody from the audience. "He's here as my guest today," Mann was saying. "Please welcome Dr. Byron Swinton, a new resident of Charlemaigne, living in the public health area. One of the world's top men in the field of scientific research. Dr. Swinton comes to us from the Center for Disease Control in Atlanta." Mann beamed and extended an open palm to Swinton, who rose from his chair and nodded around the room at the warm applause.

Beauford Decatur observed a fiftyish, slender, pale, serious-looking man in a pinstripe suit. He looked like a school principal, or a tax examiner. "Thank you for your warm welcome," Byron Swinton said. "We'll try not to let any of our bugs escape to infest your fair community." Chuckles all around, and Swinton sat down, his hand on the shoulder of a handsome teenager next to him, whom Beauford guessed was the bug man's son.

Mann was droning on, harping on the same theme, in slightly different words. "Growth, yes," he intoned, "but orderly growth. Because the alternative comes at an intolerable sacrifice. We sacrifice our heritage and, with it, our values. Our young will be compromised and, in turn, the sanctity of God and family will be trivialized. Out the window goes respect for authority, and the love and trust of our neighbors. That is a prohibitive price to pay for progress."

Mann finished with the flourish of a traveling tent evangelist. "I can say unequivocally, gentlemen, that Charlemaigne is one of the few communities left in this country where one can still find the old-fashioned virtues, the virtues that made this a great nation. They are still priceless. Put them in the vault. They are not for sale."

The crowd was on its feet, the twenty or thirty monopolists applauding wildly. Mann took his seat, smiling and nodding. He patted his head with his handkerchief. His fervor had worked up a sweat.

Mann was stopped several times and congratulated as he made his way to the parking lot. He was eager to get away. It was almost an hour's drive to New Orleans.

He spotted Decatur walking to his patrol car and hailed him. Mann guided Decatur to a private spot between cars.

"Sheriff, I've been hearing some complaints about those teenagers hanging out around Fort Street late at night. They're not doing anything, just hanging out. They mill around the party store down there, making noise all night. The folks around there are complaining."

Decatur nodded wearily. "Well, we go down there every once in a while and run them off. But they're not really breaking any laws."

Mann pursed his lips. "No? It's my understanding that folks down there find a load of beer cans on their lawns every morning. We're not only talking about an eyesore, Sheriff, we're talking about the morals of our children."

Decatur said, "Yes sir, Mr. Mann. We'll give it a little extra attention."

"Good," Mann said, moving off. "Very good, Sheriff."

CHAPTER 19

The flat at the center of the French Quarter looked like all the others from the outside. But inside it was larger, occupying the entire floor of the building, and it was sumptuously furnished. "Hello," he called as he entered.

"In here," came the response from the living room.

Mann walked toward the voice, which belonged to a lovely red-haired woman in her late twenties. Mann gave her a brotherly hug and took a seat in an overstuffed chair. He closed his eyes for a moment.

"You look tired," the young woman said.

"Maybe a little," Mann replied. "It's the heat, I think. Very warm for so early in the year."

The woman looked at him protectively. "Can I get you something to drink, perhaps a tall gin and tonic?" He smiled and shook his head. "I keep forgetting," she said. "You don't drink."

"Nor smoke," Mann reminded her. "I consider my abstinence the reason I am in such good condition for my age."

"Truly remarkable," she agreed. "You look like a man thirty years younger."

"Thank you," he said.

She walked to another chair. "You must have discovered the fountain of youth." She smiled as she said it, and watched Mann's eyes grow cloudy. "Would you like to talk of—"

"No," he said sharply. "Let's just sit quietly for a few moments." Mann rested his head on the back of the chair and closed his eyes. The red-haired woman waited patiently and listened to Mann's breathing. Had he fallen asleep?

After a time, Mann's eyelids flickered. "I think," he said, "I'll get dressed."

"Very well," the woman answered. They both got up, each walking to a different bedroom. "It's in the closet," she called after him.

When they emerged, Mann was wearing a velvet suit with short pants, a large-sized replica of the one worn by Little Lord Fauntleroy. The white shirt had ruffles at the cuffs and throat. The young, red-haired woman wore a tight black blouse and the mobcap of an English governess. She wore no skirt, but only a white starched apron that was too short to cover the red garter belt that held up her black stockings. She had exchanged her house slippers for black high-heeled pumps. She was heavily rouged. Her lipstick was more purple than red, and was smeared as though she had been eating grapes. She stood, her legs widespread, before Mann, who seemed to cower. "Horace," she asked, "what do you have to say for yourself?"

Mann looked down at his shuffling feet. "I am a bad boy," he said meekly.

"You are a *very* bad boy. Those pictures and magazines I found under your mattress are filthy." She pointed an accusing finger. "You are a filthy little boy."

"Are you going to beat me?" he asked.

"What do *you* think your punishment should be? You either take your punishment from me or I'll tell your mother. What will it be?"

"I know I have been bad, and I should be punished. Mommy mustn't know. She is not in good health."

"Very well," the red-haired woman said, walking to a straight-backed, armless chair. On the way she took a hairbrush from the top of the dresser. She sat, and slapped the back of the hairbrush against the palm of her hand. She crooked a finger at Mann.

"Come here," she said sternly.

Mann bit his lip and edged toward her, dragging his feet in the thick carpet. He whimpered as he walked. Then he draped himself face down over her lap, keeping his balance by resting his fists on the floor. "You won't have to do it to me bare, will you?"

"Yes," she said. "Otherwise it will not teach you a forceful lesson. The hairbrush on your skin will remind you of the gravity of your sin. Lower your trousers."

"Yes," Mann whined. "I have been bad. I must be punished severely." He helped her pull the short pants down to his knees, exposing his bony white buttocks. "And then you'll love me."

The young red-haired woman brought the hairbrush down smartly on Mann's bare rump. He yelped in pain, and then made a low, keening noise in his throat. "Do you know why you are being punished?" she asked, thwacking him again, this time with more force.

"Yes," Mann cried, his face flushed and eyes aglow. "I am bad. I deserve to be beaten." The brush rose and fell and the skin reddened, and then broke. A thin trail of blood trickled down Mann's leg. "Ahhh," he shrieked, his head lifting like a braying wolf.

She continued to chastise him. "You are a dirty little boy with a dirty little mind." The red-haired woman was getting arm-weary, and she had worked up a sweat. She no longer answered Mann's plaintive cries, but continued flailing the brush until she heard his long, satisfied moan, and then felt him shudder and grow limp.

When Mann had changed clothes and returned from the bathroom, they drank iced tea from tall glasses and discussed a wide range of topics. The young red-haired woman, very knowledgeable about current events and world politics, had a fine mind. Mann was always at peace during these moments, and he judged them as among his most relaxing. The conversation would gradually wind down to nothing and then after a silence, Mann would ask the question, "Well, how's your life been going?"

"Fine, no complaints," she replied, and then after a pause, "I wish it were so for my sister."

Mann feigned surprise. "Oh, and what seems to be the trouble?"

The young woman sighed. "It seems her husband has left her. Just dropped out of sight. He cleaned out the bank account, and just disappeared. And her with two little boys to look after."

Mann shook his head sadly, and clicked his tongue sympathetically. Last month, the young red-haired woman related how her car needed a complete engine overhaul. Mann rose, his hand dipping into the inside pocket of his suit coat. He withdrew a sealed envelope and dropped it on the table next to the hairbrush. "Perhaps," he said, "this will help out." He put his hand on the young woman's head and patted her red hair.

"You are so kind," she said without looking up.

Walking to his car from the apartment of the red-haired woman, H.T. Mann's lips curled at the revelers, whose public debauchery and taste for parades started a full month before Mardi Gras. Mann had been forced to park his car six blocks away since the entire Quarter was off limits to automobiles. He walked head down toward the parking garage, ignoring as best he could the hot dog vendors and whores and the barkers for the sin palaces. Mini-bars had been set up in the middle of the streets. He bumped into a young woman and she cursed him as her drink ran down her thigh-high silver boot. Mann thought that he might be the only human being walking with a purpose. Everyone else, it seemed, was strolling around drunk in the French Quarter. The sodden young woman he'd jostled had looked suspiciously at his dark suit and tie.

Suddenly, the crowd swallowed him. Mann was brought to a stop by a wall of people at St. Ann and Bourbon. A small parade was approaching the intersection. Damnable luck! His car was on the other side of Bourbon Street, and he would have to wait. People, wild, feverish, glazed-eyed people, mouths agape, painted like warring Indians, smothered him and made him want to retch. The head of the parade was abreast of Mann. It was another of the plethora of warm-up parades that preceded the real Mardi Gras.

A makeshift float, amateurishly assembled, led the procession. A maroon cloth, with silver Greek letters, adorned the sides of the old pickup truck, on top of which rode a thin, almost emaciated man on a wooden platform. He was masked, dressed in a red oversized diaper fastened with a huge safety pin. His face and body had been painted a sparkling gold. He held a three-pronged lightning bolt fashioned out of cardboard. Mann decided that the exhibitionist was posing as a bedraggled Zeus. The gaunt golden man's too-big diaper constantly appeared ready to slip to his ankles as he took swigs from a bottle of wine, much of it cascading over his chin like a mini-waterfall.

The boisterous crowd swayed and heaved, pressing in on Mann, who was starting to sweat profusely. He tried to hold himself detached from the swirling insanity, holding his breath from time to time and steeling himself until the parade passed. A young man in front of him jiggled from side to side, bouncing on his toes. His costume was a dual-colored body stocking, green and pink bisected down the middle, a court jester's outfit with huge tassels on his slippers. His spastic movements threw him against Mann, once, twice, three times. Mann angrily held his ground— the compressed humanity gave him no choice—until, his patience exhausted, he grabbed the garishly dressed person by the shoulder and spun him around. "Young man," he began to remonstrate.

The jester flipped a limp hand at Mann, and cocked his head coquettishly. "Thank you, dear," he said. "Ma*ma* would be positively ecstatic to know that I've settled on a gender." He emitted a high-pitched giggle.

Mann felt like striking the freak. Instead, he forced his way past, shoving people from his path, and threaded his way through the parade marchers to the other side of the street.

Mann's car was approaching the Charlemaigne exit when he first noticed the discomfort. An itch, which began as an annoyance on his shoulder, was crying out for attention. Driving with one hand, he groped under his suitcoat and inside his shirt to fingernail a small pimple. Perhaps a mosquito in his friend's apartment. They were very common in New Orleans, especially in that section of the city. Too bad, Mann thought, that lovely lady was forced to live there. He wished he could afford more suitable quarters for her.

CHAPTER 20

The principal knocked for a long time on Miss Lorlene's front door. He fought an impulse to turn on his heel and leave. He stared at the doorknob, knowing, somehow instinctively, that the door was unlocked. What was he doing here? He supposed it was his duty. Miss Lorlene had not reported for work or telephoned for three days. After calling in sick for over a week, she had not been heard from. Repeated calls to her home had gone unanswered. The principal, for a brief moment, felt an overpowering rage at Miss Lorlene. What right did she have, putting him in the middle of her sordid little mess? The stupid, silly woman.

The principal put a nervous hand on the doorknob and slowly inched the door open. His nose twitched. He stepped inside and called, "Hello." A foul odor struck him, engulfed him, and took his breath away. His eyes watered. He forced himself to look at the source of the odor, and his eyes settled on Miss Lorlene's body, decaying on the couch. The principal retched, and staggered back to the porch. The odor followed him. He took in huge draughts of air like a drowning man.

It was many minutes later that the principal, clutching a handkerchief over his nose, plunged back into the room. He held his breath, averting his eyes from the remains of Miss Lorlene. He walked quickly to the telephone on the desk and dialed the police. "There is a . . . there has been a death," he said haltingly into the receiver. He identified himself, and gave the address. "I'll wait for you," he told the officer. "Outside."

The principal was replacing the receiver in its cradle when his eyes fell on two envelopes propped on the desk. One was addressed simply to "Robby." The silly, silly woman. The principal fished the note from the envelope, and quickly scanned its contents—Miss Lorlene's final message to her young lover. The principal's lip curled in disgust. He looked around quickly as though another person, another living person, was in the room with him. Then he slid the note in his pocket, leaving the other envelope by the body, and bolted for the door.

CHAPTER 21

Marva Langston set about scraping the dinner dishes, though there wasn't much left to scrape. The lasagna pan was nearly empty. She rinsed the dishes and left them in the sink for later, then went to the living room to straighten up. She caught herself humming—the domesticated melody of the contented housewife, doing dishes, even on her night off. She stopped, embarrassed, and stole a glance at Howard hunkered down on the couch, balancing a brandy on one knee. He watched her as she placed a steaming mug of coffee in front of him.

"I like this house," he announced.

Marva laughed and waved her hand at the threadbare surroundings—the frayed couch, the holes in the carpet, the fading wallpaper. "This second-hand store? It'll never make *Architectural Digest*."

"I like it anyway. Maybe I like it *because* it has no chance in *Architectural Digest*. There's a warmth here."

"A seedy warmth. I never thought of it that way." She looked around. "It'll be better some day." She spoke softly, but with a fierce determination.

"I'm sure it will," Howard said.

They sat on opposite sides of the room, conversing at long distance, content for the moment to luxuriate in the postprandial ritual of coffee and brandy. They had not talked much over the lasagna, Marva deriving a kick out of

Howard's obvious enjoyment of her cooking. "Well, are you settling in yet?" she asked finally.

Howard nodded. "I guess so. It's a little strange coming back here after all these years. Funny. Things stay the same, and yet everything is different." He fixed his eyes on her. "But, all in all, a nice town. Nice people. Most of them anyway."

Marva hid in her coffee cup. "Most of the talk is that you won't stick around, that you're here on some sort of nostalgia tour, pasting up the last page of the family album before starting a new life."

He settled back on the couch and put his feet on the worn coffee table. "That could be very perceptive. I'm not sure myself." He looked at her skeptically. "Are you speaking for the community, or is that your personal view?"

Marva blushed and laughed. "I confess, I didn't take a poll."

He grunted amiably. "It's O.K. It's human to speculate. I guess I'm really not sure what I'm doing here either." He tried to smile. "Just looking for a place to lay my weary head."

His whimsy didn't come off. Marva saw in front of her a vulnerable and lonely forty-year-old man. He was no vagabond, he was holding back, not leveling with her. Marva felt herself succumbing. Tell me he's not another helpless, insecure, little-boy type, she thought. Her ex-husband had been one of those. And when she'd gotten past all that, what was left was an ass. That sweet shy boy had turned out to be a self-centered, petulant jerk. Did she wear a sign proclaiming herself a way station on the road to manhood? The silence between them was becoming unsettling. "Look, it's time to pay for your supper, Doctor, remember? The deal was I'd cook you lasagna, and you'd tell me your life story."

He shook a finger at her. "The deal was we'd both tell, remember?"

"Yes, yes, O.K." she said.

He got off the couch and walked to the bookshelves. "You first," he said. The 'bookcase' was actually two-by-eight-foot pine boards, varnished and sagging under the load. They were stacked on cement blocks and covered one wall. He browsed, pulling out one book at a time, rubbing his hands across the covers and riffling through the pages. Marva watched him nod occasionally as he handled the books gently, almost delicately, caressing them. He was good-looking, she thought, but not strikingly so. He had an appealing, unaffected slouch when he moved.

"Well?" he said, not diverting his attention from the book.

"What?"

"You first," he repeated.

She stared at a spot on the ceiling. "My life is the proverbial open book, pun intended. You can ask anyone in town and get my life story. You want to go to sleep? Try this: single parent, struggling mother, barmaid."

He laughed. "Single, struggling parent, a barmaid who studies accounting and reads *Les Miserables*." He pulled Victor Hugo's classic from its place on the two-by-eight-foot board. "I presume this is not for purely decorative purposes."

"I've read it," she conceded, smiling.

"Go on," he said.

"Not much else to say. I manage the bar for a guy in New Orleans. Started as a waitress at the Amble Inn when my husband left."

"And the accounting?"

She shrugged. "Yeah, it seemed solid, you know. About finished. Take the CPA exam next fall. I'm kinda proud of that."

He turned to her. "You should be." He replaced the book. "An accountant with a love for the classics. A fan of Victor Hugo."

She shook her head and smiled at him. "You'll do anything to steer the conversation away from yourself, won't you? O.K., I'll take the pressure off. You don't have to tell me anything about yourself, not anything." She saw his relief, though he tried to cover it with nonchalance. Careful, she told herself, don't be the eternal nurturer. She was not going to spend her entire life breaking her ass to put some man at ease.

She watched him pull out another book. "This one's in French," he said. "Now, wait a minute. You don't mean . . ."

"Guilty," she said.

He looked amazed. "You read French?"

"I read French," she said. "And speak it, though that's not entirely unique in this part of the country. My ex-husband spoke it, so I studied it after I moved here. It's a great language. The French can make 'sewer' sound romantic."

She watched him move down the bookshelves, his long fingers playing along the rows of titles. She suddenly realized how pale he was. She was used to the darker, harder French Cajun types. How did she know he wasn't just another ne'er-do-well, no different than any of the others she had come across? Just because he was a neurosurgeon from Chicago, did that give him the right to say nothing about himself? It was all the more reason for him to talk.

She stared at him. "The word is—" She hesitated but then decided to push on. "The word is you're running from something."

He was riffling through *The Oxford Book of English Verse*, and looked up quickly. "And what is it I'm supposed to be running from?" he finally said with a sad smile.

To hell with it, she thought, let him be a Sphinx if he wants to. But it was too late, she'd already started it. She shrugged. "The world out there is assuming, rumoring, all kinds of things—ex-wives, gambling debts, drinking problems, skipped alimony. The usual reason anybody runs. There have to be some dead bodies back there that . . ."

A shadow crossed his face as she used that expression, an unmistakable look of torment. He looked back down into the book and turned from her. "Oh God," she murmured. There was a devastating silence. She got out of her chair and crossed the few feet between them.

He was turned from her and his head was still in the book when she stopped beside him. She eased the book from his hands and put it back on the bookcase. His look was now more quizzical than hurt when she put her arms around his neck. She kissed him, and he was passive at first. But they kept kissing, and he joined in, the kissing deeper and open-mouthed. They finally broke apart, and she stepped back to observe him. He stood unmoving, while she tried to identify the look in his eyes. The pain was gone. She unbuttoned her blouse, and let it fall to the floor, and her bra shortly followed. Then she began to undo his shirt. She rubbed her breasts against his naked chest, and she heard his breathing. She was glad that her breasts, though not her chief boast, were firm and youthful. And finally, she was relieved to see, he became an active participant. "Here? In the living room?" she asked.

"Of course not," he murmured, "we're going to bed like civilized people."

They stood clasped together, feeling each other's nakedness, smelling each other's delicious smell as they rubbed each other. "Vicky will be home from the movies in an hour," she blurted. She laughed. "Why am I being so practical? I'm going to bed with a total stranger."

"Not for long," he murmured into her hair, "I . . . we, are going to talk afterwards."

CHAPTER 22

The chills were beginning. And within thirty minutes, no longer, the fever would follow. He'd been timing them since the illness, whatever it was, had struck. This chill was worse. His body shook, the trembling rocking the bed. H. T. Mann had never in his life had the flu, never, for that matter, remembered ever being very ill. He reached for the thick comforter, still damp from the last sweat, and pulled it up to his chin. He felt the rolling again, his stomach muttering with a voice of its own. He had lost count of the number of times he had staggered to the bathroom. The diarrhea had left him as weak and unsteady as a newborn fawn.

He looked around his huge high-ceilinged bedroom with its solemn mahogany walls. He studied the hand-carved inlaid pattern where the dark wood molding joined the ceiling. The room was centered by his four-poster bed, also made of mahogany. He had removed the canopy years ago so it wouldn't block his view of this magnificent room. After his mother had died, in this very room, in this very bed, he'd moved in here with his desk, his books, his study table, creating a combination bedroom-sitting room, all furnished with French period pieces. As sick as he was, he took the time to admire the Louis XIV chairs, the wheeled tea cart and the mammoth secretary with its fold-out writing shelf.

He checked his watch. Eleven thirty, dark, lights on. Time had passed so quickly. It seemed it was only morning a short time ago. He admired the workmanship of his Swiss Tissot watch. Nothing like it. Let them have their Rolexes and Concords. Mann took note of his long, thin fingers, remarkably pale and delicate. Mother had always complimented him on his hands; "the hands of a surgeon," she had called them. He called out to her, and she appeared at the foot of his bed. He held up his finely boned hand toward her, and imagined the small muscles with their tension pulleys, all under the control of his brain and nervous system. How well they worked! His mother smiled, and nodded.

He started to speak to her, but she had vanished, and his hand began trembling as another chill struck him. He called to his mother again, asking her to return. He wanted to ask her about Grandfather—hadn't he died of some sort of infection? Mother materialized beside the bed again, and spoke to him not in words but thoughts. Yes, Grandfather had passed on with pneumonia. Horace remembered now. It was one of his earliest boyhood recollections. Grandpa had a rigor, uncontrollable bone shakes. Now *he* was having a rigor. The word sent him into a panic, and shocked him into lucidity. Mother had disappeared again, and he recognized his hallucination. He must act quickly. The cramps would follow the chills, along with the diarrhea; then the fever would return.

He used his arms to force himself to a sitting position, and laboriously swung his legs over the edge of the bed. He paused to catch his breath, and then picked up the phone and dialed the Charlemaigne Hospital. Hearing the nurse's voice calmed him somewhat. The physician on call was Dr. Howard Fletcher, she said. Fletcher, the local boy who'd left Charlemaigne to live with the Yankees. A prodigal. But Mann had no choice. Yes, he told the nurse, he would come to the emergency room.

• • •

Horace T. Mann looked cadaverous. He was incredibly dehydrated, with sunken eyes, and mucous membranes so parched there was no saliva. Despite a temperature of over 105 degrees, he was too dehydrated to sweat. A bad sign, since sweating was the most natural and best way to get rid of body heat.

Mann was babbling the answers to Howard's questions. Though he was close to hallucinating from the fever, the history he gave was a déjà-vu from last week's case: devastating and debilitating nausea, diarrhea and fever. Again there was no history of drinking or eating anything that could be remotely considered contaminated. And then Howard realized the other similarity. The Avignon boy had been brought to the emergency room exactly one week ago, almost to the minute, Thursday at six P.M. However, he had recovered very well. Howard had discharged him just yesterday.

He started the physical exam by easing Mann out of his clothes. At first he thought Mann had come to the E.R. in a white bathrobe. But as he and the nurse undressed him he realized Mann was dressed in a long nightshirt, a throwback to another time. The nightshirt was filthy, soaked in perspiration and soiled with feces. Howard remembered seeing Mann about town dressed in a three-piece suit in the steamy climate. The guy was a nineteenth-century reincarnation.

Howard helped the nurse prop Mann to a sitting position and they pulled the nightshirt over his head. There was the gagging smell of excrement. They put on a clean gown and covered Mann's lower half with a sheet. The nurse steadied him with a hand on his back while Howard quickly examined the head, neck, chest, lungs and heart. Everything was negative except for the severe dehydration.

As he lifted the gown to examine the abdomen, he saw the spots. They were exactly like the ones he'd seen on the Avignon kid's abdomen, even in the same location. No

question about it. This time, he studied them more carefully, and realized they were not just a skin irritation or a
rash as he'd thought with Avignon. There were a dozen of
them in the left upper quadrant of the abdomen, closely
grouped, flat and macular. He estimated each one to be
eight or nine millimeters in diameter and crescent-shaped.
The color struck him. The spots were a very bright red,
incongruous in that pale dry skin, like a vividly colored
flower in a bleak desert.

He pulled the gown down, covering the abdomen, and
looked at Mann. "How long have you had these spots?"

"What spots? There aren't any spots on my clothes,
Mother."

The nurse shot a puzzled glance at Fletcher—Mann's face
was beginning to twitch, his eyes were glassy. It figured.
His temperature was almost 106 degrees! A little confusion
was not unexpected. Howard picked up the chart and added
aspirin and a cooling blanket to the orders he'd already
written, then asked the nurse to take the patient to a room
upstairs.

He stood in the E.R. doorway as Mann was being
wheeled by, and suddenly wondered if he might be gay.
Fifty-six and never married. On an impulse he stopped the
gurney cart and bent over him. "Mr. Mann, have you been
to New Orleans lately, the French Quarter?"

The twitching and babbling stopped and he seemed
suddenly lucid. "I've never been to the French Quarter!
Filth, nothing but filth and degradation."

The nurse looked at Fletcher and shrugged. Fletcher
nodded for them to take Mann upstairs.

CHAPTER 23

The family standoff had been going on for several minutes, and Marva Langston had thus far kept her temper in check. She hadn't wanted an argument, but she was about to lose it.

"Look, Mother," Vicky was saying with ill-concealed impatience, "I told you, he's new; he doesn't have any friends."

"How did you meet him?"

"Mom," Vicky whined, the word a drawn-out exasperation. "He's in my biology class. He's quiet, but very intelligent. He knows more than the teacher." She flicked her head defiantly, her light-brown hair swishing about her shoulders.

Marva raised an eyebrow. "A genius, is he? Well, I still don't like it. Going out with somebody who's new in town, someone we don't know."

Vicky's green eyes snapped. "'We' don't know him? I know him. That's all that matters. Mother, I'm an adult. He comes from a very good family. His father's a doctor at Carville. They live in those old houses the Carville doctors live in. And they came here right after New Year's so they've been here over a month. The other kids think he's just a science, bookworm nerd. But I know better."

They stared across the table at each other over their half-eaten plates of spaghetti. Marva gave a little shrug.

"Sounds to me like you're only going out with him because you feel sorry for him."

Vicky dropped her fork; it rattled off her plate. She bit off her words. "It's nothing like that at all. Besides, what difference does the reason make if it's what I want to do? I don't question why you bring your doctor friend home for afternoon interludes, do I?"

Marva had never struck her daughter, hadn't even spanked her. But at this moment, the urge was compelling. "Shut your mouth with that kind of talk," she said with lips barely moving. "That was one man, a friend of mine, thank you, and"—she paused—"and I don't have to answer to you for anything like that. I've done nothing to be ashamed of. And I've never done anything to shame you." There was no response, only a sullen scowl from across the table. Marva took note of her daughter's rigid posture, and sighed. Maybe it was *her* fault. They had so little time together, to talk, to vent feelings, given their varied schedules. It always seemed that she was leaving the house as Vicky was coming home. And Vicky was a straight A student. Enough of a brain herself that a boy like this would appeal to her. Defeated, Marva looked at her watch. "I won't even be here to meet him," she said. She had grown tired of being bitchy, and she was making no impression on Vicky anyway. Ahead of her lay another long shift: seven in the evening to two in the morning, smiling when she didn't feel like it while others had fun. Was she objecting to Vicky's date out of some perverse jealousy?

Vicky intruded on her thoughts. "I can't very well ask him to pick me up two hours earlier just so you can meet him," she said patronizingly. "Mother, this isn't the nineteenth century. They don't have gentlemen callers anymore, not even in the South."

Marva nodded, got up and emptied her cold coffee in the sink, listening to her daughter, who had softened her tone. "This place, this town, is so smothering. It's stifling me. I'll be glad when I graduate." Vicky left the table, and Marva could hear the door closing to her daughter's bedroom. Yes, she thought, graduation would solve a number of things. While Vicky primped for her date with the genius, Marva went to her bedroom to change into her dress for work.

CHAPTER 24

Howard Fletcher's office was located in an antebellum mansion at the edge of Charlemaigne. A G.P. had practiced here since the early forties, living in the back of the house with his wife and nine children, and using the front rooms for an office. A custom, Howard guessed, no longer in use anywhere in the world except Charlemaigne. The practitioner, a widower the last five years of his life, had died right in the office the week before Howard had arrived in town. He'd been able to rent the offices immediately from one of the doctor's sons.

As his practice had grown, he'd given up trying to schedule patients. They wandered in when they felt sick as they had with the previous doctor. The routine checkup—and preventative medicine generally—was considered unnecessary and superfluous. Howard had taken over many of the G.P.'s patients and had quickly realized the man he'd replaced had been very good.

The lack of scheduling left a lot of gaps in the afternoon and today Howard found himself filling the time, as he often did, wandering around the old mansion. There was a master bedroom—with a nursery leading from it—as well as countless children's rooms. Indoor plumbing had been added long after the house had been built—as had electrical wiring and central heating.

He strolled through the upstairs hallway wondering what

sort of life his predecessor had led. Probably a happy one. What would it be like to live here with a family? He thought of Ellen and then, God help him, Marva.

His woolgathering was interrupted by the phone in the office downstairs. It was hooked up to ring in the rest of the house. *That* was something he would want to change. He hurried down the stairs.

He clutched the receiver tightly as he heard the dismaying words. The duty nurse's voice was professionally cool, conveying the news as though reading a restaurant menu. Samuel Avignon, the nurse intoned, had "expired" this afternoon. Howard, stunned, slammed down the receiver and hurried to his car.

The Avignon boy lay stiff and blue on the emergency room gurney cot. His mother sat on a metal stool, cradling her son's lifeless hand alongside her cheek. She didn't stir at the sound of Howard Fletcher's footsteps. He paused in the doorway. Grace Avignon, he could see, had cried herself out for now. The silent pain floated across the room, all the way to Howard. He steeled himself and approached her. A thin film covered her eyes, which were locked in shock. She looked up at him, and Howard nodded, "Mrs. Avignon."

Sam Avignon was incredibly dehydrated, his skin dry and flaking. It was like sand. And his abdomen was strangely distended. It usually took days for the bacteria in the abdomen to multiply to the point where it became distended. Howard moved to the head of the gurney. "What happened?" he asked softly.

Grace Avignon struggled for control. "He . . ." she began, swallowing air. "He was fine this morning. He went out in the field about seven. Later, the other kids found him on the bed. They called me at school. He was having a hard time trying to get his breath. I called the ambulance." A deep sigh caught in her throat. "He was gone before they got there."

Howard's brain whirled. Had he missed something? A

healthy Sam Avignon had walked out of here under his own power just three weeks ago. His mother was staring at Howard with a questioning look of disbelief. Howard didn't have any answers for her. "Did Sam have any recurrence of diarrhea or anything, any chills or fever?"

Mrs. Avignon, her eyes welling, shook her head. "No, he was completely over that. Felt fine. Got his weight back and everything."

There was silence while Howard searched for his next question. "Mrs. Avignon, is there any family history of sudden death? Has this kind of thing ever happened before?"

She shook her head and began sobbing. "What difference does it make? He's dead. Sam's dead."

Howard wanted to ask permission for an autopsy, but he didn't have the stomach for it now. He decided to leave them alone for a while, and come back later. "I'm sorry, Mrs. Avignon," he said. "I would like to talk to you more when you feel up to it."

He left the grieving family in the E.R. waiting room and stopped at the nurses' station. He ordered the nurse to give Mrs. Avignon a sedative, instructing the nurse to have the mother wait there until the hospital social worker came down to help with the arrangements for a post-mortem. Then he headed for the record room to review Sam Avignon's chart of three weeks ago.

"I'm sorry, but Dr. Mortague, our pathologist, does all the bacteriology. You should talk to him about that."

"When will he be back?"

"You just missed him. He finished all his work today. He's only here one day a week, so he won't be back until next week."

Howard Fletcher was disappointed to find the pathologist not around and now found himself talking with the chief lab technician.

"Maybe you could help me," he said. "I was looking

through this chart." He pointed to Sam Avignon's chart, still in his hand. "I noticed there was no final bacteriology identification on a culture taken three weeks ago. Do you know if it's been done? Maybe Dr. Mortague did it when he was here today."

The technician reached across her desk for a huge ledger and began thumbing through it. This had to be the only lab in the world, Howard thought, that didn't enter its lab results into a computer.

She looked up from the book. "All this record shows is that we received the stool specimen three weeks ago."

Howard scowled. "I know that. I was curious as to what the final identification of the bacteria was. If Dr. Mortague comes in once a week to make final specimen reports, he should have been in here three times since we collected those specimens. Are you sure the report isn't somewhere else?"

The technician stared at him blankly, then a glimmer crossed her face. "I think maybe it's one of those stool specimens Dr. Mortague sends to Charity Hospital for final identification. We've been doing that for any case of suspected bacterial diarrhea."

Howard nodded. "Maybe that's it. Have Dr. Mortague call me when he comes in next week."

He was surprised to find the family gone when he returned to the E.R., and he called the social worker immediately.

He couldn't believe his ears. The family had sent the body to a funeral home. They were Seventh Day Adventists, and when the social worker had indicated that the doctor wanted a post-mortem, they wouldn't hear of it.

As he took Sam Avignon's telephone number from the chart, he knew it was useless to call, but he decided to anyway. Seventh Day Adventists did not believe in autopsies. It defiled the body—as did a transfusion. He'd seen them die rather than compromise their faith.

And there was no hope of demanding an autopsy. The parish was too small to have its own coroner. The local sheriff had to demand an autopsy if there was no next-of-kin consent. And that was done only if there was a strong suspicion of foul play. Knowing it was a waste of time, he picked up the phone and dialed Grace Avignon.

CHAPTER 25

Horace Mann let the phone ring at the other end for twenty times before hanging up. Too bad. He'd wanted to explain to his friend about his illness. And he'd wanted to see her again. A convalescent for three weeks, he'd read everything in the house and he was bored.

He threw his legs over the side of the bed and stood up, too quickly as it turned out. The room spun, and he had to wait for the dizziness to subside. He hadn't regained as much of his strength as he thought. He steadied himself, and walked slowly to the kitchen and prepared himself a glass of hot cocoa. When he had been discharged from the hospital three weeks ago, he'd been inclined to seek another medical opinion, in New Orleans, about this peculiar illness he'd had. But another doctor would mean more questions about the personal life of Horace T. Mann. And he was not unhappy with Dr. Fletcher. For a boy from the wrong side of town, Dr. Fletcher had done very well for himself. He'd arrived in town after the first of the year and had succeeded in building a successful practice in less than two months.

He suddenly felt a renewal of energy. He would telephone his friend in the French Quarter later in the day, and tell her he would visit her tonight. He reached for the phone.

And then the pain struck, just as it did three weeks ago, but much worse. This time the spasms were more painful.

They doubled him over, and took away his breath. The hot cocoa spilled onto his lap, burning his thighs through his silk pajamas. He struggled to the phone and dialed 911.

Howard Fletcher saw the nurse coming at him at a half-run, and knew the news was bad. He took the X-ray film from her and held it up to the light. Radiographs were not meant to be read this way, holding the film by hand up against a fluorescent lamp. You were supposed to sit down in front of a special view-box and study the film, preferably with a radiologist at your side. "Never read an X-ray standing up; you're more apt to miss something," the radiology professors had preached in med school.

But he didn't need to study this one. The X-ray, a flat film of Horace T. Mann's abdomen, showed an intestinal perforation! There was no question. There was "free air" high up in the abdomen. The gray and white structures familiar on an X-ray as the normal abdominal structures were pushed aside by a dark, sinister-looking area.

Howard couldn't believe it. Had he made a terrible mistake during that hospitalization three weeks ago? Had Mann's problem been something else—a perforating diverticulum or penetrating peptic ulcer? Maybe even a smoldering appendicitis that had now ruptured. Diarrhea did not cause an intestinal perforation.

He finished the examination of Mann's abdomen, noting it was becoming more distended by the minute. He could almost feel it increasing in size under his fingertips. He would have to open the patient now! The preparation would take at least an hour and he wanted to get started. An operating room would have to be reserved, the instruments sterilized, an anesthesiologist called, and pre-op medicines administered. And during this time he would have to start some antibiotics and straighten out any electrolyte imbalance or other problems that might have resulted from the perforation.

Despite his obvious pain and discomfort, Mann was

awake and alert. Howard remembered his confusion and disorientation of three weeks earlier and realized the perforation had occurred within the hour. Mann had not yet had time to go into shock.

He walked around to the head of the bed to tell Mann that he would be having surgery. Struggling with his pain, Mann rolled his eyes up at him. "What's happening?" he croaked.

"You've got an infection. And now it's spread into your peritoneal cavity."

"I've got peritonitis?" Fear widened his eyes.

Howard nodded. "Yes, you do. But with surgery and with the antibiotics we have today, we have every chance of curing you." He emphasized the word 'today,' knowing Mann was from an era when peritonitis was usually fatal. "Mr. Mann, is there anyone we should notify? Not that I expect anything unforeseen to happen. But it's routine to call the next of kin or a loved one when someone is going to have surgery."

Mann hesitated. Howard, staring at his face upside down, wondered if this might be the onset of shock and confusion.

"Did you hear me, Mr. Mann?"

Horace T. Mann seemed to be searching, thinking something over. Finally he spoke. "There is no one," he said.

As disappointed as Howard Fletcher had been about much of Charlemaigne General Hospital, he'd been delighted to find the O.R. crew especially competent. It was the first time he'd ever worked with nurse assistants. In the larger teaching hospitals in Chicago, a senior resident always stood across the O.R. table as the 'first assist.'

He now realized that a well-trained nurse was a much better assistant. Better than any of the residents he'd ever worked with. Residents came and went. The nurses around here stayed. And they knew how to assist. Residents were more interested in learning and watching, awaiting the day when *they* would be doing the surgery.

H. T. Mann's incredibly bloated belly had been cleansed,

sterilized, and draped. Howard nodded to the assistant nurse across from him and then to the nurse anesthetist on his right at the head of the table. Over his shoulder he nodded to the floating nurse who was not scrubbed. Lastly he nodded to the instrument nurse on his left, and as he did so, she slapped the handle of a scalpel in the palm of his hand. With no words exchanged, the operation began.

Howard Fletcher had always taken pride on his surgical imagination. Before a neurosurgery case he could picture with exact detail what was happening inside the patient's head. He could picture a middle cerebral artery hemorrhage the way people pictured the faces of their children.

And now as he touched the knife point to H. T. Mann's skin, he knew he would see the foul and putrid contents of the bowel spilling into the clean glistening peritoneal cavity. He could clean it, sucking and removing by hand the bowel contents as best he could. Then he would find the beginning of the large intestine, the cecum, and proceed meticulously to examine the entire length of the colon by threading it along between his fingers—'running the bowel.' And he would find a large perforation. A hole through the bowel wall caused by a cancer, a perforating carcinoma most likely, or perhaps a perforating diverticulum as part of the disease of diverticulitis. Maybe an ulcer that had eroded through, maybe even a foreign body. It would be a large and single hole in the bowel wall, a large opening the size of a penny—maybe the size of a quarter—spewing out infected gunk.

Opening the abdomen slowly and carefully, in layers, was the usual technique. One cut first through the skin, then the subcutaneous tissue, then the muscle layer, and finally the peritoneum, slowly in carefully dissected layers. But because of the severity of the infection he decided to make one large, deep incision cutting through all layers of the abdominal wall in a single stroke. He wanted to hurry this operation, give Mann as little anesthetic as possible. It would probably be safe because the X-rays showed the

bowel to be pushed back away from the abdominal wall by
gas and spilled feces, reducing the chance that he would cut
through bowel as he went into the abdomen.

In one stroke Horace T. Mann's abdomen fell open. The
scrub nurse, anticipating him, followed along behind the
moving knife, clamping off the bleeders and gently pulling
the cut edges of the abdominal wall apart with retractors.

And with the abdomen now open in front of him, Howard
Fletcher now realized just how wrong he had been! There
was no cancer or perforating diverticulum or ulcer here. In
fact there was no single lesion of any kind. The entire large
intestine was leaking! He had never seen anything like it.
Putrid bowel content was oozing its way right through
gangrenous intestinal wall.

He attempted to make some sutures through the bowel
wall in an attempt to tighten and perhaps strengthen it. But
it was no use. The bowel was too rotten and the sutures
wouldn't hold. Even handling it caused it to tear.

He looked at the digital readout of the blood pressure,
pulse and heart-rhythm strip on the monitor at the head of
the table. Mann's vital signs were terrible, and worsening
by the minute.

And he knew what he had to do. There was no suturing
through this bag of Jell-O. He had to bypass it in order to
prevent the spillage, clamp off the distal colon and bring the
proximal bowel out through the skin.

He hated colostomies, hated the sight and smell of them.
They somehow represented a failure. A failure to be able to
resect, to properly cut out, diseased tissue. You bypassed it,
you detoured around your surgical problem. The way you'd
bypass a bad accident without stopping to help.

Quickly now, he found a proximal loop of bowel that
didn't look too gangrenous and brought it through his
incision; then, using large through and through sutures, he
began closing the skin around the ugly cut end of the bowel.
He'd left a mess behind, but at least he'd diverted the

stream of contaminated bowel contents away from the abdominal cavity and out through the skin.

They were wheeling Horace Mann out of the O.R. as Fletcher pulled off his gloves and began writing orders. He ordered Mann sent straight from the O.R. to the intensive care unit. He'd written heavy antibiotics orders as well as fluid replacement. He knew that Mann, with that much infection, would soon be losing the ability to maintain his blood pressure. Rarely did Fletcher give any kind of thanks to his Vietnam experiences, but thanks to that awful war, he was expert at dealing with septic shock.

But, he realized bitterly, he didn't have to think back to the war to remember his last case of septic shock. He'd seen one just a week ago. Young Sam Avignon had died from exactly this same thing. He was certain of it, had realized it the minute he'd opened Mann's abdomen. Sam Avignon's severe abdominal distension combined with that incredible dehydration. Avignon had been pouring fluid into his abdominal cavity! *Now* he knew that. He was angry at himself for somehow not being able to help him.

It was a week ago today! Avignon had that first illness with the diarrhea one week before Mann had his. Then had later perforated his colon and died. Each of them had had that initial diarrheal illness and had seemed to recover on antibiotic therapy only to suffer, three weeks later, a blowout of the colon!

He picked up the phone outside the O.R. door and called the record room to pull the charts on those first illnesses of Mann and Avignon. He would stop there now and review them.

There was a slapping noise as the record room librarian dropped the two charts on the table in front of Howard. He began reading the charts slowly, almost simultaneously, his eyes going back and forth, and he wondered why the similarity of the two cases had not struck him before this.

Not just the similarity, the timing. Sam Avignon's first hospitalization had been at six P.M. on a Thursday. The boy had done nothing unusual except that he'd been in the French Quarter the previous Saturday night. He was treated with antibiotics, appeared to be cured, and was discharged feeling fine. A week later, also on a Thursday at six P.M., Horace Mann had been admitted to the hospital with the same illness, received the same treatment, and had seemed to recover.

Then three weeks after their initial illnesses, each of them developed an infection that perforated the intestine. Sam Avignon died of it at home because he didn't come to the hospital right away, but it probably didn't matter. Mann *did* get to the hospital right away and he was still going to die.

The charts were side by side and he had been turning the page of each chart at the same time. At the back of the charts—past the history and physical, the progress notes and the X-ray reports, were the laboratory slips. Why did it not surprise him that there was still no final report on the specimen identification? Avignon's stool cultures had been collected four weeks ago and Mann's three weeks ago.

He remembered his conversation with that lab tech after Sam Avignon had died: "Must be one of the specimens we send to New Orleans."

He'd have to see about that.

CHAPTER 26

Howard Fletcher dialed the sheriff's office, and asked for Beauford. A slow, almost sleepy voice told Howard that the "Sheriff ain't here right now. Somepun' I kin hep you with?"

Howard recognized the voice; it belonged to a beefy deputy he'd seen trailing behind Beauford once or twice, a second cousin or something like that. Beauford had casually remarked once that he had another cousin, plus a nephew, working for him. "Ah, no," Howard said. "I have to talk to the sheriff. This is Dr. Fletcher. It's important. You know how I can get hold of him?"

"Fraid you can't do that, Doc. But you might catch him over to the school if you hurry."

"School?"

"Heh, heh. Yep. The sheriff's doin' his annual heifer wrangling in the local meat contest. Should be just winding down over there 'bout this time."

"The school, you say."

"Yessir," the deputy said. He cackled. "The sheriff, he's the master of ceremonies at our little beauty contest every year. The sheriff might welcome a little help, what with all the fine young pulkertood we got around here."

"Thanks," Howard said. When he hung up, the deputy was still chuckling at his little joke.

• • •

It was standing room only at the Charlemaigne High
School auditorium. Beauford Decatur, in full uniform, was
standing on stage, smiling out at the audience as if he were
really enjoying himself. The auditorium was stifling, which
didn't seem to bother the packed house at all. They were
applauding wildly. Howard had squeezed in among some
other standees along the back wall. He looked around to see
Vicky Langston less than ten feet away from him. Vicky
hadn't noticed him and was engaged in an intense conversation with another girl. Since he was now officially
'dating' Vicky's mother, Howard was sorry he barely knew
the girl. According to the Charlemaigne gossip mill, she
was a very nice kid, popular, and a good student. He started
in her direction to say hello, when a teenage girl in a white
gown with a wide red sash strolled onto the auditorium
stage. There was pandemonium in this corner of Charlemaigne. Howard guessed that he was seeing the new Miss
Charlemaigne in the flesh. Beauford was dabbing a handkerchief on his sweaty forehead under the hot lights.
Howard edged toward Vicky but then realized it was a boy
and not a girl she was talking with. He was thin, with long
eyelashes and a handsome, almost pretty face. Howard
changed his mind and turned his attention back to the stage.

Beauford shouted the girl's name, Eunice something or
other. The last name was drowned out by the noisy sounds
of adoration. The girl's hand fluttered to her mouth to cover
an embarrassed giggle, followed by excited tears. Her
mascara began to run and Howard was afraid her eyelashes
might slide off onto the floor. He smiled at Beauford's
obvious discomfort. He was sweating like a sharecropper.
Eunice was nearly outsweating him. Howard shook his
head. These were *his* people, he thought. It took something
like this to remind him how much he loved them all.

Beauford cleared his throat. "Thank you, thank you," he
shouted. The microphone screeched a feedback that shook
the auditorium, and the crowd howled. The ancient sound

system, going back to Howard's time, had always been good for a laugh. "Eunice," Beauford began again, "congratulations. I know it must be quite a thrill."

"Yaz, it is," Eunice replied, leaning into the microphone.

"Tell me, Eunice," Beauford asked her, "what are your plans for the future?"

She bit her lip, and looked at the heavens whence all riches flow. A sweat puddle had formed on her upper lip. "Well, I would like to have a home and family, of course. That is, eventually. And I want a career. Maybe a model or a beautician."

"Fine, fine," Beauford was saying.

"But first," Eunice said, "I would like to do something for the unadvantaged." Howard coughed loudly to choke back his laugh while Beauford asked Eunice what she had in mind for the 'unadvantaged.' She wasn't sure, she said, maybe she'd join the Peace Corps.

"Isn't that great," Beauford shilled the crowd. They cheered, and Eunice brushed away a joyous tear. Nobody could make this up, Howard thought. It had been the same way when he was a kid. Beauford was laying the queen's booty on Eunice—a fifty-dollar gift certificate from Haley's Department Store, a two-hundred dollar scholarship to a business college donated by the Chamber of Commerce, a year's subscription to *People* magazine, free dry cleaning for a month, a makeover at the local beauty salon, and assorted other goodies. There were also a dozen red roses. Eunice had an armful. Fortunately, Howard thought, Eunice looked to be a strong girl. She seemed reluctant to leave as Beauford steered her stage left.

"Whew," Howard said. He elbowed his way through his perspiring Charlemaigne neighbors, making for a side exit, in a hurry to catch Beauford before he got away.

Howard sprinted across the school lawn, catching sight of Beauford just as he was reaching the black-and-white patrol car. He shouted to him, then raced on. He was puffing as he got to the car, and sagged against the door, exhausted after a fifty-yard run.

"You oughta see a doctor," Beauford said. "You're outta shape. What'n hell are you doing here, anyway?"

Howard, sucking in great gulps of air, smiled. "I wouldn't have missed this for anything."

"You sonofabitch," Beauford said. "You see what a whore I am just to keep the peace around here?"

Howard was getting his wind back. "You didn't volunteer for this?"

"You know better, you went to school right here. It's tradition. Just like everything else around here. Sheriff's been doing this for fifty years."

Howard jerked his thumb back in the direction of the school. "And Eunice? Was she really the best of the lot?"

"It was her turn," Beauford said. "Besides, she's got a great personality." The parking lot was clearing fast. "C'mon, Howard. I'll buy you a cold one. I can use a beer. Or six. I earned it."

Howard put his hand on Beauford's arm. "Not now. I need you to give me an O.K. for an autopsy. I understand this parish is so small one of your duties as sheriff is to be the county coroner."

Decatur nodded. "Who died?"

"H. T. Mann. Not long ago."

"Get in the car," Beauford said.

Beauford drove slowly. "No foul play?"

"No, hell no," Howard said. "But he's the second person to die the same way. And I don't know why. Mann's got nobody, apparently. No family, and I need that autopsy."

Decatur was driving one-handed, a cold pipe bobbing between his teeth. "You're right about that. He's the last of the Manns. His mama went a few years back, and his daddy's been gone for twenty years."

"Yeah, right. So how about that post?"

Beauford looked pained. "Jeez, I don't know, Howard.

There'd be talk. There's a fee, you know, that has to go to the parish fathers; they'd want to know why. They fly-speck the crap outta me now. There's some old boys sitting on that board who've been trying to nail me to the wall for years. It'd be all over town before you got Mann closed up." Beauford lowered his voice, and talked out of the corner of his mouth. "Can't you do it without getting my name in the damn thing?"

"How? Dammit, Beauford, here I am, the new doctor in town, wanting to carve up the pillar of the community for no apparent reason." Beauford grunted and Howard saw the sheriff's lips curl into a sneer. "What's that supposed to mean?"

"That pillar wasn't all that solid." Beauford said.

"What?"

Beauford drove in silence for a moment. "Hey, good doctor," he said softly, "we all of us got our little secrets, correct? Our dark side?" Beauford started to hum tunelessly.

"Come on, Beauford, give."

"Old man Mann had a libido that wasn't exactly dormant."

Beauford drove on, humming off-key, infuriating Howard. "Christ, Beauford, do you want me to beg?"

"Well, this is just between you and me. 'Bout two years ago the pillar of the community got rousted down in the French Quarter at some place that caters to pretty exotic tastes."

"No?"

"Yep. Some important tourist from up north got taken for a bundle, and he made a lot of noise. They went through a whole row of houses, the New Orleans P.D. did, and Mann and some girlfriend of his got swooped up in the same net. They let everybody go. New Orleans takes a live-and-let-live attitude about those things. Putting out raging libidos is part of the place's charm." Beauford chuckled. "The cops just wanted the tourist's money back. They let all the solicitees go, and gave the solicitors a talking-to on how to treat out-of-town guests."

"I'll be damned," Howard exclaimed. "How do you know all this?"

Beauford turned, the pipe canted to the side. "I'm the sheriff, ain't I? Cops got their own jungle tom-toms, just like doctors or anybody else, you know."

"Beauford, do you know, if Mann made these trips on a Saturday night?"

"Don't know. He was never arrested or nuthin'. Got no rap sheet. As far as he knew, nobody in town was in on his dirty little secret."

Howard chewed on Beauford's words for a minute. "I'd like to know exactly where and when Mann went down there," he said.

Beauford took the pipe out of his mouth, pulled the car to the curb and stopped. "Maybe," Beauford said, "I could make a phone call. Get you some names or phone numbers."

"Good," Howard said.

"I'm not gonna ask why you want to know," Beauford said.

"I appreciate that, Beauford,."

Beauford stirred in his seat, shifting his weight to look directly at Howard. "About this autopsy," he said quietly. "What I don't know won't hurt me, Howard. Like you said, Mann's got nobody left behind. Once he's in the ground—"

Howard didn't react right away. He was usually not so slow on the uptake. "Thanks, Beauford," he said.

CHAPTER 27

Vicky had been surprised when Robby Swinton took the freeway exit to New Orleans instead of driving into Charlemaigne. But Robby had assured her the movie in New Orleans would be a real treat. She had not protested. After all, it was their fourth date and Robby had been a perfect gentleman. She'd given a fleeting thought to what her mother might say if she found out they were going to New Orleans this close to Mardi Gras. But she hadn't lied. She'd thought the movie would be in Charlemaigne, not New Orleans. She glanced at Robby, his face softly illuminated by the dashboard lights. Just like in the classroom, he was so serious, so self-assured, so different from the other silly, nervous boys she knew. Robby drove the car confidently. He obviously knew his way around New Orleans.

The 'theater' turned out to be little more than a dingy basement, and she laughed when she saw that the screen was a bed sheet tacked to the wall. They sat on folding wooden chairs—Vicky guessed there were some thirty in the audience—conversing and laughing in low tones. Most were a few years older, but with Robby she somehow did not feel out of place. She glanced to her right. In the next seat was a slight, bearded young man. He was wearing a Confederate army cap and carried a tambourine. He was holding hands with the man next to him. Vicky flushed, and looked away. The smoke from a dozen shared marijuana cigarettes rose to form a hazy blanket above her head. It swirled into the cone of light cast by the projector. The film flickered to life on the bed sheet. A girl in the front row stood and turned, shushing the audience. She wore a white leather outfit with skintight toreador pants, and an old-style aviator's helmet with goggles. Slashes of what looked like green greasepaint were smeared on her cheeks. She waved for quiet with a long-stemmed pipe.

Vicky didn't know what would appear on the sheet, but she was pleasantly surprised. It was not pornography or a foreign-language film. The story was about a husband and wife who loved each other deeply, but who devoted their lives to science, working night and day, and winning the Nobel prize. The wife died, a victim of one of their own experiments. Vicky dismissed the sloppy casting that placed two British actors in the French roles. She cried softly, and whispered to Robby that she thought *Madame Curie* was a "sweet" movie.

Vicky left the theater on a fantasy cloud, nodding but not really listening to Robby, chattering endlessly as he drove. She felt secure, safe and contented. *She* was Greer Garson, working tirelessly by the side of her scientist husband for the benefit of all mankind. She glanced at Robby, so wise beyond his years, so purposeful and resolute. She was sure he would take his place in the world, and then her mother would come to realize what Vicky had sensed from the beginning.

"It's the eighth time I've seen it," Robby was saying.

"The movie?" she said, snapping out of her dream state.

"Yes. The first time was on TV, the late show. I couldn't believe it. I said, 'That's me up there on that screen.' That's what I want to do with my life."

Vicky edged closer to him on the seat. "It would be a wonderful life," she said, lightly touching the sleeve of his jacket.

"I have a treat for you," he announced grandly. "You

remember that dreary little laboratory in the movie? Well, I'm going to show you *my* laboratory where I do my experiments."

"Your laboratory?" She felt a tingle. "Where is it?" She watched the Charlemaigne exit sign fly by.

"At Carville."

She straightened. "Oh, I don't know. That'll make it awfully late."

"It won't take long," he replied. They rode in silence for a while. "I think you'll find it interesting," he said. "I had a lab in my basement in Atlanta, but we couldn't move it to Charlemaigne, so my father lets me use the one in Carville just like it's my own."

She looked up at his smooth face, and smiled softly. "I think that's exciting."

He turned to face her, his eyes wide and pleased. "Most people wouldn't call it that," he said. "It's not very dramatic or showy."

"Don't say that. It's unselfish and uplifting. There are too many showy and shallow things in this world. Anybody can be a salesman or a banker, or one of those things"—she groped—"or an accountant."

He flicked on the lights in the laboratory. The sudden brightness was blinding. He led Vicky down the aisles between the long workbench tables crammed with equipment. She walked behind him as he pointed out the different apparatus on either side. They eventually entered a glassed-in room off the laboratory. "This is my father's office," Robby announced. He went to a nearby Bunsen burner, and began to brew coffee. "Please, have a chair," he said. "Yes, a complete biologic laboratory. Except for the animals, of course."

Vicky had become totally absorbed. "Yes, of course," she answered. "But don't you have to work with mice or rats or something—like guinea pigs?"

Robby smiled at her tolerantly, offering her a mug of

steaming coffee. "Well, yes, but not here. This lab has never needed them because the leprosy bacteria won't grow in animals, only humans. And I don't need lower animals for my experiments either. I used to use lab rats, still have some in my basement in Atlanta, but I don't need them here."

Vicky caught herself nodding in agreement at something she knew absolutely nothing about. "I'd like to hear more about your experiments, but I'm afraid it would be too deep for me." She laughed self-consciously.

He looked at her for a long time, then smiled slightly. "You could learn," he said. "Anyway, you'll someday be reading about my experiments in the papers."

She was sitting in the swivel chair behind Dr. Swinton's desk, staring at a photograph of a chubby ten-year-old Robby. She smiled at it. "My goodness you were a cute little boy. Not always too thin and . . ." She reached for a word. "Serious," she finally said.

He walked around behind her, staring at the picture. "It was taken seven years ago, it seems like seventy. Before my mother died. I feel so much older now than just seventeen."

"You *do* act more mature than most of the kids," Vicky said. She sincerely felt that.

"There is so little time," he continued. "I have so much to do, I don't have time for the usual things." He slowly swiveled her chair around so that she was facing him.

"What 'usual things'?" she asked.

His face was serious as he stared down at her. "Dating, for one. I can't waste my time going out with girls or dating or 'courting' as they call it down here."

She laughed. "What do you think we did tonight? Wasn't this a date?"

He looked at her, his brow wrinkled as though in deep concentration. "No," he finally said. "This is not a date."

"What?"

His hand cupped the back of her neck, and she raised her

face to accept the expected kiss. As she had guessed, it was very satisfying and he smelled sweet and fresh.

"And why isn't this a date?" she said into his lips.

"I told you. I don't have time for that. And yet I have certain needs, certain urges. Sometimes they interfere with my work." He straightened up, towering over her, his legs against the edge of the chair, preventing her from turning it. "Have you ever heard of Friedrich Nietzsche?"

"Who is he?"

"A German philosopher. He advocated suspending your inhibitions or morals if certain needs had to be met to improve your life, and the life of your fellow man. Some temporary discomfort and sacrifice was worth anything. Do you understand?"

"I . . . I'm not sure." She made a gesture of looking at her watch. "It's late. I really have to be getting home."

He bent down to kiss her again. She tilted her face up to meet his lips. She would allow him this kiss and then insist they leave. He kissed her gently at first, as he had the first time. But then his lips mashed hers, hurting her teeth, and he began forcing her back on the chair. His hands went under her skirt. "Hey," she said, and she thought she heard him laugh.

"Hey," he said mocking her.

She was not frightened at first, only annoyed. She was sure he would stop when he saw she was angry. He was leaning across her on the swivel chair, his hand pushing up her skirt. As she tried to jackknife her legs under him they both fell to the floor. He was immediately on top of her. As she tried to roll away, she felt his fist grind into her face. He did not hit her; he pressed his knuckles along her upper cheekbone, and kept increasing the pressure. She cried out in pain. At the same time, his other hand clamped down on the inside of her thigh, and her legs flew apart. "Oh, no, please," she pleaded.

His face, only an inch from hers, was featureless. He

spoke rather matter-of-factly. "You are really rather plain-looking, Victoria."

"No," she whimpered. "I never . . ."

She listened to him snort through his nose, like a bull. "I knew it," he said triumphantly. "You are special."

The pain when he entered her was so sharp it stifled an outcry. She could only gasp, a long, shuddering intake of air. She closed her eyes tightly and kept them closed until after he had finished. In the pain and humiliation that followed, she was only vaguely aware of his presence, and never heard the hissing sound or felt the mosquito-bite prick of the injection gun. And she didn't cry. That would come later.

CHAPTER 28

Howard Fletcher, the phone to his ear, tapped his foot impatiently on the floor of the sheriff's office as he watched Beauford Decatur, with agonizing slowness, fill out the form authorizing the autopsy.

A woman's voice came on the other end of the line from the Charlemaigne Hospital. "Department of Pathology. Would you please hold?" Before Howard could reply, she clicked off, and Frank Sinatra automatically filled the dead time with "All The Way."

"What was the exact time of death?" Beauford asked. "Gotta have it right to the minute."

"Hell, Beauford, I don't know. You've already asked me Mann's date of birth, suspected cause of death, how long he'd been in the hospital and ten other things I can't tell you without his chart. I'm on hold with the hospital right now trying to arrange the post. Why don't you just sign it? I'll fill in all that information from the front sheet of the hospital chart when I go over there."

"Gotta be done right," Beauford said.

There was a click in Howard's ear that, thank God, silenced Frank Sinatra. "Thank you for waiting. May I help you?"

"Is the pathologist there?" Howard asked the receptionist.

"Why, yes, but he's just leaving. May I ask who's calling?"

"This is Dr. Howard Fletcher. Tell the pathologist to wait for me. I want to talk to him, and I'll be there in about twenty minutes."

"I'm sorry, Doctor, but Dr. Mortague leaves at five o'clock."

"Now listen closely, miss. You tell Dr. Mortague that he'd better not leave his office until I get there." Howard hung up, cutting off further conversation.

Howard's heart flailed against his rib cage. He was sweating and winded from his run from the hospital parking lot. He gripped the autopsy authorization tightly, and checked his watch. A quarter past five. That itinerant pathologist had better still be there. Howard slowed to a fast walk at the laboratory, hurrying past the startled lab technicians and secretary, and into the pathologist's office.

"How soon can you do this?" he asked as he shoved the order under the pathologist's nose. From behind a cluttered desk Pierre Mortague stared evenly at Fletcher. He was a skinny, short Cajun, whose chosen specialty had earned him the permanent nickname of "Morgue."

He picked up the autopsy authorization. "Your order to wait for you was relayed to me, Dr. Fletcher," he said with a trace of sarcasm. "As you can see, I did."

"Well," Howard said, taken aback. "It's just that I'm anxious to get this done. It's pretty important."

"Okay," Morgue said briskly. "I'll do the autopsy, provided the body is cold. I never do an autopsy on a warm body." He said it with a soft smile, and motioned Howard to a chair. "Would you like some coffee?"

Howard nodded, and allowed himself a smile. "Thanks. But I'd rather have a glass of water. Or maybe a Coke."

Morgue brightened. "How about some bourbon?"

"Sounds like a good idea," Howard replied, appreciating the cordiality. He chastised himself for assuming there would be a confrontation. Pierre Mortague was a laid-back kind of guy. Howard had met him briefly a short time after arriving in Charlemaigne. He remembered him as open and friendly, unusual qualities in a practitioner whose specialty involved daily contact with the dead.

Between sips of his drink, Howard explained the cases of Sam Avignon and H. T. Mann in great detail, telling of his frustrations at not knowing what microbe he'd been treating.

Morgue listened attentively. "Not sure I can help you with a diagnosis," he said at last. "But I can explain the delay in the final specimen reports. As soon as we collect them, we ship them to Charity Hospital in New Orleans for identification of the bacteria. It's that simple." He gave a Gallic shrug.

"Who arranged all this?" Howard asked.

"The Government. All stool cultures are to be sent there."

"Why?"

"I told you. It is the Government's way."

"You mean you send all stool specimens there no matter what diagnosis is expected?"

Morgue nodded, and mugged disdainfully. "We can talk about that later. Let's go do that autopsy. I take it you would like to be there."

Once again Howard Fletcher found himself standing over H. T. Mann, but this time he was in a basement autopsy room, not an operating theater. Instead of a scrub nurse across the table, it was a pathologist. Morgue, using the pathologist's crude circular saw, began just below the neck where the collarbones joined. The chest cavity fell away, exposing the thoracic cage, as well as the heart and lungs with their glistening pleural surfaces. He continued the midline cut down through the abdomen, following the path of Howard's old surgical incision. The sutures he had so meticulously placed were popped apart by Morgue's saw.

They both stared into the abdominal cavity. The scene presented to them confirmed that Howard had not exaggerated the scope of the infection. Morgue and Howard didn't speak, and the silence seemed to compound the horror of what they saw inside Mann. Howard reminded himself to take into account that Mann had been dead almost twenty-four hours and that since bacteria doubled their population every twenty minutes, there would be some putrefaction.

Morgue began dictating into a tape recorder with a foot-activated pedal. "The structures in the abdominal cavity are so severely infected, they are unrecognizable," he intoned. It was obvious Morgue couldn't identify what he was touching. He stopped dictating while he tried to push aside some of the organs to identify them, to get his anatomical landmarks. But each time, the tissue fell apart.

Howard broke the silence. "Morgue, I want you to take some cultures, a bunch of them. There in the abdomen, get some swabs of—whatever that is—that mess in there."

Morgue, peering over his mask, slowly nodded. He walked back to a row of glass cabinets, pulling off his rubber gloves, and returned with several culture tubes.

"You make the final bacteriological identification here in Charlemaigne," Howard told the pathologist. "I don't want these routed to New Orleans."

Morgue finished the late suture, and stepped back to admire his handiwork. He pulled off his mask and gloves. "C'mon," he told Howard. Together they climbed the stairs to Morgue's office, the odor of embalming fluid and formaldehyde trailing behind them. Morgue settled in behind his desk. "Well, Doctor, what do you suppose this case was?"

"No idea," Howard answered. "That's the reason I was so hellbent on getting the post. I was hoping you'd turn up something. You ever see anything like this before?"

"No, never. Not an infection like that one."

They regarded each other, the low murmur of the

technicians in the main lab coming to them from outside the office. "Tell me," Howard said, "the earlier cultures I took on Mann, where exactly do they go? How do they get there? Do you mail them out?"

Morgue shook his head. "I take them myself. Since I work at so many little hospitals, they asked me to deliver the petris personally. I hate to tell you, but I get paid very well, just for being a delivery boy. They want the petris there right away, so they pay more than I would get if I ran the specimens myself—saves me hours of work."

"Who's they?"

"The Government, the C.D.C., they're apparently doing some sort of project."

"They pay you for *not* examining the specimens? Where exactly do you take them?"

"To the lab at Charity Hospital in New Orleans."

"Next time you go," Howard said, "I want to go along with you, O.K.?"

"Sure," Morgue said, "no problem."

CHAPTER 29

Howard noted that people in New Orleans did not drive nice cars. Either they had no money or they didn't care. Morgue had made a half-dozen stops at small hospitals in the suburbs, collecting two or three more petri dishes containing stool cultures at each place. To Howard's surprise, Morgue kept them in a large green cardboard box in the trunk of his car. Not exactly ideal conditions for a stool culture. But he couldn't very well keep an incubator in his car, and at today's 90 degree temperature, the bugs would probably survive.

Morgue maneuvered his tiny Peugot through the maze of jalopies cluttering the surrounding streets, then turned into the Charity Hospital grounds, driving around to the rear, past the emergency room entrance, and finally stopping at the delivery entrance. Morgue grabbed the cardboard box from the trunk. "Follow me, Doctor. I'll show you parts of the famous Charity Hospital you've never seen."

Morgue carried the green box of specimens slung over his shoulder, leading Howard through a maze of connected hospital wards. Charity Hospital, Howard quickly realized, was designed with a minimum of hallways and corridors. At the time the hospital was built the famous shotgun-style homes were popular. A visitor walked directly through the front door into the living room. Another door in the opposite wall led to a bedroom, then to a kitchen, then another bedroom. There were no hallways. They were considered superfluous and a waste of space. Privacy in New Orleans was unheeded and, apparently, unneeded.

Howard slowed his pace, lagging behind Morgue. They had walked through four large nineteenth-century-style open wards. In all of them the curtains separating the beds had been pulled back, revealing the patients in every stage of undress and activity.

There seemed to be some sort of celebration going on in the first ward, perhaps someone's birthday. But as they walked through the other wards, he realized it was that way throughout the hospital. The patients, no matter how ill, seemed to lounge about their beds. Family members strolled through the wards, talking with other patients. There seemed to be no regular visiting hours. Blacks, whites, Orientals—a United Nations' hodgepodge—milled around. Portable radios and television sets blared forth a jumble of noise. In one ward, someone was playing a muted trumpet, a very talented muted trumpet. Stacks of food were piled here and there. Wheezing patients with the congested lungs of heart failure were eating spicy, salt-laden Cajun chicken. Nurses and other staff members moved slowly, always slowly, among the patients.

They were all partying in the time-honored New Orleans tradition. They were partying, literally, right to the end. Howard had seen it before when he was a med student at Tulane. Every hospital had its particular ambience. San Francisco General was known for its AIDS cases. The wards of Detroit Receiving Hospital were known for their danger, and New York's Bellevue had its freaks. At New Orleans' Charity Hospital, they partied.

He followed Morgue through the door that opened into the pathology department, and entered a large laboratory work area. It was a larger version of the Charlemaigne lab. There were the long worktables with technicians, all female, perched on stools at intervals of five feet. They all knew Morgue, and there were smiles and "how ya been's."

Leading off the main lab area was a door marked "Chief of Pathology." When they entered, Fletcher immediately noticed the smell, and soon discovered its source. The bookshelves lining three of the walls in the office were filled with boxes containing petri dishes.

A huge man with a two-day growth of beard and wearing a filthy lab coat sat behind a desk munching an apple. He jumped up when Morgue entered. They shook hands warmly and launched into a conversation about their krewes.

Howard knew about the prestigious New Orleans krewes. Krewes were social clubs that planned the floats for the Mardis Gras. At least they had started out that way. Over the decades they had become elite social clubs with names famous to the New Orleans area: Bacchus, The Zulus, The King of Hearts and dozens of others. People could join only by invitation, and a person's status in the community—and his skin color—determined which krewe he was invited to join. After Mardis Gras, each krewe began planning next year's float. The planning was done at a series of parties held at members' homes. The frequency and intensity of the parties increased as Mardi Gras approached. No one in the New Orleans area cared much about country clubs, or paid attention to the Rotarians, Lions or Elks. The krewe was the linchpin of social activity.

Morgue set the green box containing the petris on the pathologist's desk, and as they exchanged small talk, the pathologist attached a gummed label to the box, then placed it on the shelf with the other petris.

There must have been at least thirty other boxes of petris on the shelves, each carefully labeled and dated. Morgue and the pathologist, ignoring Howard, were chattering away, laughing at some private joke. Howard, who hadn't been introduced, began to wander around the office, looking at the boxes of smelly, bulky petris.

He edged his way back to the two men. Here was the Chief of Pathology of the largest hospital in the South, dressed like a longshoreman and talking nonstop about an organization whose sole purpose was to throw a party once a year. The Chief of Pathology at Chicago's University Hospital would be wearing a six-hundred dollar suit and talking about the stock market.

Howard decided to butt in. He couldn't wait; this thing was nagging him. "I'm Dr. Howard Fletcher, from over in Charlemaigne," he said, sticking out his hand.

The pathologist shook Howard's hand and apologized for ignoring him.

"Why do you have everybody send you petri-dish cultures instead of just slides?" Howard asked.

Morgue frowned at Howard.

"What's this about slides?" the pathologist said after an awkward silence.

"Yeah, slides. Wouldn't it be a whole lot easier to send slides around the countryside rather than a bunch of smelly petri dishes?"

The pathologist smiled. "Ah, I have wondered that myself. But you misunderstood. These specimens are not being sent to me for identification. This is just a pickup area. Some Government man comes by and collects them." He gave a shrug that implied, *Of course it's idiotic, but what do you expect from the Government*? He turned back to Morgue and resumed their conversation.

Ignored again, Howard began wandering around the room, checking the boxes. The date each specimen had been taken and the address of the hospital were on each box. A couple of the addresses Howard recognized as small, area hospitals, and he assumed they were all either from hospitals or small clinics or doctor's offices in the New Orleans area. He pulled a pen and a scrap of paper from his pocket and began jotting down the addresses and the dates. Morgue and the Charity Hospital pathologist were jabbering, not paying any attention.

None of this made any sense, Howard thought. It made no sense that the U.S. Government would specifically arrange for petri dishes to be shipped around the state like this. These were cultures of live bacteria, for God's sake. They were smelly, bulky, and it was far more likely that an accident might happen.

The logical thing was to send out slides. Biopsy slides, bacteriology slides, bone marrow slides, were all sent to medical centers or the Government every day. The Armed Forces Institute of Pathology received hundreds of slides of difficult biopsies each day for a second opinion.

Making up slides simply meant that each local hospital or clinic would have to prepare the slides: lift some culture material off the growth in the petri and smear an exact amount of the material onto a glass slide, and then, using a somewhat laborious procedure, do a gram stain. The gram stain would identify the bacteria and required a well-trained pathologist. Maybe the Government didn't trust the local pathologists to read the slides correctly. That made no sense either. There came a gnawing feeling, one that Howard had been trying to push out of his mind. If the slides were prepared at the local hospitals, someone was bound to identify the bacteria. It was the first time he had allowed himself that thought. He finished writing down the last of the locations of the clinics that had sent the petris and the date they had made the stool cultures.

CHAPTER 30

He, Howard Fletcher, had taken on the shapeless form of a blob, a spermatazoa-like ooze. He is a bacterium in a perfectly round pool, being tossed about in a substance with the consistency of molasses, swimming against the tide of agar, making no headway and desperately trying to avoid being swept near a large island of gray mold near him. The island is perfectly round and now he sees that it's made of paper and it is only covered with mold. Ah, the mold on it is ampicillin. The moldy island is an antibiotic sensitivity disc in the petri swimming pool. H.T. Mann and Sam Avignon, dressed in robes, their faces obscured by black hoods, peer at him over the rim of the mold. All he can see is their teeth, long and narrow teeth, their mouths mocking him as they soundlessly call to him and beckon him with crooked fingers.

He fights to stay away from the disc, pulling his arms through the thick goo. But as in many dreams, he seems unable to move, to make headway. Beauford Decatur, in the medieval armor of a knight of the Crusades stands to one side, one hand resting on the hilt of a broad-blade sword, saying, "Arrest that man," over and over. Below his metal breastplate, Decatur is dressed in red longjohns. Marva is there on the island, dressed in a long flowing nightgown, staring at him, saying nothing.

He feels himself moving inexorably toward the antibiotic

mold and panic convulses him. He's a bacterium, and the ampicillin mold will destroy him. But he brushes against it and nothing happens. Ah, he is immune to it, he is a resistant bacterium.

An uncomfortable, intrusive noise forces Howard's eyes open. His heart is pounding all the way up to his throat. It beats in his ears. He lets out a long sigh of relief at being alive, gazing down the length of his body, thankfully surprised that it is still whole. He stares dumbly for a moment at the jangling telephone until he knocks it off its cradle, and props it next to his ear. "Hello," he croaks.

"I woke you up, didn't I?" Marva asked.

"No."

She chuckled. "Why is it people always deny that they've been asleep when they really have? They always say no, even if you just got them out of a coma. Why is that?"

Howard, his heart finally back to idle, grinned. "You may have just raised one of the great social riddles of our time. We'll have to go into that in some depth at a later date. Okay, I was asleep. I mean, dead to the world, in a coma. You happy now?"

She laughed. "That's better. We have to be open with each other. I'm sorry I woke you up."

"That's all right. You broke into a dream at precisely the right moment."

"Were you dreaming about me?"

"Well, yeah, in a way. You had kind of a minor part."

"What was I doing?"

"Not much of anything, as I recall," Howard said. "Enough with my dreams, already. What is the meaning of this intrusion?"

"Oh," she said. "I don't think it's much of anything. I just got a call from the school. Vicky has the flu or something. They have her in the nurse's office at school. I wondered if you could drop by the school and see her or have them send her to your office. I'm at work. The afternoon bartender called in sick so I'm stuck here. I'd just feel better if you could go over there and peek in on her."

"Of course. Call the school back and tell them I'll be right there."

"Humor a doting mother, okay?"

"Sure," Howard replied.

"Will I see you later?" she asked.

"Of course, madam. Call my secretary and she'll make an appointment." He hung up on her laugh.

Vicky Langston lay on the small bed in the corner of the school nurse's office, while Howard sat on the edge of the bed preparing to examine her. He remembered having his own appendicitis diagnosed right here, probably on this same bed.

With the school nurse standing across from him, he used his best bedside manner to try to put Vicky at ease. She seemed distraught, her anxiety out of proportion to what was probably just an intestinal flu. He wanted her to be relaxed when he examined her, but she was tense and distracted and was responding to his questions with one-word answers—yes or no.

Howard felt slightly uncomfortable around the girl. She had never given any hint that she disapproved of his relationship with her mother. But Howard had never been in this situation before. He had only seen Vicky coming and going, their brief words polite but always somewhat strained. He was unsure of what her real feelings toward him might be. Probably, he thought—hoped, actually—she regarded him with teenage indifference. She appeared to be a likable girl, with only a little of her mother's self-assurance and assertiveness. She was taller than Marva, with long hair the color of rosewood. Her facial features were delicate, but her body had already reached the full bloom of adulthood. She was just on the shy side of being voluptuous.

Vicky was draped with a sheet, and Howard had instructed the nurse to leave her underwear on. With the nurse's help he sat her up from behind and checked her lungs. She seemed weak and had trouble taking the deep breaths he asked of her. "And you've been getting cramps?" he asked. She nodded. Howard eased her down on her back, and listened to her heart.

"The cramps about thirty minutes apart?" he asked her.

"Yes, uh-huh."

He gently pulled down the sheet, making sure her pubic area was covered. Still, Vicky turned her head and averted her eyes. Her hair fell away from her face, revealing a bruise high on her left temple just above the hairline, difficult to see. She had covered it with a heavy coating of makeup. The bruise was days old. Howard was about to ask her about it, when his eyes were drawn to her abdomen.

He recoiled, caught in mid-breath, by the sight of the flaring red spots. No, he thought, as he stared at the spots that seemed to grow before his eyes. He fought off the panic that came in a rush, grunting noncommittally while the reality of the spots closed in on him.

For a brief moment, Howard worked mightily to conjure up another, benign medical explanation for the spots. He did a superhuman sales job on himself. An innocuous rash, he told himself, the skin eruption of some food allergy, even, laughably, the measles. But even as he toured fantasyland, he knew with certain dread that the spots were identical to those he had seen on two other people. And they were both dead!

He could see her behind the bar, smiling, singing along with the jukebox. She was lip-synching with Loretta Lynn's rendition of "Stand By Your Man." How could he have fallen in love with this woman, this place? But in love he was, he was absolutely certain of it. He knew how she would react to what he was about to tell her and he loved her so much he could feel her pain, had already felt it over the last two hours.

Howard had just taken Vicky to the hospital in his car. He'd done another physical examination, taken the blood counts, the cultures of the stool, blood, and urine, ordered x-rays, and started IV feedings. And he'd started the antibiotic ciprofloxacin—the same antibiotic he'd used on H.T. Mann and the Avignon kid. It was simply the strongest and best antibiotic available. And, he told himself ruefully, it had worked just fine on them—for a while.

Marva saw him and smiled and waved. He'd started over to the bar to talk to her, but she motioned for him to sit down in their favorite corner booth, and so he did. He'd waited this long to tell her, a couple more minutes wouldn't hurt. He told himself he'd come here to tell her in person, rather than calling her, to keep her from racing over to the hospital alone. He knew of too many accidents caused by patients' relatives racing to the hospital after phone calls from doctors. But that wasn't the reason. He was too upset to sit around the hospital. He was in a frame of mind that was familiar; he could think clearly and concentrate as long as he was working. When he'd admitted Vicky to the hospital just now, he'd been in his practicing medicine mode, calm, with perfect concentration. But as soon as he'd finished, the butterflies had begun, a tightness in his gut, a tension mixed with frustration and anger. He couldn't sit still, too agitated to call Marva and wait around the hospital for her.

He watched her, still singing behind the bar. She patted her hair, took off her apron, drew a beer for him, and headed for the booth. In the two hours since he'd seen Vicky he'd been debating how much to tell her.

"Our steaks are cooking. How's Vicky? Did you stop off and see her?" She stopped abruptly when she saw his face.

"I admitted her to the hospital," he said quickly, forcing his voice to be light. "Her stomach was upset, vomiting, headache, diarrhea. Probably just a bad dose of the flu, but she was getting dehydrated and I thought she'd be better off there. I can give her some IV fluids and some sedation and she'll get more rest." He was amazed at how well he could lie. His voice was controlled, and it hadn't been a *total* lie. Vicky had all those symptoms; he'd just shifted the emphasis, mentioned the diarrhea last and down-played it. There would be no conversation about red spots.

She stared at him. "Are you sure that's all it is?"

He took a deep breath and nodded quickly, meeting her eyes squarely. He was committed now to the obscene lie. "Sure, just the flu."

"How long will she be in the hospital?"

"Just a few days. We'll get her hydrated and she'll feel better."

"But this is so strange," Marva said. "Where would Vicky get something like this?"

"I was going to ask you. Has she done anything unusual, been anywhere?"

Marva shrugged. "No. She's been in school. . . ."

"She hasn't gone out of town? No, uh, field trips to New Orleans or whatever?"

Marva stared at him. "She's been home. I'm positive."

They were interrupted by one of the waitresses bringing over two thick steaks, still sizzling. They looked nauseating to Howard. Marva looked at them, then at him. "Let's get over to the hospital—now."

He nodded.

Marva peppered him with questions on the drive to the hospital. Howard thought that, for the most part, he had parried them quite deftly, though he didn't trust himself to look at Marva directly to see if she was swallowing his line.

"It's just precautionary," he said. "I told you, she needs some IV fluids and antibiotics and I'd prefer that she get some rest in the kind of setting where I can watch her for a couple of days."

"Poor kid," Marva said. "I bet she's scared. She's hardly been sick a day in her life, except for the usual childhood stuff."

"And that's probably all this is," Howard said. He had said it too quickly, not a desirable attribute for the accomplished liar. From the very moment he had discovered the red spots, he had wrestled with the painful knowledge that he would have to tell Marva the truth. There was no reason not to. She had a right to know. He knew he was stalling, probably because he selfishly didn't want to feel his own pain when he would have to see Marva absorb his bleak prognosis and know he was helpless to do anything to change it.

"Howard, what the hell?"

"What?" He had driven past the entrance to the hospital parking lot, and now had to make a sweeping U-turn to double back. From the corner of his eye, he saw Marva shoot him a perplexed look. Howard shrugged, and faked an embarrassed chuckle.

As they entered the room, Marva hurried to her daughter's side, drawing up a chair. "How do you feel, honey?" she asked. Howard stood in the background. The girl, he thought, had gotten some of her color back. The bloom of false health.

"I feel awful weak, Mom," Vicky said in a small voice. "I feel crampy. I must have eaten something bad, or something."

Marva smiled tenderly. "You'll be okay, sweetheart. It's some old bug that's floating around. Dr. Fletcher just doesn't want to take any chances." She looked at Howard, who nodded in agreement. Marva gently rearranged a few strands of hair that had tumbled over Vicky's face. "We'll have to get a bright red ribbon to keep that in place. A little lipstick and an antibiotic, and you'll be walking out of here as bright as ever." Vicky was able to muster a smile.

Howard, feeling somewhat the intruder in this family setting, eased himself into the conversation. "Can you tell us, Vicky, about anything unusual that you may have done in the last week or so, maybe gone someplace or been around anybody that, uh, may have passed something on to you?"

The girl shook her head firmly. "No," she said.

The answer had been so abrupt, so defensive, that Howard knew instinctively that the girl was hiding something. And he saw Marva give her daughter a questioning look. Doctors, over time, acquired a sixth sense in computing a patient's veracity. If the man with a bad liver admits to "a couple of belts," the physician multiplies by five; when the cigarette smoker admits to a pack a day, "more or less," the studied indifference and shifty eyes tell the physician it is closer to two packs, or maybe more. "Have you had any siege of vomiting or been drowsy during the day?" he asked. Howard, in a way, was groping, but it was not altogether an idle question.

"No, nothing like that," Vicky said.

"I see. Still," Howard said, "we might send you for a CAT scan just to make sure you don't have a concussion."

Marva whipped around. "Concussion?" She looked back and forth from Howard to Vicky. "What are you talking about, Howard?"

"Well, that bruise on her left temple," Howard said. "It doesn't look like much now, but she must have taken a pretty good rap. When did you get that, Vicky?" he asked. Marva pushed back her daughter's hair, and Howard saw the girl's eyes widen.

"Vicky," Marva said, "what happened?" Vicky bit her lower lip, but said nothing. Her face reddened. Tears started forming in her eyes, and she turned her face and buried it in the pillow. The pillow muffled a sob. Marva put a hand on her daughter's shoulder. "Vicky, what is it? Talk to me." Vicky slowly brought an arm up to encircle her mother's neck and draw her close. Howard watched as she whispered in Marva's ear.

Marva's face bore a look of shock when she at last looked at Fletcher. "We'd like to be alone for a few minutes, Howard."

• • •

Howard paced the corridor outside Vicky's room, now and then stopping to lean against the wall opposite the closed door. Marva had been alone with her daughter for a full twenty minutes. Howard shifted his weight from one foot to the other, and resisted the urge to break in on them. He glanced at the large clock above the nurse's station. He would give them five more minutes. He had made up his mind. He had to tell Marva the truth about Vicky's illness! What he hadn't decided was what his answer would be when Marva asked him the mode of treatment. While he waited, Howard rehearsed a number of speeches, each of them ending with the same cruel conclusion. He didn't know if Marva, a woman of immeasurable strength, would have the strength for that one. He looked at his watch; the hands were flying around the dial, and he tried to will them to freeze in place.

He hadn't heard the door open, and he looked up to see Marva standing in front of him. Her face was strained and white, the skin stretched taut against her cheekbones. The artery in her neck was jumping. When she spoke, her lips barely moved, and her voice was cold. "Howard," she said slowly, "Vicky's been raped."

Howard felt his jaw drop. "What?"

"Yes," she hissed in a controlled fury. "On a date. Last Saturday."

"Five days ago," Howard said distantly, almost to himself.

"You have to drive me over to Beauford's office," Marva said.

"You want me to look in on her again?" Howard asked. He started for the room but she caught his arm.

"Vicky's all right for the time being," she said sharply. "Drive me downtown. I've got to tell Beauford." Howard hesitated, trying to fit the pieces together. "Come on," Marva said. "I'll tell you all about it in the car."

• • •

Sheriff Beauford Decatur nodded gravely. "That's a serious charge," he said.

"Well?" Marva said impatiently.

"You say the perpetrator was this Swinton kid? What did you say happened again?"

"I told you, Beauford, Vicky was raped. Beaten and raped."

Beauford was combing his mustache with his fingers. "The Swinton kid, huh? Bad business, bad business. At least maybe we could get him for assault. You say he beat on her and put her in the hospital?"

"No. Not really. I mean he beat her up, but she's in the hospital for something else. She's sick."

Decatur put down his pen. "When did she get admitted to the hospital?

"This afternoon. That's how we found out about the rape. When she was in the hospital we got talking. . . . You know."

Decatur sighed. He ran his hand through his sparse brown hair. "When did the, uh, assault occur?"

"Last Saturday."

"Marva, you tellin' me this happened five days ago and she just told you today? After she was examined in the hospital for something else?" He looked painfully uncomfortable.

"Beauford, she was embarrassed and humiliated. She felt like everybody would condemn her."

"Uh-huh," he mumbled.

Again, Marva waited while Decatur turned things over in his mind. "Well?" she said finally.

"Well, if she'd come forward right away, we could have taken pictures of the injuries and have her, uh, checked to see if there was any . . . you know."

"No, I don't know, Beauford, for God's sake."

"Uh, penetration. A, uh, special medical examination. Very important, but it's too late for that now. Suppose you give me the story just like your daughter gave it to you. We'll have to interrogate her too, you understand."

"Yes, of course," Marva answered. She paused briefly. "Well, it's simple, really. They were out on a date—it was only the fourth time she's ever been out with the kid—and he drove her to the leprosarium at Carville. Then he assaulted her."

Decatur raised his eyebrows. "They were out on a date?"

Marva hesitated, then became furious at the implication. "Dammit, Beauford, it's still a crime, isn't it? Or does he have to jump her from behind in an alley?"

"Whoa, calm down," Decatur said. He got up and sat on a corner of the desk close to Marva. "I didn't mean anything by it. You just have to understand, Marva, what the girl could be letting herself in for if she has to testify in court. She will testify, won't she?"

"She'll testify," Marva said. "I'll see to it."

"Well," Decatur said, "just so you understand what she'll probably face. These defense attorneys are pretty doggone clever at twisting these kind of cases around. They can make it come out like the girl's at fault. Like she led him along, or maybe like she consented, you know, and then cried rape when she got scared later if somebody found out. Or to get the kid in trouble."

"That's crap, and you know it," Marva said heatedly.

"Marva," Decatur said gently, "I know it, and you may know it and your daughter may know it, but it wouldn't be the first time the gal has been made out to be a floozy in these kind of cases. Now you're talking real humiliation. Public humiliation." Decatur's gaze was steady on Marva. He took an oversized blue bandanna from his back pocket and soaked it in the sweat from his face. He felt the ceiling fan move the tepid air around the room. The air conditioning had broken down two weeks ago, and the parish fathers wouldn't authorize the repairs until their next monthly meeting.

Marva shook her head slowly. "You mean you're not going to do anything?"

"Didn't say that," Decatur said quickly. "Didn't say that at all. I'll go pick up the kid for questioning, go out there tonight. But you have to sign a formal complaint. We should get a picture of your daughter as soon as we can.

"Yes, O.K.," Marva nodded. "Whatever you say."

CHAPTER 31

The pretty red-haired woman's walk-in closet stretched along two entire walls of the bedroom, and was divided into two sections—one containing her personal clothing, the other the costumes she wore to accommodate the tastes of her gentlemen callers. Her 'clients,' as she listed them in her account book, were confident and successful men, men of culture and sophistication, men of purpose and unassailable pride. They were particular and very specific as to their requirements, and it made the red-haired woman happy when she saw they were pleased.

She walked along the closet, fingering her extensive wardrobe, running her hand over the expensive material before pausing in front of a tasteful scooped-neck green sheath. Black pumps and handbag, she thought, to complement the dress. Perfect for shopping. She lifted the dress from the rack, holding it against her body as she stood in front of the full-length mirror. She also checked her image from another angle in the huge mirror over the bed, and nodded approvingly.

She replaced the dress in the closet, and went to draw her bath, slipping out of the silk DeLaurente robe and letting it fall to the floor. She studied herself in the bathroom mirror. Was her lower abdomen protruding just a little? She sucked it in, then slowly exhaled to see how far out it extended. She was not in the least narcissistic, she reminded herself. She had to look her best; it was simply good business.

She checked the water temperature with her toe, then slowly descended the Florentine-tiled steps into the mammoth sunken tub just as the bathroom telephone began ringing. The phone, along with remote controls for the stereo and television, was attached to a specially built, electrically grounded headboard panel at the end of the tub. She'd spared no expense here, the second-most used room in the flat. She settled into the tub, leaning back against the headboard. After six rings, the answering machine cut in. She switched on the speaker system that conveyed the caller's voice to the bathroom. "This is Dr. Howard Fletcher," came the voice. She smiled. It was probably his real name. Men rarely gave fake first *and* last names. "I wondered if we, that is, might meet. Uh, we have a mutual friend who speaks very highly of you."

It was the line she always waited for—the reference line, the word-of-mouth recommendation from a pleased client. She insisted upon it before conducting a face-to-face interview. "I live in Charlemaigne," the man said. "I hope you will call me as soon as is convenient." He broke the connection.

How fortuitous, she thought. She submerged herself until the bath water lapped at her chin. Stephen had been promoted—a vice-presidency at I.B.M.—and would be moving to New York. He had been a generous man, but his demands had been extraordinary. The Civil War officer's and nurse's uniforms and the red Georgia clay had been relatively easy to obtain; the black dwarf, quite a bit more difficult.

And then poor, sweet Mr. Mann, dying so suddenly. It just went to show, the red-haired woman mused, how tenuous life was. She had read of his demise, a small article, in the *Times Picayune*. She should have guessed something was terribly wrong. He had always been so punctual, and then he missed two Saturdays in a row. Death was so unfair, she thought, and so final. She thought back to a year ago when that attorney from Memphis had died on top of her. The pretty red-haired woman shuddered. That had been messy.

She pushed a series of buttons on the headboard panel of the tub, then listened carefully while the answering machine replayed the message. Only then did she realize that the caller hadn't left a phone number. His way of letting her know that Howard Fletcher was his real name. A nice touch, she thought, as she dialed information for Charlemaigne.

No cars were allowed in the Quarter this time of year, so Howard parked in a garage on Basin Street and made his way to the address he'd been given. He was to meet her at two o'clock, but was early and decided to take a detour along Canal Street. He had been here a few times as a kid. At least one high-school graduation party had ended up in one of the strip joints on Bourbon Street. He strolled along the familiar rough-brick streets. The crowd was large, especially for this early in the day. People started coming down here for Mardi Gras shortly after the Christmas holidays, for God's sake. The place looked good, though there were some who complained about the gays taking over the French Quarter. Howard had little use for such opinions. The Quarter looked clean and safe. The art shops along Canal Street were beautiful without sacrificing the motif of nineteenth-century France.

The address was dead center in the French Quarter at the corner of Bourbon and Saint Ann. From the outside, virtually every structure was the same. They were built of wood and plaster, three stories high with flat roofs, the balconies with wrought-iron railings around the second and third floors. People milled around on the balconies as though at some unending elevated cocktail party. Howard stood for a minute, took a deep breath and rang the bell.

She stepped outside to meet him, closing the door behind

her, and he realized he would have to pass an initial inspection before he would be permitted to enter. She looked him over for a moment, then tilted her head back and smiled. "Please," she said, "do come in." She was certainly striking, her hair a bright red, natural, he thought, with soft blue eyes. She was tall, five foot nine or so, with a trim waist and broad shoulders, and the highest cheekbones Howard had ever seen.

If the outside of the place was unimposing, the interior was spectacular. The low ceiling, common to all these flats, seemed to exaggerate its length and width. The living room was French Provincial, the colors coordinating pastels that were enhanced by the narrow cones of light that streamed in through the floor-to-ceiling windows. Howard caught a glimpse of a courtyard garden outside.

She motioned him to a hard French loveseat, one of those delicate pieces that defied any effort to lean back. He sat hunched forward, his arms resting on his knees.

"Coffee or sherry?" she asked.

"Coffee will be fine," he said with a smile.

She returned quickly, balancing a sterling silver tray. A trace of heavy musk perfume mixed with the coffee's keen aroma as she bent over him. She sat down in a delicate bergère chair, settling back into the cushion, and crossed her legs. "And what kind of a physician are you?" she asked.

"I'm in family practice," Howard answered.

"And *your* family?"

"I'm a widower."

"Ahhh," she sighed, pouting understandingly. "And you're from Charlemaigne, I understand. A very good friend of mine came from there. Perhaps you heard of him—Mr. Mann? He passed away recently, a tragic loss."

"Yes, tragic," Howard said. "As a matter of fact, I knew him well. I was his doctor."

There was a long silence. It left Howard feeling awkward, but she looked totally at ease, twirling her sherry glass by the stem and moving one leg up and down. "I see," she said finally. "Then this is how you happened to call me?"

"Yes," Howard answered quickly.

"You and Mr. Mann were quite close?"

"Yes, you see, I'm a native of Charlemaigne. Our two families have been in town for generations."

She was studying him over the top of her glass. "Yes," she said at last, "professional men do tend to gravitate toward one another, don't they?" She put her glass on a marble-topped stand next to the couch. "The basic fee will be four hundred a week," she said. Her smile was provocative, scarcely lewd. "Extras, well, are extra." She patted her red hair. "I trust that will be satisfactory."

"Oh, yes," Howard said, relieved that nothing was expected of him today. It dawned on him that he had been called here for an interview to see if he passed inspection. He chose his words carefully. "As a physician, of course, my free time is limited. I wondered if Mr. Mann's spot— that is . . ."

"An opening?" She nodded and smiled. "Saturday, six in the evening would be fine."

Howard stared at her, hiding his relief. He wanted to shout, "Are you sure that is when Horace Mann came to visit you?" He had to be absolutely certain of the time of Mann's visits, without putting her on the defensive. "Yes, yes," he said. "Mr. Mann spoke fondly of his Saturday evenings here." Howard paused, then frowned. "I recall Horace, that is Mr. Mann, telling me about his difficulties getting here. I mean, with automobiles not allowed in the French Quarter on Saturday evening."

She shrugged. "That's true. As I recall, he parked in that garage on Bourbon, at the edge of the Quarter, then came down Bourbon to Saint Ann and . . ."

"Yes, yes," Howard said quickly, rising from his chair. "I'm looking forward to, uh, next Saturday, then."

She shook her head. "I forgot to mention—sorry—I will

be out of town the next two Saturdays. A little vacation—
going skiing. We could begin in three weeks if that's
agreeable."

Howard tried to appear disappointed. "I see. All right.
I'll call you first." He laughed. "Skiing? Around here?"

She shook her head. "Colorado. I always go this time of
year. Get away from the tourists for a while."

"Aspen or Vail?" he asked.

"Snowmass. I always go there. Vail is awful. Too
pretentious. It's overbuilt with new money. Too plastic.
And Aspen is worse. Everytime I go there some man tries
to pick me up."

Howard searched her face for a trace of irony. There was
none. He said goodbye and walked out into the clamor of
Bourbon Street.

CHAPTER 32

Beauford Decatur had to knock twice at the Swinton home, waiting several minutes before the door opened.

"Yes?" The woman who stood in the door was attractive, though older than he'd expected. Immaculately groomed, she looked cool and crisp in a smart silk-print dress.

In contrast, Beauford was sweating like a hippo having a baby. "I'm Sheriff Decatur, ma'am. Wonder if I can come in for a minute?" Her eyebrows arched. "Official business," Beauford said.

The woman nodded. "Of course." She stepped aside to admit him.

Beauford took off his cap, and gave her a courtly half-bow. The woman stood fast in the foyer, an obvious signal that the sheriff could conduct his business on the spot. Beauford fiddled with his cap. "Mrs. Swinton?"

"Yes?"

"Is your son home?"

"You probably mean Robby. I'm his grandmother, his father's mother. Robby's mother is dead. Is there any trouble with Robby?" The question came unruffled, casual, almost bored.

"Don't know if there's any trouble, ma'am. Just want to ask him a few questions."

Mrs. Swinton sighed. She spoke quietly, obviously unintimidated, and fixed Beauford with a stern gaze. "Sheriff, what about, please?"

Beauford took a deep breath. "Well, there's this girl in town." His voice trailed away. "She says, well, she says that your grandson, that is—"

"She says what, Sheriff? What did she say about Robby?"

"Well, ma'am, she told her mother that Robby, the other night, that he assaulted her."

Beauford waited for the shock to register on Mrs. Swinton's face, but it never came. Nothing! She folded her arms in front of her. "Assault?"

"Yes'm. Uh, the girl said they were out on a date."

"He raped her," she cut in. "Is that what you mean?"

"Yes, ma'am. That's what the girl says."

"I see," she said after a moment. "Well, you have to do your duty, Sheriff. But Robby isn't here. He left with his father, and I can't tell you where they went. They didn't inform me."

Beauford shuffled his feet. "I see. All right. Now, this thing hasn't gone very far yet, Mrs. Swinton. We just want to get the boy's side of the story right now. There'll be nothing else done until we talk to the boy, you understand. If he'll just come into the office. On his own, I mean."

"I understand," she said. "I'll tell him. I'm sure he'll cooperate."

It was the end of the interview. Beauford was momentarily at a loss. He had come prepared to handle outraged denials from hysterical parents.

Mrs. Swinton opened the door. Beauford hesitated. "Is there anything else, Sheriff?"

"No, nothing else," Beauford said. "For now." He tipped his hat, and backed out the door. "Thank you, ma'am."

She smiled back at him. "Have a nice day," she said.

• • •

Beauford sat in the patrol car for a moment before pulling away from the Swinton home, shaking his head. Talk about your stiff upper lip. Have a nice day? "Whew," he said.

As promised, Morgue was waiting for Howard in the pathology office of Charlemaigne Hospital. He sat behind his cluttered desk, eyes buried in a microscope and didn't acknowledge Howard's presence. Fletcher, standing across from him, rapped his knuckles lightly on the desk between them. Morgue looked up, blinked a few times and rubbed his pink, watery eyes. The microscope seemed part of the desk, protruding out of the center like a periscope. Morgue leaned back in his chair, then gave Howard a tight-lipped nod and motioned him to look.

Howard, somewhat awkwardly, bent over and stared into the unfamiliar domain of the bacteriologist. When his eyes had adjusted, he could see hundreds of bacteria. They were colored blue with gram stain and were unmoving, apparently dead, and their shape was deformed. He began searching his medical school memory banks thinking he at least ought to be able to differentiate between the rod-shaped bacilli and the rounded cocci. These were somewhere in between, many of them club-shaped, vaguely familiar but he couldn't bring it back. He moved his head to one side, taking his eyes from the eye-piece, and looked, with his naked eye, at the slide under the barrel of the scope. It looked like a glob of clear jelly on the slide, meaning it was a 'wet mount' and the bacteria should have been alive and swarming. Morgue's silence was unsettling and Howard could hear him tapping his fingers on the desktop, apparently waiting for Howard to render an opinion.

After almost five minutes, he straightened up, arching his back to get the kinks out, then looked at Morgue and shook his head. "You've got me. I'm not sure what they are. They're gram-positive, took up the stain very well, but they have a peculiar shape with irregular borders, and appear to be dead." He forced a faint smile. "You're talking to someone who had bacteriology a long time ago."

Morgue scowled and began nodding slowly. "It took me a long time to realize what they are—it's most unusual—they're spores. And they're not dead. Like all spores, they're dormant." He paused dramatically, raising a finger. "And they're from your patient, Horace Mann. I'm preparing another slide from Vicky Langston—probably find the same thing."

Howard stared at him. "Are you positive?"

Morgue leaned back in his chair behind the desk and rubbed his eyes again. "I'm going to culture Vicky Langston this afternoon. I'm sure she's got the same thing. Yeah, I'm positive, and it's making it impossible to do antibiotic sensitivity studies. Every time we try to grow the bacteria in a petri dish with antibiotic discs, it forms spores. Can't find out which antibiotic to use, can't even identify the bacteria."

Morgue was still leaning back, the fingertips of his right hand doing a nervous drumroll on the desktop. His scowl had deepened. "Sorry to have to dump all this on you."

Howard said nothing for a minute, then spoke softly, nodding his head. "At least it explains why my patients have been getting better for two or three weeks and then relapsing."

They could hear the paging operator's voice echoing through the halls. One of the technicians in the lab next door started a centrifuge, and a soft whirring noise filled the office. Finally Howard spoke. "Which antibiotics did you use in your sensitivity tests?"

"All of them," Morgue answered.

Howard shook his head. "This makes no sense to me. How could this bug suddenly become resistant to every antibiotic? Did you test every one?"

"All of the commercially available ones. We get the sensitivity discs from drug companies; everybody does.

That bug, whatever it is, was resistant—formed spores—with every antibiotic we used."

Howard stared around the office. For the first time, he noticed a copy of the textbook, *Zinzer's Bacteriology* next to the microscope, the page open to the section on spores.

"Howard," the pathologist said, "the only way we could find out for sure what this bug is, would be to stop all antibiotics, let the spores stop hibernating, revert back to their natural state, start multiplying, and then maybe we could reculture and treat her before . . ."

"No!" Howard shouted, starting forward, and Morgue flinched.

The pathologist stood up quickly and snapped off the light under the stage of the microscope, then stared at Fletcher. "You going to keep her on antibiotics the rest of her life, Doctor? Have her live at the hospital, be a carrier, harboring spores?"

"Goddamn it, Morgue, it's too dangerous. As soon as you stop antibiotics, that bacteria—spore—whatever the hell it is, it takes off. When that bug gets going—I mean, there wouldn't be time . . . You did the autopsy on Mann for Chrissakes! Yeah, I'm going to keep her here until I find out what the hell is going on!" He stomped out of the office.

Beauford Decatur had about decided he didn't like big-city cops. They were always busy and Beauford didn't trust busy people. A different breed, very macho, always talkin' about their arrests, their "collars." Hellsfire, arrestin' people was easy; any fool could make an arrest. It was *not* makin' an arrest that took some doin'.

(*Now look here, Timmy LaFleur, I know where that bicycle come from. I saw the Turbineau kid ridin' it day before yesterday. His daddy told me he'd just bought it for him and it got stole last night. Madder'n a wet hornet he was. And no, I'm not arrestin' you. We ain't goin' to the station, we're goin' to your house and talk to your daddy, and then I'm takin' you to the Turbineau kid's house and*

*we're talkin' to his daddy. After that I figure there won't be
enougha you left to arrest.)*

"I'm too busy," the lieutenant in Atlanta was saying. "I
don't have the time now. Let me switch you to my secretary,
see if she can run a computer check for you." There was a
click. "Your secretary, huh," Beauford said into the dead
phone. "Cops in Atlanta got secretaries? You got valet
parking at the precinct?"

"May I help you?" a young female voice said.

"Well, yes, ma'am, I wonder if you got a record on a kid
named Swinton, Robert Swinton?"

There was silence except for the muted clicking of a
computer keyboard. "Yes we do. We have a Robert
Swinton, birthdate of 1973. That about the right age?"

Decatur hadn't expected this and he gripped the phone
expectantly. "That's him." He hoped to God the kid was
wanted for murder, rape and arson. Anything to get a little
justice for Marva here.

"Umm yes, it's coming up on the screen now. Here it is,
a coroner's case, a Miss Lorlene Davis. This Robert
Swinton was mentioned as 'Robby' in a suicide note found
at the scene. He was only questioned about it, never any
charges. You see, Sheriff, the computer cross-indexes
everybody's name, even non-suspects who are interviewed
about . . ."

"I understand." Decatur sighed, disappointed. "You
probably got the relatives of jaywalkers on that computer."

"Well," she chuckled, "almost. You want me to send a
hard copy of what we've got?"

Decatur started to tell her to forget it, but changed his
mind. At least he'd have something to show to Marva—
prove he'd at least tried. "Yeah, send me everything you
got," he said.

Marva was busy behind the bar when he walked in. She
gave him a tight-lipped nod and motioned him to have a seat
in the corner booth. A waitress arrived at his table and

Beauford held up one finger. He wished Howard were with him. Damn but he was beginning to wonder about his so-called friend. He'd been acting stranger than an owl with insomnia. Secretive he was. Fletcher would hardly talk to him, and now he was "too busy" to help him break the news to Marva. Bad business, bad business. Any rape was, but this one was hurting all of 'em. He stared at Marva. He loved coming in here. She'd always give you a wave as she sang along with the juke box. He reminded himself not to get jealous about her. Funny. When she'd been married to that worthless Langston fella it hadn't bothered him nearly so much. He *knew* that wouldn't last, that she'd be free again. But now Howard Fletcher was a different story.

A beer was slammed down in front of him, spilling foam over the edge, and he looked up to see Marva scowling at him. "Well now, that's personal service," he said with a sickly grin.

"Move over, Beauford," she said, sliding into the booth and sitting next to him. "So tell me what you've been doing."

Beauford avoided her stare. "Oh, you know, Friday night, so I got to rattle a few doors and make the store owners feel they're gettin' personal attention. Story goes the city fathers insisted on the sheriff checkin' every store on Friday night since the Cunningham girl went into a dressing room at Jackson's Toggery and they forgot about her and locked the store and she was there all weekend. Tried on everything in the store, so they . . ."

"Goddammit, Beauford, you know what I'm asking. I know in these parts you're supposed to answer a question with a story. I know all about us 'Loosianans' starting off on a tangent and working our way back toward an answer. Now tell me about the Swinton kid!"

Beauford stared into his beer as if the answer might come bubbling up from the bottom of the glass. Painfully she drew out the story of his visit with Robby's grandmother.

"And the Swinton kid's not showing up at school," he finished lamely.

"Not showing up at school? Not showing up?" Marva shouted in the now-silent bar. "You mean the poor kid may not make it to the spring prom? Jesus, Beauford, what kind of a cop are you?"

Beauford laid a placating hand on her arm, but she shook it off. "I know how you feel, but the evidence, the lab report were inconclusive. I mean it was, uh, five days later and then it got found out because of this other, uh, medical problem." Beauford drew in a deep breath, shaking his head. "So far, the prosecutor won't back a warrant."

"No, Beauford, you don't know how I feel. You haven't got the goddamned remotest idea how I feel. Not showing up in school! His grandma doesn't know where he is! This is rape, not truancy. Why don't you go up to that laboratory where the little bastard raped my daughter, and sweat the kid's old man, collect some evidence, whatever you're supposed to . . ."

"Laboratory? What's this about a laboratory?" Howard Fletcher had sat down across from them without their noticing. Marva stared at him, then looked around the bar. The other patrons quickly turned their heads away. "You said Vicky told you she was raped in an office chair," Fletcher persisted. "What's this about a laboratory?"

Marva shrugged. She lowered her voice. "When I talked to her that first time, alone, she did say she was raped in the chair in the father's office, right behind his desk. But there was some laboratory in the next room, or something like that."

There was silence. A waitress came over to take Fletcher's drink order. "Get out of here!" Marva snarled. Their waitress slunk out of sight.

Finally Fletcher spoke. "Beauford, the lady's right. We should go up to that laboratory or office or whatever the hell it is and look around."

Beauford was about to mumble something about Federal

property and jurisdiction and search warrants, but he could feel Marva's shoulder touching his and was sure he could feel the heat from her. And he saw the way she was looking at the man sitting across from them. "First thing in the morning," he said.

CHAPTER 33

They had traveled first on a magnificent causeway built over the swamps and bayous. It wound out from New Orleans, past Charlemaigne, then narrowed down to a cracked macadam road which led to Ascension Parish and the leprosarium at Carville. Having been a medical student at Tulane, Fletcher knew all the stories about the famous leper colony, and he remembered the drive, since all med students were required to spend two days there while on the infectious disease service.

"Always wondered why the doctors who work up in the leprosarium live in Charlemaigne," Decatur said. "Must be a ten-mile drive for them."

Fletcher sighed. "Nobody wanted to live near a leper colony in those days, Beauford. Nobody even wanted a Carville mailing address. Public Health Service had to buy those houses in Charlemaigne to get anyone to work here."

Decatur's Camaro had reached a stretch of blacktop that followed the Mississippi, winding past the Hunt Correctional Center. Beauford slowed the car, studying the prisoners, all of them black, working or leaning on shovels along the levee. He waved to them. "Still drainin' swamps out here," he said. "Gives 'em something to do, I guess." One of the prisoners recognized Beauford and returned his wave.

"The patients were five men and two women," Fletcher

said. "Brought them ashore from a quarantine ship on a coal barge and put them in a slave cabin. Eighteen ninety-four, I think it was. They were the only people in the barge and they used twenty-foot poles to push the barge up the river. Nobody wanted to get closer than that."

Beauford slowed the Camaro as they passed a sign that read "The Gillis W. Long Hansen's Disease Center." He steered the car through an unguarded gate that led up to what appeared to be a large antebellum mansion, which another sign announced as the administration building.

The scene was almost pastoral. The buildings sat on fifty acres or so of manicured grounds, the outbuildings shaded by cypress. He and Beauford left the car and paused for a moment on the steps of the building. People were meandering on the grass or riding bicycles. They were all dressed in street clothes. There were no hospital pajamas or wheelchairs and nobody looked the least bit sick.

Beauford made a reluctant and unlikely sneak. "You sure this is the way to do it, Howard? Just walk up there in broad daylight?" Beauford's head swiveled like a sparrow's. He looked out of place without his uniform and wore an ill-fitting suit which was too heavy for this weather. He kept dabbing his head with an outsized handkerchief.

Fletcher kept up his guided-tour prattle, hoping to calm him. He pointed to a huge stable barn about two hundred yards away. "Slaughterhouse and a dairy there," he said. "Place was entirely self-sufficient for a lotta years. Had to be."

The receptionist behind the desk was a well-dressed attractive woman not much past thirty. She immediately recognized Dr. Byron Swinton's name as "one of our visiting doctors from the C.D.C. in Atlanta." She handed them a map of the premises and a brochure and told them to find the "outbuilding Dr. Swinton was using."

Beauford made a mournful clucking noise. "I wish I could convince myself that this made any sense. You sure there won't be a lotta people there?" he asked.

Fletcher grinned tightly and stared at his friend. "Byron Swinton works alone, I'm sure of it. Remember what Vicky told us about the kid? Had his own key, lets himself in late at night. He tells Vicky he has the run of the place and rapes her, for God's sakes, without a worry anybody's going to drop in unexpectedly."

Byron Swinton hurried through the hallways of New Orleans Charity Hospital happy to be heading back to his lab in Carville and thankful that he did not practice clinical medicine. He detested these smelly, noisy wards.

He wished Robby were here. Robby usually came with him on these specimen-collecting trips. Since many of the cases were admitted to Charity Hospital, the Surgeon General himself had arranged to have the specimens sent here, then picked up and sorted at the station in Carville before being forwarded to Atlanta for identification. It put an intermediate step between the hospitals where the cases were found, and Atlanta, where the specimens were being studied. Tracking the epidemic had been given the code name "Operation Swamp." Robby had loved that and knew more about this epidemic than anyone. To Byron's delight, Robby had come to appreciate the excitement of epidemiology even more. Each week, before they'd even left the Charity Hospital parking lot, Robby would be ripping into the boxes of petris they'd just collected, anxious to find out how many new cases there were and where they'd come from. What a terrible injustice having to send him away, just when things were going so well. The poor kid, up there alone in Atlanta, everybody picking on him like this. Even Robby's grandmother seemed to have some doubts about his innocence. Byron Swinton remembered that it was not a lot different when he was Robby's age. He too had been quiet, studious, and had had to endure the taunts of his classmates.

• • •

The building was similar to others on the grounds, with an outer layer of hand-fired bricks, probably dating to the turn of the century. It was the size of a small ranch house. "God, I feel out of place," Beauford said. "No gun, no badge. In this damn civilian suit. Ain't had a suit on since my cousin Amanda's funeral."

Howard laughed. "Beauford, you've never had that gun out of the holster. A gun is exactly what we don't need."

"I know, I know. It's just become a part of me. I feel lopsided."

They knocked on the door for a full five minutes. Fletcher gripped the screwdriver in his pocket which he had brought along in case he had to break out a glass panel. But the doorknob turned easily and the door swung open. He stepped inside, and Decatur, after a nervous full circle, followed him.

The laboratory was one large room, probably 30 by 40 feet and at the far end was a glassed-in office with the name "Byron Swinton, M.D, Ph.D." stenciled on the door. Along each wall at intervals of about six feet, were holes in the plaster, cavities where fixtures used to be. Howard suddenly realized they stood in a makeshift laboratory that once was a small medical ward. He'd read about these small infirmaries with rows of beds spaced closely together along each wall, leaving only a narrow aisle in the center. Swinton's office obviously had been a nurses' station that afforded a clear view of the patients. Fletcher could imagine the stern night nurse, in her Florence Nightingale habit, watching over her charges who lay in beds illuminated by oil lamps. And the doctors, what did the doctors do? They did damn little, unless you could count purges, blood-letting and mercury vapors, which probably did more harm than good.

Beauford Decatur let out the breath he'd been holding. "Guess you were right, there's nobody here. Hope you find out what you're looking for fast."

Fletcher didn't have the heart to tell Decatur he didn't know what he was looking for. And Beauford hadn't asked.

"Beauford," Fletcher said, "why don't you check out Swinton's office; see if you can find his Atlanta address in there someplace, and any letters from Atlanta or the C.D.C., anything. I'm going to look around the lab." Decatur nodded and shuffled off.

Fletcher began walking slowly around the benches and tables. In one corner there was a special vent called a "hood." It was used by chemists and bacteriologists to get rid of noxious fumes. Fletcher threw the switch on the hood to activate the blower. It sputtered, and some smoke, mainly dust, came out. He quickly turned it off.

Strange that there was only one of these in such a big lab. And it was obviously unused. He counted ten bacterial incubators. Ten! But there were no autoclaves for sterilizing equipment and no beakers or even test tubes. The only Bunsen burner was in the office, not in the lab.

He began going through the incubators. They were stacked neatly, with carefully labeled petri dishes. Fletcher pulled them out one at a time, reading each label. They seemed to be in some sort of code. One read "F.Q-7" and another "F.Q-9." As he went through the petris, the smell of stool samples began to pervade the room. Why the codes? He was fingering a petri dish the size of an ashtray, rolling it over in his hands when Dr. Byron Swinton came through the door of the laboratory.

Swinton was carrying a large green box on his right shoulder, blocking his view. With hurried strides, he moved past Fletcher without noticing him. He headed straight for his office, where he bumped into Beauford Decatur coming out the door.

Decatur jumped like a jack rabbit, then stood perfectly still, almost at attention. His appearance was that of a naughty little boy caught by his mother, or maybe a recruit about to be chewed out by his drill instructor. "Dr. Swinton," he began. "I'm . . ."

"I know who you are, Sheriff," Swinton said as he brushed past Decatur, entered his office, put the green box on a shelf and sat in the chair behind his desk. "You're a little bit out of your jurisdiction, aren't you?"

Beauford sucked in his stomach, threw back his shoulders and tried to look official. "It's about your son, you see. There's been a complaint." Beauford hooked his hands in his belt. "Quite a serious complaint I'm afraid."

"I know all about it, Sheriff." Swinton nodded, smiling slightly. He cradled the back of his head in his hands. "Robby's grandmother told me all about it and I spoke with him. It was nothing, nothing at all. A teenage lovers' quarrel, and you have no right to go out to my home and interrogate my mother."

Howard, who had been eavesdropping in the laboratory unnoticed, entered the office and was at Decatur's elbow. Neither man seemed to notice him.

"A little more than a teenage lovers' quarrel, I'm afraid. The girl was beaten pretty badly. She's charged that she was raped."

Swinton came forward in his chair, his smile fading. "That's a serious accusation, Sheriff. I hope this, uh, girl can back it up."

Beauford flushed and Howard could sense he was being intimidated. "The girl, the family, well, they have a pretty good standing in Charlemaigne, Doctor. The girl has never been in any trouble before. Quiet kid, honor student."

Swinton seemed to notice Fletcher for the first time. He shifted his eyes from Beauford to him, then back to Beauford. Then he began speaking slowly, in a soft, condescending singsong as though lecturing small children. "My son is in Atlanta, you see, because that's where he belongs. And I can think of no conceivable reason why he should ever return to Charlemaigne." Swinton's eyes narrowed, his thick, pale eyebrows coming together.

"You mean," Beauford said, "that he ran away?"

Swinton came slowly out of his chair. "I mean, that I drove him there myself."

"I see," Beauford said. "All we'd like to do, Doctor, is talk to him. To get his side of this."

Swinton smiled tightly. "Do you have a warrant, Sheriff?"

Beauford shot a quick look at Fletcher. "No, but I could get one." Beauford looked unblinkingly at Swinton, trying to play out this monumental bluff.

Swinton sneered at Decatur. "Fine, Sheriff, then you get one. And *if* you do, see that it's processed in the proper manner, not skipping all over every parish in Louisiana like some nineteenth-century bounty hunter. The boy's in another state. He would have to be extradited, you know. And I would move heaven and earth to see that that doesn't happen."

Howard Fletcher found it hard to breathe. Swinton's voice seemed to be coming from a distance, hollow, echoing as in a cave.

"I never should have brought him here, never let him leave Atlanta," Swinton went on. He had turned slightly away from his visitors as though addressing an unseen audience. "It is a place of culture and refinement. As for Charlemaigne!" He snorted. "Ancestors of the settlers of New Orleans, slopover inbreeding, descendants of misfits, criminals, whores and pirates." He turned back to Decatur. "This girl who is making up lies about my son—bred from the same colony, no doubt. Trash! and her mother, a barmaid . . ."

Swinton didn't finish. Later, Howard Fletcher would remember only a guttural noise coming from his throat, and then a blur. He wouldn't remember his fingers around Swinton's throat, buried deep in his neck. His first recollection of that moment would be Decatur grabbing him from behind, trying to pull him free of Swinton. "Howard, let go," Decatur had said and he would remember Beauford's grunting with the effort to pry him loose. He would remember Swinton's contorted face, his mouth open wide in a noiseless scream when he let go and Beauford pulled away.

He had allowed himself to be pushed toward the door. "Get outta here, Howard, and wait for me in the car," Decatur had said. He could hear Swinton shouting behind him. "You, Sheriff, I should swear out a warrant against *you*. That thug, whoever he is, tried to kill me."

They had gone several miles back toward Charlemaigne before either of them made a sound. Then Beauford began beating the steering wheel with his fist. "Damn Sam," he muttered, "he sure shoved it up our ass. What in the hell did we think we were going to do down there anyway?"

Howard had been kneading his knuckles together, amazed at his red-rage assault against Byron Swinton. He was also appalled, appalled at the transiently satisfying warmth that had come over him as he was squeezing the breath out of Swinton. He shook his head, staring at the long bony fingers, noting the hair on the back of the fingers, the wormy veins coursing down to the knuckles. How many lives had he saved with them? He'd just come close to giving one back.

Beauford growled, "We were totally out of bounds. I could get my Cajun ass in a very large sling. That wasn't no low-life retard back there that you tried to commit homicide on. He could cause trouble."

They rode in silence for a long time, Fletcher watching the familiar landscape slide by. "My God, Beauford, I almost killed him."

Beauford sighed. "You almost did. I mean, he didn't know for a minute, did he?"

"What?"

"Whether you were going to kill him or not." Beauford chuckled. "When he was turning blue and his eyes were popping out of his head, he thought for a minute that he was going to meet his maker."

Fletcher found himself smiling. "Yeah, at least he stopped bad-mouthing Charlemaigne in a hurry."

Decatur began chortling. "Yes, do get your warrant, Sheriff, and see that it's properly processed."

And they both started laughing, each one's glee feeding on the other's. Soon, tears ran down Beauford's cheeks, and Fletcher was doubled over the dashboard. The car had slowed to a crawl, and was weaving back and forth across the highway.

Byron Swinton tried to settle into the chair behind his desk in the lab at Carville. He swiveled nervously. Despite his restlessness, he was totally drained and his body seemed depressingly heavy just turning with the chair. He reached into the right-hand desk drawer and took out a tube of Neomycin ointment, then went into the bathroom adjoining his office. He stared into the mirror, undid his shirt collar and rubbed a thin layer on the bruises on his neck. He felt the area slowly with his fingertips. The skin wasn't broken and there would be no infection.

Who was that man with the sheriff? His assistant or some sort of deputy? He acted more like someone who knew the girl, though he and Robby had discussed the entire matter on the drive to Atlanta, and Robby had said the girl's mother was single, and the girl some backwater tart trying to make trouble for a rich boy's family.

He walked back into his office and stood in front of his desk, staring at his swivel chair. His mother had told him the girl claimed Robby had beaten and raped her in that very chair. No, it wasn't possible. Byron was struck by a surge of guilt for the years that he had not been closer at hand to guide Robby. But the boy had always seemed so self-sufficient, not wanting help or advice, stubborn and proud, qualities that Byron had looked upon with a quiet paternal pride. He remembered how puffed up he'd become when he heard his son's first cries after Joan's long and painful labor. And then Joan had died. And Robby had become distant, had drawn into a shell and begun spending endless hours in that basement laboratory. Byron admitted now that, in a sense, he had done the same thing, had poured himself into his work, traveling around the globe and working seventy-hour weeks.

But these three months in Charlemaigne seemed to be a watershed. Robby was changing and seemed closer to him, so fascinated by this epidemic. Robby's grandmother, who had constantly reproached Byron for being an absentee father, had recently been fretting that they were now *too* close, that Robby had no friends. Byron had told her that Edison, Pasteur and Einstein had not been exactly social butterflies.

Impulsively, Byron reached down and grabbed the telephone from his desk and dialed the Charlemaigne Hospital.

After about eight rings the operator came on the line. "Patient information," Byron said.

There were several more rings until another voice answered. Byron could feel his hand gripping the phone. "Uh, is there a . . . Miss Langston in the hospital?"

"Yes, I'll connect you to the nurses' station on her floor." Byron felt his heart racing. He was afraid of this; she had been hospitalized.

"Two West," a bored voice answered.

"I'd like to inquire about a patient that was admitted last week. Name of Langston."

"Are you immediate family?"

"No, just a . . . friend. I wondered about the extent of her injuries."

"Sir, you must have the wrong patient. Miss Langston is not a trauma patient."

"What? Well, uh, could you tell me what the problem is?"

"I'm sorry, sir, we're not allowed to give that out. Only the admitting diagnosis on the front sheet of the chart and her status."

"Fine. Could I have those?"

"Her admitting diagnosis was diarrhea with dehydration. Her status has just been upgraded from critical to serious."

The surge of relief caused him to slump against the desk. "Thank you," he croaked, barely able to replace the receiver.

CHAPTER 34

Howard Fletcher was nagged into wakefulness. Something left undone during the day had been filed away in his subconscious and was gnawing at his sleep, turning it into a fitful nap. He slept in one of the smaller bedrooms of the antebellum mansion. It had probably been one of the children's bedrooms. The bed was too short. He had to either curl into a fetal position, or let his legs dangle over the edge. He avoided the huge four-poster in the master bedroom. It was too large for one person.

A television set next to the small bed flickered. It had been on all night, a sentinel of his insomnia. He had rarely watched television before Ellen had died, but in those weeks alone in Chicago he'd developed the habit of switching it on as soon as he walked in the door. Tonight he found himself waking frequently and watching segments of old movies, evangelists on small budgets, and fascinating public service announcements from the U.S. Agriculture Department.

It was 3:15 A.M., and talking to him now was the weather girl from New Orleans. She was reassuring him that the approaching rain would not be nearly as heavy as the three inches that "soaked the Action-Eyewitness News viewing area last week."

From the lips of the TV girl, the weather was never really bad, even when it was ferocious. It took on a benign, even lovable quality. She was saying that "the storm pattern was not very aggressive," and that it was only a "teeny, low-pressure system." She pointed to a symbol on a map and identified it as a "shallow, cute little isobar."

It almost made you want to cuddle that isobar. Howard turned his back to the weather girl, and started counting the dots in the faded pattern of the wallpaper. He closed his eyes, but knew that counting wallpaper dots or sheep would not work. He sighed and roused himself, getting out of bed quickly. Still in his pajamas, he walked downstairs and outside to his unlocked car. He pulled the map from the glove compartment and took it back to his office. He spread out the "Tourist Map of the French Quarter," then ran back upstairs and got the list of addresses of the hospitals, clinics and doctors offices he had copied from the boxes of petri dishes at Charity Hospital. He couldn't find any pins, so he straightened a bunch of paper clips and began sticking them in the map.

With growing excitement, he watched as the makeshift pins clustered and formed a perfect circle around the corner of Bourbon and Saint Ann's Streets. All on the same corner and all became ill on the same day of the week—Thursday!

She was sitting up, reading a book. She wore a trace of lipstick and her features were fuller. The awful parched and sallow complexion of severe dehydration was gone, and she smiled as he entered the hospital room. "I'm feeling better," she said.

"What?"

"Better," Vicky said. "I'm feeling better." Another smile, "Thanks to you."

Howard Fletcher felt a pang of guilt. Over the past three days, he'd come to know Vicky Langston. She was mature, intelligent and brave, and she had indeed improved enough that he had been able to take a more careful history from her. As tactfully as he could, he'd quizzed her about everything that had happened on her 'date' with Robby

Swinton and had asked repeatedly exactly what she'd had to eat and drink. She remembered the name of the art theater where they had seen the Madame Curie movie, the irony of that not escaping him. He had looked up its location and then called the theater to double-check. It was nowhere near the corner of Bourbon and St. Ann—it wasn't even near the French Quarter and, as far as he could determine, they had not been near that area.

He'd stopped by to take another look at the spots, and stepped to the side of Vicky's bed. The spots looked different. Was it the light? He'd examined the Avignon kid and Mann at night under artificial light. With the afternoon sunlight pouring through the window the spots looked different, a deeper red, maybe a touch of violet, less like a rash and more like a painting. The red blotches formed overlapping circles each about one inch wide. They spread out from a central point and seemed too arranged to be real, like some sort of mystical *au naturel* tattoo. Each circle was a paler shade of red until the outer circle was a pale pink, barely darker than the canvas-skin beneath it. It reminded him of Cézanne's incredible paintings of flowers, and of fruit so realistic that when he painted outdoors, birds flew to the picture instead of the fruit trees, so it was said. Howard could still picture those pears.

Bizarre that these sinister spots would remind him of Cézanne, except they were more like Cézanne's flowers. Especially the roses. Preoccupied, he drew up the sheet, and without a word to Vicky left the room.

As usual the place depressed him. It wasn't even a decent doctor's lounge, and not close to being a medical library. But people with problems tended to drift to some sort of beacon: some went home to talk things over with their fathers or spouses, some went to their lawyers, some to their psychiatrists, some to a priest. Howard Fletcher had always sought out the medical library to sit and think. It dated back to medical school, when indeed a lot of the answers to his problems *could* be found in a medical library.

He expected no answers here. His thoughts were too jumbled, and he found himself doodling on a scratch pad and sipping stale doctors'-lounge coffee out of a huge urn replenished only once every twenty-four hours.

The pathetic two shelves of outdated textbooks and bound journals were dusty. He rolled his fingers across the oily attenuated bindings, seeking reassurance, as though the outdated knowledge they contained could somehow help. He pulled out a volume of *Pillsbury's Textbook of Dermatology*, looking through the R's under Rashes, although the subheading under that listing, as in any dermatology textbook, were several pages long and seemed to take up one third of the fifteen-hundred-page volume. A review of the indexes of *The New England Journal of Medicine* and *The Annals of Internal Medicine* were of no help. He suddenly felt ridiculous, rummaging around blindly through books under the heading of "Rashes." He would call a dermatologist friend of his in Chicago, or have someone here in consultation from New Orleans.

He was about to leave, when his eye fell on a 1962 edition of *Kent's Physical Diagnosis*, and he, once again, turned to the Rs.

His breath was drawn in and he felt lightheaded. It was one of those surprises that appeared too suddenly. The terror of the unexpected, as when people open certain closets in horror movies.

The index of the book did not direct him where to look for the answer to his problem—instead, it *gave* him the answer, gave it too soon, before he was ready. Though he was looking in the Rs for "Rashes," his eye caught another listing in the index: "*Rose Spots—See Typhoid Fever.*"

For once, the Charlemaigne Hospital doctors' lounge and library seemed more than adequate. For the first time since he'd been in Charlemaigne, there was a plethora of information on a subject he wanted to look up. Maybe there was an advantage to being in a library with outdated journals and textbooks: there was plenty of information about an old-time, outdated disease called typhoid fever. The 1955 textbooks were full of it.

Usually reading calmed him. He was reassured by it. A live, breathing, talking human person, mortally ill, was frightening—a kind of intolerable pressure. It was hard to think, to be objective. But a medical problem—no matter how difficult—laid out in a textbook always seemed easier, manageable, controllable. The cold, lifeless pages were objectively reassuring.

But not in this case. As he read, his initial apprehension approached panic. It was all there: the five-day incubation period, the mode of transmission, its symptoms and prognosis. And the textbook description of the disease left no doubt as to what Vicky Langston had. The chills, fever, diarrhea, dehydration, were all there.

And he knew he should act—should do something. Not only for Vicky's sake but for others who surely were infected. There had to be other Horace Manns out there. He stared at the phone in the doctors' lounge. He should be calling someone, 'notifying the authorities' as the saying went. But who? The C.D.C.?

He was suddenly aware of his name on the overhead pager, and he picked up the phone.

"Howard?" God, it was good to hear Beauford's voice. "Howard, we need to talk about this whole mess."

He found himself nodding, the phone still to his ear. Not a bad idea, he thought. He needed to talk—and to think. "I'll be right there," he said.

CHAPTER 35

The ashtrays were full of cigarette butts, and the bottle of Wild Turkey was three-quarters empty. The cigarette smoke had turned Beauford Decatur's small living room into a pale shade of blue. Howard watched as Beauford sailed playing card after playing card at an upturned hat in the middle of the floor. More than a little drunk, Beauford had missed his target more often than not. Cards littered the rug. "Used to be good at that," Beauford said. He threw the last card with a quick flip of his wrist and watched as it, too, sailed past the hat. Beauford muttered an obscenity and looked around, seeming to notice for the first time the cloud of smoke that hung in the still air. "Place looks like a poolroom," he said sourly.

Howard wasn't listening, and had only intermittently glanced over at Beauford and his solitary game of card-pitching. He had never felt so impotent. Marva was someplace right now trying to cope with her rage over her daughter's rape. And since she was expecting them to call her, naturally they were proceeding to get drunk. The rock in Howard's belly was the reality that he would have to tell Marva that the rape would prove, in a very short time, to be inconsequential. Would have to tell her that Vicky had a blood smear that looked like a trip to the zoo, and that he was keeping her alive, but not curing her, only forcing her bacteria into a temporary retreat from which they would eventually emerge.

It reminded him of the first case he had cracked. He'd been a senior medical student and one of the cases assigned to him had been an elderly lady with back pain. Except she hadn't really been elderly—maybe sixty years old—considered elderly at the time by most of the twenty-four-year-old senior medical students. And it hadn't been the usual back pain; it was excruciating and had baffled her attending physicians. But with hard work—a diligent history and extra reading—Howard had made the diagnosis of multiple myeloma. He'd accepted the congratulations of everyone connected with the case. But there was absolutely no meaningful therapy for the disease and he'd had to stand by—somewhat cynically—and watch the woman suffer a painful, lingering death.

Now he had diagnosed Vicky Langston. And he knew he had cracked what had to be a good-sized epidemic. The bacteria known as *Salmonella typhosa* had somehow developed resistance to all antibiotics. Instead of rolling over dead when exposed to the wonder drugs, it rolled up into spores and hibernated. Then when the patient seemed to be getting better and antibiotics were discontinued, it reverted back to its virulent form and caused the disease known as typhoid fever.

Big deal. What good would his discovery do? He would notify the public health people and the C.D.C. But, he realized, somewhat bitterly, they were already in on it. They knew there was an epidemic of spore-forming bacteria in the area and had sent Dr. Byron Swinton here to investigate it! He now realized what had bothered him about the lab in Carville; all those bacteriology incubators, but no bacteriology equipment. It wasn't a lab, it was a collecting station. Did the C.D.C. know their spores were typhoid bugs? Probably not, since all the specimens they received were from sick people—patients who were receiving antibiotics! By the time the C.D.C. received the petris, the bugs had already formed spores and couldn't be identified.

He'd notify them first thing in the morning. At least they could send out a public health bulletin and notify physicians to keep their cases on antibiotics indefinitely, as he was doing with Vicky.

He'd started Vicky on ciprofloxacin, the same antibiotic he'd used on H. T. Mann and Sam Avignon. Ciprofloxacin, the newest and most potent. What a cruel joke. But, like all the other antibiotics, it would at least change the typhoid from its invasive state to the inactive spore form and buy some time.

And he was using the time—Vicky's precious time—to get drunk because he didn't know what the hell else to do. He drained the bourbon left in his glass and slammed it angrily on the end table, startling Beauford.

Beauford leaned over, almost losing his balance, and pushed the Wild Turkey towards Howard. "Enough in there for a couple more good belts. Finish her off."

Howard turned slowly to stare at Beauford, amazed that his own mind was the least bit clear. Perhaps the adrenalin of anger had a way of diluting the effects of alcohol. He wondered how close he had come to killing Swinton, and what if he'd been alone—without Decatur there to stop him? Love, hate, jealousy, everybody knows about them, but not anger. Definitely not enough written about anger. Where were are all the psychiatrists when you really needed them? Maybe his mind wasn't so clear, he thought as he reached for the bottle. "Might as well," he said.

Beauford leaned back, rested his head on the back of the chair and closed his eyes. "That Marva," he said after a time, "she's a stubborn woman." His words, slowed by the liquor, were coming at the pace of syrup. "Jesus, she's gonna be madder than hell when I tell her I couldn't get my hands on the Swinton kid. Promised her I'd call her tonight. How am I going to tell her?" *We've both got a problem that way*, Howard thought. "Yeah," Beauford was saying, "a good woman, damned good woman, but stubborn. I'd do anything for her, she knows that." He started to say something else, but he swallowed the words. "I guess she figures I'm just an errand boy. I guess," he continued, "maybe I am."

In the heavy silence that followed, Howard felt a sinking feeling, and, for the second time tonight, guilt sat on him like a lead weight. Of course he'd suspected it—no, known it. It had been all out there in front of him, the way Beauford hung around the Amble Inn, nursing a beer and getting cow eyes every time Marva came close, instantly protective when any drunk even looked like he might slobber over her. Yeah, he'd known it, he just hadn't known it was this bad. God, the best friend he'd made in this town and they were both in love with the same woman. And Beauford had to know which way that was likely to go. Howard felt sorry for Beauford; he felt sorry for Marva and Vicky; he felt sorry for himself. He raised the glass to his lips, hoping to drown the helpless feeling.

Beauford was snoring softly, his mouth open, lips slack. His chest was rising and falling rhythmically. He still held his empty glass in a limp hand draped over the armrest.

The sudden ringing was accentuated by the still room; the noise seeming to bounce off the walls. It jangled louder than any phone Howard Fletcher could remember.

Beauford's eyes flew open, his glass falling the short distance to the carpeting, where it bounced without breaking. Howard cleared his throat. "You taking a little nap, Sheriff?" he said. "Now who do you suppose would be calling us at two A.M. just when the Amble Inn closes?"

Decatur got woozily to his feet and shuffled for the phone in the kitchen. "My mouth tastes like dirty socks," he said, coughing.

Though Howard was sitting over ten feet away from the telephone, he could hear Marva shout at the other end of the line. "Atlanta! The bastard's up in Atlanta? Goddammit, Beauford, you let him get away!"

Decatur shifted the phone in his ear so Howard couldn't hear her. Howard thought he'd never felt so sorry for anyone in his life. Beauford stood there wiping the sweat from his face with a large red handkerchief, half drunk and half hung over, while the woman he loved belittled him. He tried to explain, and told her about Howard's half-strangling Byron Swinton, as though that had exacted some measure of revenge. Although Howard couldn't hear her now, Marva was obviously having none of it. Beauford's explanations seemed pathetically inadequate as she kept interrupting him. "Marva, now we just can't go up there and drag some kid back from another state. . . . Yes, I told you I talked to the Atlanta police right . . . right after, afterwards. . . . The kid's got no record. . . . No, I told you, it was just some teacher committed suicide . . . I don't know why she did it. . . . Look, Marva, I got the report on that right here." Decatur, the phone still to his ear, walked back into the living room, trailing the extension cord. He picked up some papers from a folder on the coffee table and waved them in the air as though Marva could see through the phone. There was a loud click as she hung up.

Neither man spoke for a long minute. "Now she wants us to go to Atlanta and get the kid," Decatur finally grunted.

Howard Fletcher stared at his friend. "What's this about the Atlanta police? I thought you said the kid had no record."

Decatur shrugged. "He don't. There was a teacher of his up in Atlanta who committed suicide. Guess old Robby was her favorite pupil, and when she did herself in, she willed him a couple a rare books in a suicide note. Atlanta police questioned him about it and he turned up on their computer."

Fletcher stared at the sheaf of papers in Decatur's hand. "That's a long suicide note," he said.

"Nah," Decatur said, "note's only half a page. This here's the autopsy report on the teacher. They sent everything in the file from Atlanta." Decatur tossed it into

Howard's lap. "Nothin' in it much. She died of cyanide poisoning, no foul play."

Howard let the report lie there, then picked it up and put it back on the coffee table. If there was something he wasn't interested in at this particular time, it was another autopsy report.

"That poison sure made a mess outta that lady," Decatur said.

"What's that?"

"The poison," Decatur said. "Sure tore up her insides."

Howard shook her head. "Cyanide? Nah, it's an enzyme inhibitor. It works through the blood stream."

"That's not what this here report says. It tore her up pretty bad."

"Toss it back, Beauford." Howard frowned and began reading the first page. It was the usual description of the body. Though something—even in that ordinarily mundane description—bothered him. "The gross appearance of the body reveals it to be greatly dehydrated." He felt suddenly absolutely sober. Quickly, he turned to the back part of the report and began reading the part under the heading "Gross Description of the Intestines." He turned to the microscopic section of the intestines and sped-read it, then turned back and read it again. And then again. He leaned his head against the back of Decatur's couch and closed his eyes, willing himself to be calm. He needed to concentrate, to think it through, that relaxed concentration he'd learned to attain just before doing surgery. And he began recalling all that had happened these past few weeks.

He looked up to find Decatur staring at him. "Beauford," he said, "did you say Marva wanted us to go to Atlanta?"

Decatur shrugged. "Yeah, well, ya know she's upset, and . . ."

"Beauford, we don't have to go to Atlanta, Atlanta is coming here." He gave a slight smile as he said it.

"What the hell you talkin' about, Howard?" Decatur asked.

The smile began spreading on Howard's face. "I'm talking about it being five days from Saturday night to Thursday night."

Decatur squinted at his friend and cocked his head to one side. "It's late, Howard, and I guess we both had enough to drink. And I—we—well, maybe we both got Marva under our skins, upsettin' us. Let's get some sleep and . . ."

Fletcher spoke slowly, softly, enunciating each word perfectly as though it would help Decatur believe it. "The Swinton kid is going to be in the French Quarter on the corner of Bourbon and Saint Ann Streets Saturday night—tomorrow night—at six p.m."

Decatur continued staring. "Howard, the Swinton kid's in Atlanta. His old man said so."

Howard was still smiling and now began nodding his head slowly. "You're right, Beauford, the Swinton kid's in Atlanta, but at six tomorrow night, he'll be in New Orleans. I'm certain of it. As certain as the sun will rise tomorrow, the kid will be there." He checked his watch. "Tomorrow, hell, it's past midnight. He'll be there tonight. Beauford, get some rest. I'm going back to the hospital now to check Vicky and tomorrow we're keeping our appointment with Robby Swinton."

CHAPTER 36

Byron Swinton had never been able to toler-
ate fools or frightened sycophants, and the high-school
principal was clearly one or the other, probably both. He
made indecisive clucking noises in his throat, seemed to
have chronic sinus trouble, and was partial to incomplete
sentences.

"Mr. Swinton . . . That is, Dr. Swinton, I suppose you
wonder why I came all the way down from Atlanta. . . . I
know your time is valuable . . . but then. What I mean to
say . . . I wouldn't have asked to meet with you if it
weren't a matter of extreme importance."

The principal—Byron hadn't caught the last name, and
he didn't particularly care if he ever learned it—was a
sniveler. "Suppose," Byron said, looking at his watch,
"you just tell me what this is all about."

"Hmmm, yes, right you are." The principal twisted in
anguish and gathered himself. "We've never had anything
like this happen before. You understand, I want to be fair to
Robby. To everybody. But I seem to be caught in the
middle. And then I thought Robby had moved to Louisiana
to finish his senior year, so I was going to let it go. But now
that he's back in school in Atlanta . . ."

Swinton felt his patience slipping away. Robby had only
been back in Atlanta a few days. Was there trouble already?

"Your phone call was a little short on facts," he told the principal sharply. The principal's phone call had come two days ago, and Byron had been impatient with the man, who seemed vague and secretive and, Byron surmised, given to melodrama. But he had agreed to meet him halfway, in this little restaurant off Interstate 10 near Biloxi. "What about Robby?"

The principal approached his subject cautiously, as though defusing a bomb. "Dr. Swinton, a few weeks ago, shortly after Robby left school—after you moved down here—one of our teachers took her own life."

Swinton felt a chill but kept his face a mask. "Go on."

The principal shifted his eyes rapidly as though looking for a trapdoor. "This is a very delicate situation."

"What has it to do with Robby?"

"It came to my attention . . . That is, there was talk among the students—I was even approached by a member of the school board—that Robby had been tutored by this teacher in her home." The principal manufactured a cough. "It seems, Dr. Swinton, that it had been going on for some time. I investigated, of course. My job."

"And?"

"The boy, that is, Robby, and Miss Lorlene, the teacher—it seems they were carrying on an intimate relationship. As I say, I was willing to let it pass, but with Robby now back in Atlanta, there is a lot of talk . . . and . . ." His voice trailed off.

Swinton recoiled. "This is absurd."

"She left a note," the principal said.

"What?"

"Miss Lorlene left two notes. I was the one who discovered the body. One of the notes was addressed to your son. I took it without telling the police. You understand, the poor woman was gone. I was only trying to protect the reputation of the school and, ah, your son. Miss Lorlene couldn't be helped by divulging anything more than was already known." The principal wrinkled his face in pain. "I could be arrested for withholding that note. I was only trying to minimize the repercussions. You understand?"

Swinton's mind whirled, his thoughts swinging from irritation at the hand-wringing demeanor of the principal to a dread of what was to come next. He forced his voice to a level of calm he didn't feel. "You still have the note?"

The principal nodded. He reached inside his suit jacket and extracted a single sheet of white stationery, folded in half, bordered with tiny purple flowers, violets perhaps. Glancing at it as the principal handed it to him, Byron could see the beginning: "My Dearest Robby."

He read it slowly, presetting his mind into a skeptical mode. He tried to shape the words into an innocuous scenario, one in which the writer was a hopeless romantic living out a fantasy. He tried to bend the words to those of an ingenuous spinster, time passing her by, creating a one-sided love affair until the fantasy became real. It didn't work. The letter was too honest, a heartfelt outpouring, nothing held back.

And then he read, and reread, the closing. ". . . You will always be that brilliant, inquisitive boy whose single-minded purpose will be to use your rare intellect to prolong life, to enhance the nobility of life. I am sorry for nothing. I was flattered and proud to share a part of your life, share your mind as well as your body, share in your science, your experiments. I say good-bye to this world without regrets. Love forever."

He crumpled the letter, then for a time stared out the window at the parade of passing trucks on Interstate 10. He couldn't concentrate, and the restaurant noises, the rattle of plates and dishes and the conversational hum intruded on his thoughts. He deliberately smoothed the schoolteacher's note out on the table, flattening out the dogeared corners. He looked once more at the signature of the woman who, in a few weeks, had become closer to his son than he had in seventeen years. Finally he looked at the school principal. "You say this woman committed suicide?"

The principal nodded, not meeting his eyes. "There is something else . . . that is a source of rumor at the school . . . One of the main reasons I wanted to talk to you about this." He leaned forward, the cheap restaurant chair creaking. He spoke just above a whisper. "At the autopsy—I think you should know—they found that Miss Lorlene was two months' pregnant."

At the second blow of the day Byron sucked in his breath. But he stiffened, willing his emotions to stay hidden. Curiously, for a moment, he thought of his dead wife. And he also thought of how he would like to strangle this man for bringing him such news. The moment passed. "You say," he asked the principal, "there was another note?"

The principal leaned forward as if sharing a conspiracy. "Yes, but it didn't mention her—relationship—with your son. It was about her personal effects—and about, uh, the arrangements . . . well, that is what to do with her body. . . . She left Robby some books . . . but nothing was made of that. . . ." The principal's hands fluttered nervously and he leaned even closer. "It might make you feel better to know that Miss Lorlene was going to die anyway."

"What?"

"Yes, yes, it's true. If she hadn't killed herself . . . would have lasted only a week or so . . . heard that from the doctor myself."

Byron was leaning back in his chair as far as he dared, backing away from this loathsome little man. "What on earth was the matter with her?" he asked.

The principal shrugged. "Some sort of terrible intestinal infection . . . very serious. Apparently no chance of recovery. Poor thing, she must have been suffering. And so now you see, Dr. Swinton, now you know why I . . . and the school board . . . that is, with Robby back in Atlanta . . .

living there alone and attending our school . . . well, we wanted some assurances that . . ."

Byron Swinton had been folding and unfolding the letter, watching the purple flowers turning in and out. Finally, he put it in his pocket, rose from his chair and, with the principal still talking, walked away.

Byron turned the key in the ignition, sparking the car to life. He planned to drive home slowly, willing himself to think, to concentrate. But as he swung the car out of the restaurant parking lot, he suddenly jerked the steering wheel hard and stabbed at the brakes. A small dog had shot from the curb into traffic, and he'd just missed mashing it to a pulp.

An image of long ago forced its way into his head. A couple from the neighborhood—Byron hadn't bothered to learn their name—had appeared on his doorstep one day when Robby was twelve. The man seemed ready to explode; the woman was sobbing hysterically. They'd stood at Swinton's door, pouring out a bizarre story of their dog—Cuddles or Puddles, or something like that—having been set afire. Ablaze, the dog had run in terror and pain until it died. The woman, who Swinton later learned was childless, kept wailing that the dog had been her "baby." And they had accused Robby of committing the cruel act.

Byron slouched behind the wheel, remembering how he had ordered the man and wife away, dismissing the accusation as preposterous, even calling the couple mentally unstable. The police were called, but nothing ever came of it. The episode had upset him for days, but he'd eventually put it behind him. He recalled that at the time he had casually asked himself the question, What kind of a person could do such a thing?

He slowed his car as he approached the expressway, finally coming to a complete stop at the entrance ramp. He stared up at the huge green and white sign with arrows that read, "West—New Orleans, East—Atlanta."

He was suddenly aware of the blaring of the horn of the trailer truck behind him. How long had he been here blocking the ramp? He stared up at the sign one last time, then quickly pulled his car into the eastbound lane.

CHAPTER 37

Robby Swinton dragged the cot down from the attic and installed it in a corner of the basement. He sat down, breathing heavily. The task had exhausted him, and he decided to rest for a while before returning upstairs for some blankets and a pillow. He was sweating, although the cellar was cool. He put it down to the excitement of being back in Atlanta alone. His father, or rather, his philistine grandmother, would never have allowed him to sleep down here. He hummed as he made the final loading of the injection syringe. It was good to be back in his old Saturday night routine.

He surveyed his laboratory. It was just as he had left it when they'd moved to Charlemaigne two months ago. Most of the rats had survived. His father had told him to destroy them when they'd moved, but of course he hadn't. His father would never understand. The white rats were his friends; more than friends, they were partners in a noble experiment. He knew that he would return and would need them again, so he had freed them from their cages and left sacks of food and several pails of water around the lab. They couldn't escape, though the food was gone and about half of them had starved. But the strong rats had survived by cannibalizing the weaker ones, as with any life species. It was the natural order of things. Robby listened to their high-pitched squealing, and laughed. He thought that maybe his next experiment would be one using *Pasteurella Pestis*, the bubonic plague bacillus. Maybe he would reward the surviving rats by using them in that experiment. But at the moment, he didn't have the energy to even think about future experiments. He must renew himself, get some sleep, and then come back with his usual vigor.

He pulled his favorite epidemiology book from the shelf, lay down on the cot and snapped on the overhead light, balancing the book on his chest. It fell open to where it was most often read, to the chapter on "Demographics and the Initial Infection." The chapter outlined the requirements for the start of an epidemic: the weather, the sewage management, the types of food and how they were cooked. But mostly it was about people, about their habits, their average ages, their style of living and how they interracted on a daily basis. There was a long section on crowds. How often crowds formed and their density. Robby congratulated himself. New Orleans had been perfect.

He closed the book and glanced around the room, his eyes growing heavy. The squeaking of the rats seemed to fade. For a moment, just before sleep came, he considered the irony of his father—indulgent, stolid and guileless Dad, trying to solve a puzzle created by his own son. Robby, contented, smiled at the image. Someday he would let his father in on it, and he would be so proud. Someday.

Robby's dream was a familiar one. It was as though it occupied a privileged place in his subconscious. It always came to him in the twilight of sleep, as he was about to awaken, making it even more vivid. But it was even colder this time. He was speaking to the General as the snow swirled and the wind howled. Robby towered over the little General, who was gazing around the drafty command post in his three-cornered hat, his arm under the shoulder strap he wore diagonally across his chest. His hand was tucked into his waistcoat. "But, *mon général*," Robby heard himself imploring, speaking perfect French. "It is neither the Russians nor the Russian winter that is defeating you. It is typhus. The French army is being crushed by typhus. I can show you how to control it. A few simple measures will stop it." The General smiled, and bid him continue. Robby was always puzzled by the brilliantly colored uniform and polished brass buttons. One was not supposed to dream in color. "And your navy, General. It is being decimated by scurvy, and will be defeated by Nelson at the battle of Trafalgar. The British fleet has learned to conquer scurvy by eating limes, but your staff only ridicules the English crews by calling them limeys. But they will win unless you let me help you. Disease and epidemics change the course of world history."

The General smiled and seemed ready to embrace him, calling him a genius and proposing they join forces. But as in past dreams, Robby went too far and angered the General. Though he knew what was coming, Robby could not help himself. "And there is another reason. We can save the life of my mother! She died of Lyme disease, a painful, lingering condition that can only be discovered by the work of epidemiologists. It is a terrible infection that was unknown at the time of her death. Only later--too late—did anyone know the cause or treatment. If I can start researching the disease now, I can save her. You are the most powerful man of the nineteenth century. By combining forces in this century we can save her life a hundred and seventy-two years from now. You support my research now and I will prevent you from losing your troops to disease."

The General's face darkened. "I've told you not to talk about the next century," he said. "We can't be discussing things that haven't yet happened."

"But I can help you take over America also," Robby said. "The colonists are conquering the Indians by spreading tuberculosis and measles, not with armies."

"That hasn't happened yet," the General shouted. "This is only eighteen twelve! I don't covet the American wilderness. I've already sold the Louisiana territories to raise money for my armies."

The General began stomping his foot on the board floor of the small cabin that served as a command post. His heavy boot crashed through one of the floorboards, and the leaden cold of the Russian winter enveloped them.

Robby's eyes flew open to take in the familiar basement laboratory. He was drenched in sweat which had soaked through his clothing. The sound of the General's stomping still rang in his ears until he realized the noise was that of someone pounding on the heavy basement door. Robby struggled to a sitting position. It was a superhuman effort to drag his senses back to the present. After a moment, he slowly made his way to the door through the rat food and feces.

Byron stepped back when he heard the tumblers click in the door's mechanism. He shook his hand, which he had skinned trying to rouse Robby. For a moment, he thought no one was there. He and Robby, working side by side, had installed the heavy steel door years ago when Robby was about thirteen. Robby could never keep the rats in their cages, and one or two would occasionally gnaw their way through the old wooden door. Robby's grandmother would have a fit when one made its way upstairs.

But Robby, Byron Swinton now knew, was not like other kids. All during the drive up to Atlanta, Byron Swinton rationalized, telling himself that the circumstantial evidence, taken one piece at a time, could have several plausible explanations and that, strung together, the most likely conclusion was absurd. It was incomprehensible, he told himself, while all the time a chilling horror sat on his shoulder and itemized the missing petri dishes, the dead teacher, the sick girl in the hospital.

The steel door opened a crack, creaking on its hinges, and then wider as Byron stepped into the room. The musty subterranean odor· hit him, and the scurrying commotion along the floor and the agitated, unending screeching told him the rats were running free. The figure that backed into the middle of the room framed itself in the puny glow of a single lamp on a stand next to the cot. Byron recognized the form as that of his son, but the boy was thinner, almost emaciated. He must have stopped eating the day he left Charlemaigne. His eyes shone like a deer's caught in a car's headlights.

"Come in, Pa*pa*, come in," Robby said, putting the accent on the second syllable.

Robby had never before addressed him in that manner. "Robby, what are you doing here?" Byron asked, striving for a conversational tone. He watched a slow, sly smile cross his son's face.

"No, Pa*pa*, the question is, what are *you* doing here? You are trespassing on private property here, hallowed scientific ground, if you will." Robby's laugh, a maniacal cackle, set the rats into a renewed flurry of activity, and froze Byron Swinton. "Look around," Robby said, expansively sweeping his arm before him. "You have failed as an epidemiologist. You let your wife—my mother—die of a curable disease that other, more brilliant epidemiologists later uncovered. That will not happen to me. This laboratory will someday be a shrine, spoken in the same breath with Edison's Menlo Park and Pasteur's laboratory."

Byron sagged in anguish. "Oh, Robby." Byron Swinton, who in his entire life had never considered religion a viable aspect of the human condition, wished with all his heart that an unseen hand would reach down and pluck them both off the face of the earth. "Robby," he began, pacing his words carefully, "what you have done here is ingenious." He was mocked by his own words. He had helped Robby set up the lab, instructed him in the techniques of bacteriology. The incubators, autoclaves, animal cages and test tube stands were as familiar to him as his own face in a mirror.

"Yes, ingenious," Robby said gleefully. "Culturing the bacteria, nurturing them, coaxing them to form spores to grow in petri dishes soaked with antibiotics." Robby's weight loss seemed to accentuate the smooth, fragile face and sweeping eyelashes. Byron watched his son jiggle his feet in place like an inattentive five-year-old. Robby leaned back coyly, and put a hand to his lips to squelch another laugh. "I might as well tell you," he said. "The whole world will know about it soon." His voice dropped to a whisper, although the words were clear, if disembodied, as though spoken inside a marble mausoleum or empty gymnasium. "Do you know, I even developed one strain so potent that it formed spores faster in the presence of ciprofloxacin. Did you hear me? It grew even faster when exposed to the most powerful antibiotic."

Byron Swinton could feel his eyes burning wetly. He watched his son swagger, and swallowed hard, trying to choke back his revulsion. He hoped he would grow numb. "That's quite an accomplishment, son." Byron took a step toward Robby. "A brilliant piece of work."

Robby broke into hysterical laughter. "I'm glad you agree, *mon général.*"

Byron felt that his head was about to explode. "Stop that," he said, his voice rising. "Stop that goddamn laughing." He found it difficult to breathe. Robby shrank back at the outburst, shuffling sideways, his eyes narrowing warily. Byron brought his voice under control. "Yes, what you have done here is remarkable. But, you see, you have . . . You have jeopardized innocent people." He couldn't bring himself to use the word 'kill.'

Robby shook his head vigorously. "But I needed human subjects. The lab experiments had to be validated." He snorted disdainfully. "French Quarter scum. Perverts, without a single redeeming quality. They should be grateful. My experiments have made them a footnote in scientific history.

They should look at it as an honor." Robby crossed his arms, wrapping them tightly across his chest. "It is getting colder, *mon général.*"

It occurred to Byron that he had never physically laid a hand on Robby, had never once spanked him when he was younger and defiant. Would it have made a difference? Now, it was of no consequence. The system would take into account that the boy was not mentally responsible, wouldn't it? Wouldn't it? Byron tried to soothe his son without talking down to him. "But you haven't gone far enough," he said gently. "The next logical step is to effect a cure."

Robby snickered. "All in good time. When I have a broad enough database, that's when the world will have to acknowledge my work." He took a small black book from the workbench and waved it over his head. "You see, I left one antibiotic out. It's all in here. Everything is recorded. At the proper time, they will come begging me for a cure."

Byron held out his hand. "May I see it?"

"Certainly, *mon général,*" Robby said. "Take all the time you want. Just put it back in the same place. I must leave, you know. I have work to do."

"What?"

"Yes. In the Louisiana Territory. It will be good to get out of this cold."

Byron tensed. As Robby made for the door, Byron moved to block his way. "I can't let you do that, Robby." Up close, his son looked like he'd aged twenty years. Byron put out his hand. "Come with me, Robby."

With amazing strength, Robby charged him, sending both of them crashing against the door. Byron heard himself cry out. They grappled, and it was quickly clear to Byron that he was no match for his son. "Please, Robby." Byron fought for breath, and he could feel his heart racing, pulsing in his ears.

Robby momentarily released him and Byron collapsed against the door. He caught only a glimpse of the metal rat cage before it crashed into the side of his head. He felt himself falling, his face coming to rest on the cold wetness of the basement floor among the rat droppings. Byron Swinton felt blood fill his mouth but, strangely, little pain. He tried to rise, but saw the rat cage raised again, coming at him.

CHAPTER 38

A sign marking the New Orleans city limits flashed into view, and Beauford slowed as they neared the exit leading to downtown and the French Quarter. The car went rapidly from cruising to a crawl. The traffic, human and vehicular, clogged the streets. Picking his way, Beauford finally nudged the Camaro to the side and killed the engine. They were still more than a mile from the Quarter, but pedestrians surrounded the car. "We'll have to hoof it from here," Beauford said.

They sat in the car for a minute as Beauford eyed a bare-chested man walking by in an oversized purple jacket and red slippers adorned with small gold bells. The sheriff seemed in no hurry to leave the car and join the cadre of freaks strolling towards the Quarter.

Howard stared at the dashboard clock, which said ten after five. "We've got to get to Bourbon and Saint Ann by six o'clock," he said.

"So you keep sayin'," Beauford said. "And we're gonna find the Swinton kid there? Jesus, how'd I let you talk me into this. Chasin' a kid for rape when I ain't got enough evidence to give him a parkin' ticket."

They watched a crowd of people dressed like court jesters swirl by. They were followed by some fey men in lipstick and rouge, surrounding a woman in a Marie Antoinette gown balancing a bird cage with a live parakeet atop her head.

Beauford reluctantly pushed the car door open. "You got any idea," he said, "how many people are in the French Quarter this time of year?"

"I know," Howard said.

"They're like fleas, a couple million of 'em."

"We'll find him," Howard said. "If we're at the corner of Bourbon and Saint Ann between six and eight, we'll see him."

The taller Howard pushed off with long strides, forcing Beauford into a half-trot in an effort to keep pace. "How about slowing it down a mite?" Beauford puffed. "Hell, once we get there we'll be lost in that swarm anyway."

Howard didn't answer. As they approached the Quarter, they ran into a wall of noise. They entered from Basin Street, and began elbowing their way down Saint Ann. Howard slowed his pace somewhat and felt a sinking sensation. Maybe Beauford was right. The street was carpeted with people and they were being literally carried along with the crowd, jammed into a beehive of half-naked, sweating drunks. Many of the women were bare-breasted. Howard looked up to see a huge float, as wide as the street and, he estimated, a third as long as a football field. Sitting and standing in various poses were men in identical rubber masks depicting a pockmarked face. Many of them had large-bowl pipes jutting from mouth holes in the masks, and as Howard watched one of the men light up, he saw the bowl spark and crackle. They were all smoking crack—the real thing. At the back of the float was a mock-up of a church with windows large enough to see inside. Women, stripped to the waist, hung from the windows, while some could be seen inside in provocative poses. Another woman and a man rode at the head of the float, simulating sex. A sign on the church proclaimed, "The Holy Catholic Church of Panama." Howard saw Beauford stop and stare, then roll his eyes and shake his head.

Then Howard remembered. The church was a model of the one in which Manuel Noriega had hidden with his mistress before he was taken into custody by U.S. forces. All of the men on the float wore rubber Noriega masks, and they were tossing masks to the screaming crowd. Half the people on the street, it seemed, bore a resemblance to the deposed Panamanian dictator. Howard remembered that he had heard someplace that the theme of this year's parade was drugs.

He looked up at the street sign marking the corner of Bourbon and Saint Ann. Through the haze of tobacco, marijuana and crack he now recognized the apartment of the hooker he had talked to earlier in the week. No wonder she had gone skiing.

"Must be a thousand people just on this here corner," Beauford shouted in his ear. Howard nodded. The crowd was so thick, just three or four faces took up his entire visual field. He could have held up a sign saying, "Anybody on this corner will die from typhoid fever," and it wouldn't be noticed. Or maybe he'd win a prize.

Howard motioned Beauford over and shouted directions. "We'll make laps in opposite directions around the four corners and meet back at this same spot. If you see him, wait until you see me before you do anything." Decatur gave him a don't-you-trust-me? look, then nodded.

Howard found it hard to breathe as he squeezed between bodies. Getting through the crowd was like swimming against a strong current and he began to feel a sense of futility. It would take an army to sort out this legion of indistinguishable revelers.

It reminded Beauford Decatur of his days as a halfback at Charlemaigne High School, in the days when there were two halfbacks, one quarterback and one fullback. They

didn't have running backs and tailbacks and tight ends.
They lined up the same for every play. If you needed to
make more than two yards, one of the two halfbacks got the
ball. If it was under two yards, either the fullback hit the
line or they tried a quarterback sneak. It was simple. Now
he was back to broken-field running, picking his holes in
the crowd, dancing sideways, sometimes stopping dead and
running in place, then bounding ahead, hopscotch fashion.
He crashed into someone—gender unknown—dressed like
the Tin Man in the Wizard of Oz, sporting an oilcan with a
spout in the crotch of the metal suit, but Beauford righted
himself and moved on.

He had just reached the corner diagonally across from
where he'd left Howard, when he saw Robby Swinton. He
watched as the kid donned one of the Noriega masks and
made his way through the crowd. Knowing he would not
see his face again, Beauford quickly memorized the kid's
outfit, from the red-and-blue-striped polo shirt down to the
white sneakers.

He figured Howard would be coming along from the
other direction, and stood on his toes, swiveling his head
like a sparrow, trying to look for Howard as he watched
Robby Swinton disappear into the crowd.

There was a sudden break in the crowd and Howard saw
the sheriff signaling him frantically. He plunged through the
teeming mass, pushing people aside. Beauford was breath-
less. "I saw him, Howard. He's walking down Bourbon
Street. I'm sure it's him. He put on one of them masks, but
I got a look at his face." Howard started to move off, but
Beauford grabbed him. "Wait a minute; I'll have to go first.
You don't even know how the kid's dressed."

"O.K., lead the way, Beauford."

They hadn't gone fifty feet when Beauford pulled up
short and pointed. Howard saw a slim figure in a polo shirt,
jeans, sweat socks and an old pair of Nikes walking slowly,

appearing to scout the crowd. The sight of the kid saunter-
ing down this carnival street while Vicky lay in a hospital
bed enraged Howard.

Robby disappeared from view momentarily, and Howard
guessed that he had turned into one of the courtyard alleys.
He and Beauford quickly doubled back and entered the
alley, almost stumbling over three derelicts sleeping it off in
a sitting position, their backs propped against the side of a
building. They caught sight of Robby, and Howard, with
Beauford trailing, quickly closed the gap between them.
Howard clamped a hand on Robby's shoulder. "Robby," he
said sharply. "Robby Swinton." The boy turned. "You're
coming with us, Robby. I have the sheriff with me. You've
got some explaining to do."

Slowly, almost lazily, Robby turned to face them. In one
motion, Howard ripped the mask from the boy's face and
looked into a face with dead eyes. Robby stood motionless
for a moment, then a noise, a rattle, came from his throat.
He lunged forward, his fingers closing around Howard's
throat. Howard reflexively clamped his hands around Robby's forearms, trying to pry them off him. But suddenly,
Robby's grip was broken. Beauford was behind him, an
armlock around the kid's neck. Robby was flailing his arms.

Beauford was grunting, losing his struggle with the boy.
"Jesus, I wish I had my cuffs," he ground out. Howard
cocked his fist, aiming it at Robby's midsection, but then
saw a metallic glint as Robby pulled something from his
waistband. He twisted, put the injector gun under Beauford's chin and pulled the trigger. Howard heard a swishing
sound, and saw the fine mist spray from the barrel.
Beauford recoiled. Robby wriggled free, and bolted down
the alley and out into the street. Howard was only four steps
behind him.

As Robby reached the street, he found his way blocked
by a long float carrying several huge black men in
spangled loincloths, poised like statues, holding spears,

bows and arrows and tom-toms. Their bodies glistened under the multicolored lights arrayed in profusion along the street. An overhead banner supported by two poles proclaimed the float to be sponsored by "The Zulu Krewe."

Robby slowed for an instant, with Howard only inches behind, and then with amazing agility leaped aboard the float. He stood on the edge, teetering before regaining his balance, and brandished the injector gun in the air.

Howard threw one leg onto the moving float and hoisted himself on the deck. Robby pranced down the length of the float and, almost playfully, pointed the injector gun at a gleaming, muscular black man. But the man swiped at him with a hard forearm, catching Robby on the side of the face. Robby pitched over the side. Howard could hear screams from the crowd as the float ground to a halt.

Howard jumped to the street. A circle of people stood unmoving, struck dumb by the sight of Robby Swinton under the float. The rear wheels had passed over his chest. With each shallow breath, a froth of blood bubbled from his lips.

Beauford was at the center of the crowd, shooing people away and flashing his badge pinned to his wallet. Howard bent over the broken body. Robby's legs were still twitching, but his eyes were staring past Howard, fixing the sky with a gaze Howard had seen many times in hospital emergency rooms. Howard felt with his fingers along the carotid arteries, then shook his head at Beauford. Howard took the injector gun from Robby's hand as a siren wailed up the street.

And then Howard saw the key ring that had fallen from Robby's pants pocket. It lay there shining in the dirty street. Howard covered it with his hand just as a policeman appeared at his side. "O.K.," the cop ordered officiously. "Let's make way for the ambulance."

Howard palmed the key ring, and got to his feet. "You won't need it," he said wearily. Beauford turned to the cop and was about to say something, but Howard pulled him away.

"Damn, Howard, what in hell we doing bugging out like that? That cop back there deserved some kind of an explanation." They were sitting in Beauford's Camaro where they had first parked it, a mile from the Quarter.

"There wasn't any time. As far as the cop knows, it was a simple accident." Howard held the injector gun in his lap, and was fingering the set of keys, staring at the address stamped on its metal disc.

Beauford rubbed the puncture wound under his chin, and nodded at the injector gun. "Is that what the kid hit me with?"

Howard nodded.

"What the hell is it?" Beauford asked.

Howard ignored him. He was muttering to himself. "That lab at Carville *was* just a collecting station," he said to no one in particular. "The lab that started all this is in Atlanta. Damn, why didn't I tumble to it sooner? The father was sent down here to work on an epidemic started by his own kid!" Beauford was talking, but Howard wasn't listening. "Let's trade places, Beauford. I'll drive. We've got to get to Atlanta."

"Atlanta?" The sheriff gathered a fistful of Howard's sleeve. "It's just about time you tell me what's going on here."

"Tell you later. We have to hurry. Trust me, Beauford."

Beauford didn't budge. "Trust you?" he said sarcastically. "Why in hell wouldn't I trust you? All I did this past week was help you break into a building, the property of the Government of the U.S. of A., I might add, then stand around—me, a duly-sworn officer of the law—and watch while you beat up a guy, and then come all the way down here to put the collar on some kid, outta my jurisdiction, without a warrant, and he ends up dead, and I run away like a striped-ass ape. Hell yes, why wouldn't I trust you? Can I trust you to come see me on visiting days?"

Howard regarded his friend for a moment, then smiled. "You're right, Beauford. Let me get behind that wheel. I'll tell you all about it on the way. Promise."

CHAPTER 39

The Swintons' Atlanta home was a large rambling structure set back from the road about a hundred feet in one of those tree-shaded suburbs of endless cul-de-sacs. The neighborhood was one of well-kept lawns, except for the Swinton place, where the weeds had taken over. Howard Fletcher and Beauford Decatur approached the front door on a walkway overgrown with oleander and bougainvillea.

They paused at the door. No sign of light came from behind the draperies that covered the windows. The evening breeze rustled through the high bushes fronting the house. Beauford nudged Howard, and pointed. The door was open a crack. They exchanged glances, and Howard shrugged. Slowly, he pushed the door open.

They stepped into a darkened foyer. With Howard in the lead, they began moving from room to room toward a faint light that proved to come from a ceiling lamp in the kitchen. Plates in the sink were encrusted with decaying scraps of food. An open half-gallon of milk on the table gave off a sour smell. The light above the table seemed to be the only one on in the house. The living room, library, bathroom and a family room, all on the first floor, were dark. They were about to mount the stairs to the second floor when an undercurrent of sound came to them. They followed it back to the kitchen, where it seemed to come from beneath their feet. "The cellar," Howard whispered. Beauford nodded.

They slowly made their way down the short flight of stairs until confronted by a large metal door that looked thick enough for a bank vault or a commercial meat locker. Howard wrinkled his nose at a putrid odor. The strange noise grew louder, an indistinct mewing chatter, not unlike the excited squealing of small children talking all at once at a birthday party. Howard pushed open the door, and they got the full effect of the odor. Howard gagged. He and Beauford stepped into the room, guided somewhat by the kitchen light at the top of the stairs which faintly illuminated shelves and workbenches against the wall. They stopped and looked down at the small moving shadows at their feet.

"Keeee-rist!" Beauford said. The floor was thick with white rats.

"Yeah," Howard said. "Lab rats." He began making out different objects in the room. He edged forward carefully, trying to ignore the frantic scurrying at his feet, the brushing against his pant leg, the shrill chorus. He could pick out a light switch against the wall, and he flicked it, activating the fluorescent lamps over the workbenches.

Beauford, who had stayed near the door, beckoned to Howard. "Over here." Howard walked through the legion of rats until he could make out the outlines of a human form on the slimy floor. He bent over and looked down into the face of Byron Swinton. Howard grimaced. A large red stain covered one side of Swinton's face. The blood ran down behind his ear, spreading down his shirt and pooling behind his head. Swinton lay on his back, his feet turned slightly outward. His face was in ghostly repose.

Howard groped with his fingers to confirm that there was no pulse. "He's dead."

"Somebody sure gave him a working-over," Beauford said.

"Robby," Howard said.

"No shit?"

"I'll bet on it."

Swinton's hands were clasped over his chest, clutching a notebook bound in imitation leather. Howard tugged at the book, having to literally pry it from the stiffening fingers. As Beauford watched, Howard moved to the workbenches and under the glow of the lights he thumbed through the pages, scanning the handwritten notes. It was all there. For all his craziness, Robby Swinton had observed the first rule of research. He had kept flawless records, and had carefully documented everything he had done. A careful entry had been made each day. It didn't take long for Howard to form a mental picture of Robby Swinton's daily routine in that basement tomb he called a laboratory. He had started months ago, culturing the typhoid bacillus in the presence of low levels of various antibiotics, then slowly and gradually increasing the amount of antibiotics in the petri dishes, allowing the bacteria time to develop resistance to each drug. Only one drug, albamycin, had not been used in the cultures. One of the early groups of tetracyclines, albamycin had long ago been replaced by other, more potent drugs, but now was the only antibiotic that would kill this strain of typhoid. The people trying to break the epidemic had undoubtedly been testing newer, more powerful antibiotics against the bug, never realizing an outdated drug was the key.

Beauford moved over next to Howard. "I better call the local police."

Howard looked up. "Not now, Beauford. We'll call them as soon as we get back to Charlemaigne. We've got to scare up an old drug and get back to Vicky. And you're going to have to have the same treatment."

EPILOGUE

Robby Swinton had been a busy boy over the space of a few short months. The final toll was fifty-one cases. Not included in the count were whatever number may have fanned out across the country before manifesting symptoms, only to be misdiagnosed and mysteriously succumb. Twelve had died on the record, and it was probably inevitable that the whole thing would get out. A nurse, some hospital staffer or somebody at the local health department, had leaked it to a reporter. The wire services had picked it up and there had been a few days of scare headlines about a typhoid epidemic 'raging' through New Orleans, until the Surgeon General had gone on television to calm the fears—a freak, he had said, a medical fluke that was now under control.

Dr. Howard Fletcher had given the health authorities and the C.D.C. the name of the effective antibiotic, and most of the hospital patients had been discharged, including Vicky Langston, who was busily preparing for graduation day. (She had made a point of inviting Howard Fletcher.) Beauford Decatur hadn't even gone to the hospital.

Howard had fallen back into his regular routine in Charlemaigne, his patient load not much heavier than it had been before, nor any more challenging—fevers and coughs, a few broken bones, an appendectomy. Howard wasn't complaining. Some quiet time was just what the doctor ordered. And it left evenings free for Marva, when her schedule permitted.

The newspapers, which had never tied Robby Swinton to the epidemic, had more fun with Byron Swinton's murder. They poked into the 'whys' of the death of a highly-regarded scientist at the hands of his scholarly and seemingly devoted son, without ever reaching a definitive conclusion. Even the Swinton saga proved to have a fleeting shelf life, disappearing from the front pages after some mawkish accounts of the double funeral in Atlanta. When Beauford had delivered the news of the deaths to Robby's grandmother, all she said was that "he was always a rather odd boy." She then smiled a chilly smile, and turned away.

Howard was between patients and the waiting room was empty. He turned his chair to the window and spent a few minutes taking in the signs of late spring coming to Charlemaigne. Mrs. Touhy had hung a bird feeder on the low limb of a tree, and it had attracted quite a clientele. It reminded Howard that in two hours he had to pick Marva up for dinner.

He swung around at the tapping at his office door. Mrs. Touhy stuck her head in the room. "Doctor, there's someone to see you," she said, breathless and a little wide-eyed.

"We don't have anyone scheduled, do we?"

"No," she said, her voice fluttering in excitement. "It's him," she stage-whispered.

Howard got to his feet. "It's who?"

She pushed the door open and backed deferentially out of the way like a servant bowing to royalty. The energetic and robust figure of the Surgeon General of the United States strode into the office with a smile and a courtly 'thank you' to the awed Mrs. Touhy. He stuck out a huge hand to Howard. "Dr. Fletcher, it's a pleasure meeting you."

"Well, yes," Howard agreed stupidly, and realized he was a little awestruck himself. "I mean, thank you. It's a privilege meeting you, sir." The Surgeon General stood waiting to be offered a chair. "Please," Howard said finally, "have a seat."

"Thank you." He settled his bulk into the chair. "I've wanted, for some time now, to stop down here and express my gratitude for your fine work."

"Thank you, but—"

"Yes, a fine piece of work," the Surgeon General said. "As a matter of fact, we want to recognize your, uh, contribution in a more tangible way."

"I don't know what to say," Howard replied.

"Don't say anything; you deserve it."

Howard squirmed. "The whole story is—"

"We have an award," the Surgeon General interrupted. "It's for civilians, outside of government, who perform meritorious service in the area of public health. Not generally publicized." He paused for a moment. "A generous check goes with it."

Howard raised a hand. "I don't know if you understand what went on down here."

The Surgeon General smiled. "I think I do."

"Sir, what I've been trying to say is the antibiotic that worked on that strain is an old one. It's been around for years."

The Surgeon General combed his salt-and-pepper beard with his thumb and forefinger. "Well, yes, that's true." He paused as though choosing his words carefully. "But we don't have to make an issue of that, do we? I can't see the advantage in shaking the confidence of the public, do you? All right, the antibiotic has been around for years. The fact of the matter is, the boys over at the C.D.C. were looking at the stars, and the solution was right under their feet. And the fact remains that *you* were the one who figured it out. Good, logical approach. That's what medical sleuthing is all about."

Howard caught himself nodding in agreement with the Surgeon General's flattering rationale. Good, logical medical sleuthing, he mused, such as interviewing high-priced call girls, following petri dishes around the countryside and breaking into Government labs. Not to mention that he couldn't tell a spore from an eggplant. The Surgeon General was on the edge of his chair, and Howard could see he was getting antsy to leave. "Well, I certainly appreciate your coming way over here to see me," Howard told him.

The Surgeon General got to his feet and offered his hand. "Not at all, Doctor. I apologize for the haste, but I'm due back in Washington. I also apologize for telling you about your award in such an informal manner, but there never seems to be enough time to do things properly. . . ." His words trailed away. "You understand."

"Of course," Howard said, amused at the chief medical officer's transparent wish to see the whole episode go away. Howard could not resist tweaking him. "I was just thinking, sir. Would you like me to put something on paper, you know, a synopsis of how the disease manifested itself and the procedures I used in arriving at my conclusions? Ah, just for your records?"

"No, no, that won't be necessary." He gave Howard a comradely pat on the arm. "I doubt that we'll ever again see the type of thing we saw down here in Louisiana."

Howard nodded. Unless, he thought, that someplace out there, by chance, there was another Robby Swinton.